Olive Envy

Other Titles by D.R. Ransdell

Fiction:

Campanello Travels

Amirosian Nights
Thai Twist
Carillon Chase

Andy Veracruz Mysteries

Mariachi Meddler
Island Casualty
Dizzy in Durango
Substitute Soloist
Brotherly Love

Additional Mysteries

Party Wine
Dervla Alarms the Nanas

Non-Fiction:

Secrets of a Mariachi Violinist

Olive Envy

D. R. Ransdell

Author's Note:
This is a work of fiction. Any reference to real persons
is coincidental.

Dedicated to Anna Spallaccia,
her wonderful daughters Elda and Claudia,
and their beautiful kids: Viola,
Angie, Valentino, and Fili

Thanks to them and their lovely friends,
I always feel at home in their delightful
jewel of a city, Orvieto

Chapter One

The woman regarded me with droopy beige-green eyes. "Gina, you'll be one class short. There's no way you can graduate on time."

I assumed that my University of Arizona advisor was literally glued to the chair behind her desk. She probably needed twenty minutes at the end of each working day to extricate herself from the stacks of papers she'd collected from pre-electronic years. The shelves behind her were stuffed with tchotchkes, mostly porcelain Beagles, that hadn't been dusted in decades. She sported a hint of a smile, though. A secret part of her enjoyed telling hopeful college juniors that they would continue as seniors for at least two more years.

This did not coordinate well with my plans. After knocking out spring finals, the idea was to loaf through the summer. A busy fall semester would be followed by a December graduation, which meant I was finishing after four and a half years, one semester late, even though my mother had funded me for four. It was high time for me to get out of school and get on with my life. Also, Grandma had offered to take me, my sister, and my mom on a cruise over Valentine's Day. The idea was to celebrate my graduation, but my relatives wouldn't wait if I were stuck taking more classes. They would vacation without me.

I swished my dishwater-blonde hair out of my face. "Don't you have any suggestions?"

Dr. Klein regarded me as an anomaly, a student who expected an advisor to know something useful. Although she sighed as if auditioning for a dramatic role in a play that no one would want to see, she spent the next precious minutes helping me review my limited options in useless detail.

I could hardly take more than twenty-one units a semester, which was already an overload, but the classes I needed were only offered in the fall, and only one was offered, in a pitiful online version, during the summer. That left me short by one semester of Italian.

I hadn't planned on taking a foreign language sequence. After all, my "home" Spanish was adequate even though I didn't know the rules and couldn't navigate complicated tenses. The year before, I'd taken Italian 101 just for fun. I would have left things at that. A few conversational skills for a future trip to Pompeii couldn't hurt.

Now that I'd changed my major again, this time to Global Studies, I needed to fulfill a two-semester language requirement. I needed to complete Italian 102 whether I wanted to or not.

"I don't know what to tell you," Dr. Klein said, "but your session is up. Next!"

Another would-be senior tumbled in the door. Obviously, he'd eavesdropped on my little conversation with Klein. Since he towered over me, clogging up the narrow space in the room, he'd evidently decided that his problems were more important than mine were.

Out of spite, I took extra time packing up my laptop and hoodie before I vacated the room.

*

My grandmother looked up from the ground beef she was frying on the burner. "You still haven't figured out how to graduate? I think you like being in school."

She hadn't attended college herself. She'd grown up in Mexico at a time when most women went from their parents' houses to their husbands' houses, where the chores increased along with other expectations.

"It's complicated, Grandma. You have to chalk up the right number of credits. You also have to satisfy certain requirements. It's hard to explain."

She poked at the beef as if it had misbehaved. "You have to stop changing your mind about which degree you're actually going to finish."

I knew better than to argue. No matter the points in my favor, I never came out on top. "No more changes. I'm headed straight for the finish line."

"We'll see."

Although I didn't appreciate her lack of confidence, I couldn't blame her for doubting me. I'd started off in journalism before the department disintegrated. Then I'd drifted to psychology (too serious) before trying out finance (too cutthroat).

My sister Rachel waltzed into the room and over to the cupboard. She lived with her fiancé, or rather, he lived with her, but on Thursday nights she dined with us. "You guys look like you've been discussing politics. Lighten up! And tell me, salsa verde or sriracha?"

My favorite Thai hot sauce was not the point. "I've got a serious hiccup. Now that I changed my major, I can't graduate on schedule. I need a second semester of Italian."

"Good idea," Rachel said. "I'll need a tour guide when I travel to Italy. They say the Amalfi Coast is to die for."

That was my sister, not only positive, but pragmatic, which was why she pulled out both sauces. But that didn't mean she'd considered this troubling issue from my point of view.

"The problem is that they're not offering Italian 102 over the summer, and I can't fit the class into my schedule in the fall. I'm already signed up for five classes."

Rachel retrieved dinner plates from the dishwasher. "So?"

She was kidding. Sort of. She'd worked hard to complete her degree in violin performance within four years. Since she was thirteen years older than I was, her college days were in the distant past. Certainly, it was harder to achieve a degree nowadays. Social media was so much more attractive than it used to be.

"Why wouldn't they offer the class over the summer?" Grandma asked. "That's when people have time for stuff they don't need."

I selected silverware from the drawer. "It's too hard to learn a language online, so not enough students sign up for it."

"They're probably all headed to Italy instead," Rachel said. "Doesn't U of A run a summer study abroad program near Rome somewhere?"

Travel was my middle name. But even if I stuck to hostels and takeout meals from grocery stores, I couldn't afford the luxury.

My mother strolled in with flowers she had cut from the garden. "Who's studying abroad?"

My sister patted my shoulder. "Gina is."

I bopped her with the closest dishtowel.

"That's very interesting," my mother said. "Thank goodness she makes so much at her night job."

The comment was passive aggressive. Mostly aggressive. I did not have a night job. My mother had told me three times that I needed to find something productive to do in the summer. Maybe it was ten times. I'd lost count.

By then I'd lost control of the conversation. Rachel thought I could apply for scholarship money. Grandma said my absentee Italian-American father could pay expenses. My mother claimed I could pay for them myself. Who didn't finish college with a bit of debt? Either way, the three women in my life were keen on deciding my fate. Not only did they have more life experience than I did, but they all had a lot more resources.

"You need to study abroad," Rachel said. "You can have a blast and earn credits at the same time."

"You probably have Italians cousins somewhere. You could search for them," said Mom.

Years ago I'd attempted a genealogical project, but I'd been thwarted by dead ends.

"You might have several choices," Rachel said. "Everybody's pushing study abroad these days."

A few quick taps on my cell phone confirmed that the university was offering a study abroad fair within the month.

"Go talk to the representatives," Rachel said. "Chat with former students. Get a feel for your choices."

"I'll do that," I said. "Completing Italian 102 in the summer would really help me out. It was so nice of my advisor to mention it."

"What do you think you have a big sister for! Who knows? Maybe I'll come visit."

"You could even learn to cook something," said Mom. It was another passive-aggressive attack. I never cooked if I could avoid it.

Grandma turned off the burner. "We know Gina won't waste her time cooking. But maybe she could figure out how to use olive oil. My friends all swear by it. They claim it's an anti-inflammatory that lowers blood pressure and prevents diabetes. It's like a miracle drug that you can buy at the grocery store."

My head was already swimming with possibilities; it seemed everyone had a clear vision of my trip except for me.

"No matter what you do, the experiences will be invaluable," Rachel said. "Like my going to Greece."

"You fell in love with that country so hard you almost didn't come back," snapped Grandma. She was suspicious of travel because once she'd been stranded in Austin and couldn't find a hotel.

"Look how much I learned in Greece," Rachel said. "And the friends I made! I can go back to Amiros at any time. I might work there again this summer."

"Andy would like that," my mom quipped.

Rachel smiled. "He'll get over it. Or come along! But never mind about me. Let's fix you up, Gina. One study abroad trip coming right up."

"Let's have tacos," said Mom.

That was the end of discussion. But as I bit into a jalapeño, I thought about pizza.

*

Two weeks later, I zigzagged among promotional tables at the study abroad tent. Rachel was correct; I could have fulfilled my language requirement several different ways, but the program I chose was run by the U of A itself. It was held in Orvieto, a small town in Umbria that was smartly located between Rome and Florence. A quick three-week course would allow me to keep my December graduation date and join in on the family cruise. More importantly, my grades were high enough to grant me a partial scholarship. I borrowed the rest of the money from Grandma and bought an economy plane ticket to Fiumicino with an open return. Who knew what would happen?

My fellow students, all nine of them, seemed worried during the orientation meeting, but I became more and more excited the closer we got to the departure date. I read up on pastas and truffles. I learned that extra virgin olive oil meant that the product was extracted without heat or chemicals. I memorized the ingredients in tiramisù, which included lady fingers and mascarpone.

I prepared linguistically as well. I tended to sprinkle Spanish into my Italian if I let my attention drop, so in between classes, I completed rounds of Duolingo. At night I listened to Matteo and Katie explain colloquial phrases on YouTube before listening to Jane Fonda and

Lily Tomlin shout at each other in Italian on Netflix. I spent a weekend with Rachel crying over *Roman Holiday* and laughing over *Bread and Tulips*.

Up until now, my life had included a fair share of missteps. Wrong majors. Disappointing boyfriends. Ugly hair styles. Choosing to study abroad didn't seem like a mistake in the least. It seemed exactly like what I was meant to do. I loved the excitement of travel, and Italy should be easy to manage through the hands of a university program. What could possibly go wrong?

Chapter Two

As we bumped along the runway, all I could think of was how mad I was at my sister. *If you're tired enough, you'll sleep on the plane*, she lied. Instead, I squirmed for five hours. Then I gave up and watched *Barbie* in Italian. Even though I'd seen the film three times, the only words I caught in the target language were ones the actors kept repeating: *Sono, sei, siamo,* I am, you are, we are.

That was something else I could be irritated about. Rachel had assured me that the longer I studied Italian, the less I would mix it up with Spanish. Instead, I'd spent the whole transatlantic flight trying to remember which language used *me* rather than *mi*. Even though I knew that *e* meant "and," I kept spitting out *y*, which was Spanish. Linguistically, I was a mess.

I had other problems. I was prepared for the lines at passport control, the airport bathrooms, and the ATMs. I was smart enough to avoid the train ticket line by buying ahead of time, but after I wheedled my way through the crowd to reach the automatic gate leading to the Leonardo Express that should take me from Fiumicino Airport to Roma Termini, the train station at the heart of downtown Rome, my precious electronic bar code refused to work.

I stepped aside, rebooted my phone, and re-joined the airport Internet network. When I attempted to get through the turnstile, the dratted sign still read "ERROR" in big letters, as if it reflected my state of being.

By that point, I was done. I'd traveled all the way from Tucson to Rome, but now I would be stuck at the airport for the rest of my Italian study abroad experience.

"Maybe you have arrived too early for your ticket," said a tall man standing nearby. His accent was Northern European, and his hiking pants suggested he was a fellow tourist; they would be too practical for Italian men.

"We had that same problem," said the tall woman next to him, probably British, also wearing practical but unstylish hiking pants. "You're allowed to go through half an hour early but not sooner."

It took me another moment to decipher the European time clock, but then I realized, eureka, my ticket should be valid in another two minutes.

"Of course," I said as lightly as possible. "I should have known."

But why should I have? And how closely could I calculate the exact time I'd reach the station? Never mind. Together, the couple and I assisted the next three confused travelers who had the same problem. Meanwhile travelers hurried inside the gates or outside of them, trying to make sense of things.

A simple sign would have streamlined the process. *Don't worry,* that louse of a sister of mine had said. *Ask people to help you. They will.*

That much was true, but once the couple and I finally conquered the turnstiles, we were still bewildered. We faced three tracks. The first had a digital sign next to it that said, "no service." The sign for the second track read, "Roma non-stop." The sign for the second track had no indications whatsoever.

"I guess it's this way." The tall man headed down the platform, but the overhead offered some mumbo-jumbo before offering a nearly incomprehensible message: "The Freccia Rossa train is displeased to announce a delay of twenty minutes."

"Oh, no," the woman said jokingly. "We've been in transit forever!"

"Or at least since this morning," said the man. "But we're nearly there. Then we can relax."

Relax, nothing. I doublechecked my ticket, which clearly read "Leonardo Express."

"I think this is the wrong train," I said.

"In Italy, you have to be patient," the man said.

While he was right, passengers carrying a lot more luggage than I was willing to piled onto the middle platform and spread out.

Something felt wrong. "This isn't our track," I said. "It can't be."

"No worries," the man said. "It doesn't matter which train we take."

While I didn't want to offend the poor man, when I saw a uniformed employee, I ran over to her, stumbled through incorrect Italian, and showed her my digital ticket.

She indicated the other track. "*Veloce!*"

Fast!

The couple and I laughed as we ran for the other side, flopping down in the nearest compartment right before the doors shut.

"Thanks a lot," the woman said as she slid her suitcase between the seats. "We love traveling in Italy, but it's always a challenge."

"I try to tell myself that's part of the fun," I said, not sure I believed what I was saying.

"You should come to the Netherlands," the man said. "We have a tremendous country, and it's easier to navigate than this one."

The woman patted her companion's arm. "And the men are very romantic. Once you find the right one, you'll be set for life!"

For life? Really?

"I should have considered visiting the Netherlands ahead of time," I said. "But I'm here for a study abroad program. Heritage and all that."

"Wonderful," the woman said. "Do you speak the language?"

"I should! But it's more like Spatilian or maybe Italish. My dad is Italian American, but he moved away before he taught me anything. My mom's Mexican, and my grandma lives with us, so I hear Spanish all the time even though I don't always use it when I should."

"If you want to learn a language that's easy for you, try Frisian," said the man.

The woman play-hit him with the back of her hand. "But there aren't many speakers," she said. "Logically, you should learn Dutch instead. There are plenty of nice young single men to go around. You might find one. Maybe even two!"

I laughed as if that were exactly what I wanted, but they would have never believed me if I'd told them the truth: a Dutch friend of mine kept trying to set me up with his brother. "I'm not here for the men, but do you have suggestions for touring Rome?"

I'd already made an ambitious list myself, one I wouldn't be able to complete, but I listened politely as the couple mentioned museums I hadn't read about and restaurants I wouldn't spend the money to visit by myself. I was still taking notes when we pulled into Termini, but that was the beauty of the Leonardo Express. Boarding it was a challenge, but once it stopped, you knew exactly where you were.

*

"No eating," said the guard. *"Non mangiare!"*

I turned away from the magnificent Baroque fountain where Oceanus looked out over his mythical horses. Even though I knew how famous it was, I still wasn't prepared for the monument to beauty that covered the back side of a palazzo.

I also wasn't prepared for the crowd. It seemed that everybody in Rome was at the Trevi Fountain at the same time. We squeezed onto the ring of stone seats that surrounded the fountain and dodged people who blocked our views. No wonder the locals had threatened charging tourists to visit the zone. They probably couldn't sleep through the noise: the clatter of silverware from the many surrounding restaurants, the high pitches of excited female tourists vying for the best spots along the edge of the fountain, the people who got lost trying to find their way into the famous square and then couldn't remember how to get out again.

The poor guard had a thankless job, shooing people away with their gelati and droopy panini. Eating in front of the fountain was not allowed, and the rule was enforced to the extent that the one guard could make his way among the transgressors before a new group came in and began the process all over again.

I couldn't blame the authorities for worrying that crumbs would fall into the water. The tourists were worse than spectators at a football stadium. Used food wrappers dotted the ground along with soda cans, water bottles, and even a pizza box. I didn't understand how visitors could arrive at one of the most iconic sights in the world and leave their debris. I wanted to think better of them, that they were so overcome with a sense of arrival that they didn't notice their errors, but I knew better. They weren't considerate. They didn't recognize the wonder of where they were because they were all about loading shots onto their Instagram accounts.

In the guard's shoes, I would have been cranky. I would have yelled at anyone I saw scattering crumbs. Yet the lanky uniformed fellow didn't seem to mind. He was persistent and stern without being mean. Maybe the job of monitoring tourists wasn't so bad given that half the women wore slinky tank tops that couldn't control their cleavage.

Given the chill in the May evening air, I offered no such exciting sight myself. I wore walking shorts that nearly touched my knees and a blouse that covered my bra straps. I'd wrapped a light jacket around my neck in case the wind picked up. Since I didn't even sport ridiculous high heels or a designer haircut, I enjoyed the status of being completely uncool. In case any fashionistas weren't already alarmed by my appearance, I wrestled an Android from my non-designer purse whose ancient stitches were unraveling. I melted into the background so well that nobody noticed me, which was perfect. That way I could observe the crowd in peace.

The scene was a snapshot of Modern Italy: couples with strollers, groups of women, lone men pretending not to be looking for company, photographers hoping to sell their work, flower vendors unloading wilted roses, screaming kids, sleeping babies, and, most of all, lovers. The area was a mecca for romance. Sweethearts held hands, kissed with their backs to the fountain, tossed coins over their shoulders, kissed again for a photoshoot, and smooched as if the world belonged to them. Maybe at that moment it did.

Was I envious? A little. I hadn't dated the spring semester or the fall semester either. Yes, I'd been busy, but mostly I'd turned down the opportunity for one bad date after another. I lived by my sister's maxim, *Mejor sola que mal acompañada* – Better alone than in bad company. Did I need a critic to explain that soft drinks were for kids and therefore I should drink beer with him instead? Not particularly. Did I need to be cloaked with gorilla arms as a sign of possession? Not one bit. Did I need a lizard to slide his long tongue into my ear during dull moments at movie theaters? Absolutely not. So what that romance surrounded me? Falling in love was a lot of trouble, and usually the process backfired.

No, never mind the men. I was here to learn Italian. That was my main important goal, and I had to keep it at the forefront. I had less than a month to advance my Italian, and language learning, while fun, was never easy. I needed to focus. I needed verbs.

On the other hand, I was in the Eternal City, which was the land of dreams. If I couldn't have my own little fantasy here, where could I have it? After carefully waiting for the perfect opportunity, I went over to the tanned guard, who had already been photographed a hundred times in the last half hour, and asked if we could take a selfie together. He smiled as if he were an actor with a box office hit and happily complied. An American gal offered to take a photo for me, so I wound up with two perfect shots. I was on a roll. On my first night in Italy, I scored a handsome man to post on my Instagram account.

Oh, wait, I didn't have such an account. No worries. I still had plenty of adventures to dream about, and for one jetlagged tourist, that was enough.

Chapter Three

The next morning I kicked myself out of bed early with the intention of knocking out some essential sightseeing before taking the late afternoon train to Orvieto. I had a couple of weeks to spare at the end of the program, but I hadn't decided where to spend them, so what better time to explore Rome than the present? But the hordes at the Colosseum deterred me so much that I walked around the structure without fighting my way in. Who knew that you needed a skip-the-line reservation? Where were we, Euro Disney? Instead, I circled the perimeter, imagining the arena inside. The early Romans might have battled crocodiles and tigers, but today's lone tourist battled hordes of groups from South Korea and China, all of whom wielded a tour guide as their shield.

The ticket line for the Roman Forum was not as daunting, but its ticket was coupled with the Colosseum, so it was double or nothing. Instead, I walked along Via dei Fori Imperiali, imagining Ancient Rome as I looked out at the ruins. I paused long enough to identify the Temple of Vesta, but no matter its importance in the ancient world, now it consisted of three columns on top of some rocks.

A better tourist might have felt more respect for the past. Instead, I silently cursed the fact that the city's metro didn't pass straight through the center of town because archaeological digs always slowed construction. If I'd had all day, I might have figured out a way to take the bus, but instead I strolled the three and a half kilometers to St. Peter's Square. To my naïve surprise, you could only tour the Sistine Chapel by paying to visit the Vatican Museums, so I settled on visiting St. Peter's Basilica. Passing through security required another line, but at least it moved quickly, and the symmetry of Bernini's piazza drew my eyes in all directions.

None of my family was religious. Even though my grandma was raised Catholic, she hadn't raised my mother that way. Grandma was suspicious of institutions run by men, so we attended mass for weddings, baptisms, and funerals. Yet when I finally passed through St. Peter's doors, I stepped into a Baroque marble fantasyland. Chapels called from both sides of the nave, but I crept forward in slow motion, drawn to the altar as if by a magnetic field that gently drew me into its circle. High on the back wall, the dove of peace flew in eternal hope surrounded by yellow beams of anticipation.

After my sweater slipped to the floor, I noticed the stream behind me. Although a few visitors took pictures, others crossed themselves. One started praying. Two women cried. I wasn't used to seeing such outbursts of raw emotion, and I suddenly felt inadequate. I'd come to the Vatican to check the site off my master list. Others experienced a spiritual homecoming.

I tried to imagine how I could turn my language study into a similarly significant experience. Maybe this was why I'd come to Italy, to ride a wave that was bigger than I was, to find my place in the universe's overall design. St. Peter's suggested that I had one.

After I reached the altar, I made a loop around the whole basilica, noticing the bronze columns, the marble, the priests, and the people. What I liked most were the comparisons: small indications on the floor that showed how other churches measured up. The cathedral in Milan was bigger than the one in Seville that was bigger than the one in Florence, for example, yet I was sure they all felt just as huge.

When I finally returned to the piazza, I leaned back against one of the wide stone columns, silently thankful for the beauty and majesty of a place I couldn't yet understand. Maybe I never would. Maybe my journey wasn't spiritual.

I hadn't counted on jetlag. I might have only slept for ten minutes, but when a tourist stumbled over my out-stretched feet, he apologized profusely in a language I couldn't understand. What I caught onto right away was that I had less than an hour to return to my hostel, grab my stuff, and catch my train to Orvieto. That's when my every thought of peace and tranquility disappeared right into the sky with the dove.

*

I caught the metro to Termini, ran to my hostel, and panted so pathetically that the sleek Danish twenty-year-old be-hind the desk immediately retrieved my luggage rather than asking polite questions. I sprinted back to the train station. I prided myself on passing through the station gates at 4:47, a solid ten minutes before my train left.

Then I checked the *Partenze* billboard. Not a single train went straight to Orvieto. I saw the listing for a train to Bologna, but it only stopped in Florence. The train to Venice stopped in Florence and Verona.

"Orvieto?" I asked an elderly woman passing by.

She pointed to the top of the billboard. The *rapido* to Florence was the train I needed. It departed from Track 1EST, meaning 1 East, but I was standing in front of Track 10. I raced left until I reached Track 1, but 1EST wasn't next to it. I whirled around, panicked.

High above my head, small orange letters announced 1EST and 2EST. Arrows pointed down a walkway that bor-dered the edge of the station.

"*Uno est?*" a man asked.

My thoughts exactly. I turned in time to see a train official wave his hand. "*Ávanti!*" Forward.

I hurried behind the man, worried I was headed the wrong way but unsure what to do about it. Then I noticed a sign: 1EST, 2EST, 450 meters.

I picked up my pace. I didn't remember how long a meter was, but my track wasn't in sight.

Three teens skipped past in flashy tennis shoes. They weren't much younger than I was, but they weren't burdened by a backpack and a bulky carry-on.

"Orvieto?" I called out. One turned and nodded.

If the track was so far away, how did anyone get there? I started run-walking. I didn't dare check my watch because I figured that knowing the exact time would make me panic. *Keep going!*

I came abreast of a man tugging a heavy suitcase. An even heavier woman lumbered beside him wearing sandals with two-inch heels.

"*Non posso!*" she shouted. *I can't!*

"*Dai!*" the man shouted back. *Come on!*

I looked back; the woman's face was flushed, and her cheeks were red. She favored one foot, and her left knee was twice the size of the right one.

"*Ce la facciamo!*" the man cried.

Leaving the couple behind, I jogged at my fastest pace, the one I reserved for catching a plane at an airport. Surely there were other trains, right? All I would have to do was figure out how to change my online ticket. That should only take an hour or so, which might be when the next train departed.

No. I had strict instructions. Lucia, the program's supervisor, was meeting my scheduled train. I had to be on it.

Dai!

Finally, the track came into view.

Faster!

The conductor, a 50s-something man in a wrinkled uniform, stood near the first compartment, waiting to give the "go ahead" to the engineer. Then he noticed me charging towards him like a madwoman.

"*Aspetti!*"

I'd remembered the word for "wait" at exactly the right moment, but I assumed it was my look of horror that convinced the man to give me a few extra seconds. He stepped aside as I flung my goods onto the train.

I held up two fingers. *"Altri due!"* I gasped as I climbed in. *Two more!*

By then we could hear the man's footsteps even though he was still out of sight.

"Per piacere, aspetatevi!" he shouted. He might have been at an important soccer match, one he'd bet his kid on.

The conductor checked his watch and shrugged. Seconds later, when the man reached the train, the conductor helped him lift the suitcase up the steps. By then his companion, drenched in sweat, caught up as well. As she lunged for the steps, she grasped the conductor's arm so tightly I thought they'd both fall, but he steadied her enough that she managed the steep climb.

By then her companion and I were both waiting with outstretched hands. As the train jerked forward, we helped her take the first empty seat.

The poor lady panted so hard that I insisted she drink my water. I might not have known where to find a hidden track that lay halfway to the next town, but I did know it was important to hydrate. I worried the woman might have a heart attack. Her husband fanned her while she held a handkerchief to her forehead and sobbed.

"Mi dispiace, cara," he said over and over. *I'm sorry, dear.*

She wasn't listening. She was focused on breathing.

A few minutes later, the conductor stopped by to check on his late arrivals. I assumed the rapid-fire conversation he exchanged with the male passenger concerned the hidden nature of the track. The conductor probably witnessed the same scenario a few times a day. Repeat visitors would know better. Newbies would be taken by shock.

By the time we were halfway to Orvieto, the woman graduated from near hysteria to misery. Her ankles were so swollen they were bursting through the straps, she'd sweat through her blouse until it became a sponge, and she was so done in that she might have tumbled from her seat to the floor. As far as I knew, at least she wasn't suffering from jetlag.

As the woman regained her breath, she regained her voice. She transformed from victim to interrogator. Where was I going all alone? Why wasn't I traveling with a friend or a relative? My explanation of studying in Orvieto was met half-heartedly. Why wouldn't I study in Rome or Florence instead? They were bigger cities. They offered more options.

I just wanted to study, I said. No distractions. But at that the woman and her partner laughed. It was Italy. Of course there would be distractions! But in a little town such as Orvieto, I wouldn't find anything exciting to do. That's why they would never move away from Rome. Now, that was a city! Always something going on, day and night. Presentations, rallies, parades! Exhibitions, protests, scandals! That wasn't to mention fashion shows or celebrities or concerts or soccer!

I would find Orvieto too limiting and too boring. I tried to explain that I couldn't change my program now, but they were adamant that I'd made the wrong choice and needed to jump trains as soon as possible. They insisted that the only important aspect of Orvieto was the work by Luca Signorelli in the Cathedral, but who spent all day in church?

I didn't dare mention that I didn't much care about churches anyway, but the couple had distracted me with such dire warnings that I didn't notice we were approaching my destination until we pulled into the station. I barely managed to gather my things quickly enough to tumble off the train.

For a moment I worried Lucia hadn't come for me. Then a fifty-something with wild hair, a tight red tank top, and a black skirt hiked up to her thighs waved both hands as she approached. "Gina from Tucson!" she shouted as if I were deaf. "Come to me now!" Her thick Italian accent resonated throughout the platform even though it was open air. She wrestled the carry-on from my hand as if stealing it and marched me outside the train station where three cars were honking at the once-white Cinquecento that was double parked.

Somehow, I wasn't surprised that the offending vehicle belonged to my supervisor. Welcome to Orvieto, I thought. *Benvenuta.*

Chapter Four

After hustling me up three flights of stairs but refraining to help me with a single bag, Lucia shoved the key into the lock. "You have your apartment until two days after your final exam."

"Thanks."

"*Grazie!*" She twisted the handle until she fought the door open. "Your job is to learn Italian! You must start immediately."

She handed me a single silver key and escorted me into my new living room, which was the size of a shoe box. "Here is your beautiful apartment," she said breezily, as if she'd never heard of claustrophobia. Then she stopped short. A row of cosmetics governed the coffee table. A suitcase big enough to hold a dead body took up most of the floor space while the loveseat displayed clothes as if they were for sale.

"What is going on here?" Lucia stomped past the loveseat, swept the clothes to the floor, and kicked the suitcase. "*No, no, e no!*"

My new roommate stumbled her way out of the bedroom. Strands of wavy blonde hair dangled before her pale face like a bead curtain from the 60s while her loose navy-blue shorts might have been pajamas. Her right breast peaked out from between layers of a disheveled blouse.

I recognized Henrietta vaguely from orientation back in Tucson. She'd attended the mandatory meeting after making a spectacularly late arrival. She'd elbowed her way into the crowded conference room, disrupted the speaker as the man explained how to call +112 for emergencies, sighed because all the seats were taken, and sunk to the floor at the back of the room, from which angle she couldn't see the instructional slides.

I hadn't chosen her as a roommate, but three sorority sisters had claimed the triple while two genuine sisters had claimed the other double. Henrietta and I were the two loners. Or maybe losers.

"Henrietta! For what is all this confusion?" Lucia demanded.

My roommate tripped through her mess and landed on the loveseat. "Like, what's the matter?"

Henrietta was the type to start each sentence with "like" as if she were making a fashion statement. I was pretty sure her Italian would be, like, awful.

Lucia stomped her feet. "You share this apartment! You do not leave your wardrobe in the common area! I have told you this!"

Lucia calmed down a notch but still punctuated every sentence with an exclamation point. I admired her energy; after all, she wasn't yelling at me. She picked up a blouse and shook it. "Take these things to your room. Now."

"But—"

"There are no 'buts.' Do this now. And say 'hi' to your roommate, Gina Campobello."

"Campanello," I said, daring to correct her.

"Yes, yes, Campomello," Lucia said, pronouncing my name wrong in a different way. She tossed a bra at Henrietta. "Do this now as we are waiting."

With the speed of a turtle, Henrietta made the first moves to straighten the room by picking up a pair of yellow panties.

"Sbrigati!" Hurry up!

Startled, Henrietta picked up a pair of jeans.

I resisted the urge to help her while acknowledging that I'd been spoiled my whole life. At home I'd always had my own room. Most of my travels had been with my sister Rachel, a minimalist when it came to packing, let alone unpacking. Sharing a small space with someone who immediately filled it would be a challenge. Sure, Lucia was there to protect me for the moment, but she wouldn't be living with us. I already knew what would happen: Henrietta's possessions would creep back into the living room. And linger. Then they would sneak into my room as well.

Lucia flounced over to another door. "Gina, this will be your room."

I was prepared to hold my breath due to a lack of oxygen, but the room was at least twenty by thirty. A twin bed hugged one wall. A window admitted strips of sunlight onto the desk that hugged the opposite wall. Nobody would accuse the space of being luxurious, but it was easily acceptable.

"You see? You have the lovely room."

Certainly, my roommate had been awarded a bigger room with a bigger bed, but she'd gotten herself to Orvieto before I had. Power to her. At least I'd arrived a full day before the program started. That would give me a chance to acclimate.

"See here?" Lucia asked. "You have a beautiful bathroom."

I peeked inside. Beautiful was a stretch, but at least there were two towel racks even though Henrietta's t-shirt took up one and a wet towel took up another. A tiny window looked out at the hills beyond the town.

"Do we have a balcony?"

"Ha, ha! You don't need one! You go outside and you have all of Orvieto."

Lucia was wrong about the balcony. I felt claustrophobic already, but I let her hustle me back into the living room, where Henrietta had paused in her possession-gathering long enough to sink into the couch.

"Now, I must show you how the things work," Lucia said. She flicked Henrietta's hair. "Up! Up!"

I followed Lucia to a kitchen so compact it might fit into a pantry. It boasted a mini stove, a mini refrigerator, and a mini freezer. Even the table was mini, and the two small stools would only accommodate short slender people. What commanded my attention, though, was the huge picture window. Lilies pushed against it from outside. A faint scent suggested spring, and when Lucia yanked the window open, the scent plunged in.

"You must take advantage of the beautiful weather. Now, you see here?" She tapped a metal machine in the corner of the kitchen. "This is a washing machine."

I'd never seen one so small. My clothes would fit in perfectly as long as I washed one blouse at a time. Now I understood why Italian men came short; otherwise, they wouldn't be able to wear long pants or long sleeves. Lucia ran her index finger under an array of dials with explanations in tiny letters.

"This you will have to study," she said. "There is the book." She opened the top cabinet and pointed to a manual next to a neat stack of plates. Evidently my roommate hadn't found the time to mess up the kitchen yet. Maybe she hadn't stepped inside.

"But this," Lucia continued, "this is more important." She opened a wide drawer under the sink that held four plastic containers. "You must do this correctly. You see, in Italy, we believe in the recycling. We know it is right for our environment, so we are happy to do it. You will be happy, too."

She pointed to the white container, which was lined with a thin plastic bag. "This? For *indifferenziato*. The trash you cannot recycle." She pointed to the green container. "This is for *organico*." She fingered the thin lining. "It's better you use double bags so that your greens don't break through and land in the hallway." She tapped the yellow container. "This is for plastic and metal, but there are no bags." She straightened the blue container, which was slightly misaligned. "This is for *carta*, and here too, you don't need a bag. Why? Because the animals aren't interested for the *carta*. You see? It's so reasonable this system.

25

Anybody can understand it. You take one minute to study it, yes? This you must do. Yes?"

"Yes. *Sì*."

"Now, the important part." She pointed to a laminated weekly schedule that was taped to the counter. "This chart shows you what bins to put outside. But you see, the bins have a label." She pointed to the bar code on the blue container. "If you put the wrong things, the collector takes a picture. And guess what happens?"

I was still trying to remember what she said about the first container. If everything in Italy was as complicated as the garbage collection was, I wouldn't have time to study language. Sure, in Tucson we recycled, or did we? I always suspected that half the material ended up in the landfill anyway, and recycling glass had become so complicated that I'd given up on it.

"What happens?" I asked.

"If you make something wrong, you will get a fine. *Anzi*, the owners of your apartment will get a fine. And then what happens? They will complain to me. And then? I will have to pay. After I pay, now you can guess what will happen?"

"Then I pay."

"That is exactly right. So be careful when you throw your things. Any questions?"

"Not right off."

"All right. I give you more advice tomorrow. Be on time for the introductory meeting that precedes our classes. Otherwise, I have to repeat everything twice."

"Nine o'clock?"

"This is correct. You will set your alarm? Sometimes the jetlag makes some trouble."

"I'll set my alarm."

"All right. Then I go for the next students. They arrive at the train station in ten minutes."

With a swoosh, Lucia was gone.

I breathed easier. Too much information spat out too quickly meant that I hadn't retained more than the idea that garbage was important.

At that point I might have engaged my new roommate in conversation, or at least asked about her journey to Orvieto, but she had retreated to her room and shut the door.

I didn't worry that she had immediately decided that she didn't like me or that I wasn't cool or that we couldn't be friends. Even through the door, I could hear Henrietta snore.

*

Since I had all of Orvieto at my disposal, I opened my suitcase enough to let my squashed clothes breathe before making my escape. As a matter of orientation, I trotted over to Corso Cavour, the town's main artery. I'd studied the route ahead of time, so I knew the street led from the funicular on the east edge of town to a fork culminating in the west end.

I headed towards the sunset as if pulled by gravity. I meandered down the hard stones while eyeing the three- and four-story buildings on either side. The ground floors consisted of small specialty shops that sold items of every kind: olive oil, wine, clothes, ice cream, pasta, bread, fast food pizza, kebabs, souvenirs, more olive oil, and more wine. I assumed that apartments filled the subsequent levels.

A flower shop, mostly outdoors, hugged the edge of the next piazza. I was trying to catch the street sign so I could remember where I was when a car rattled by and nearly wiped me out. The passageways were so narrow that I assumed I was in a pedestrian zone, but instead I was in a much-shared space. Before I could catch my breath from a near-death experience, three more cars shot by. I was glad I wasn't driving. Walking could be complicated enough.

I continued past a few small grocery stores, a hardware store, and even a bookstore. When I came to a fork, I rose up to the right. But I wasn't having lofty thoughts about where I was going or the layers of history I was walking on top of, or even about the workmanship that must have gone into creating a city on top of Etruscan caves. My thought was whether or not my Tevas would survive three weeks on such rough surfaces or whether I needed to order another pair.

No wonder my roommate was tired. Although it looked like she'd brought a lot of clothes, I doubted that she'd packed appropriate footwear. How could you know, as you prepared your suitcase back in Tucson where the temperatures were already over a hundred degrees every day, that what you needed in Italy was a solid pair of running shoes?

After the road curved past a few residential streets and an old church, it stopped short at a lookout point. At least around Orvieto I would never get too lost. You could only go so far before reaching the edge of the cliff. The panorama included fields and scattered buildings and a ribbon of a road, all dotted with a harmony of greens and yellows. As I sat on the stone wall and felt the breeze rustle through my hair, I felt strangely calm. Orvieto offered neither the glamour nor the chaos of Rome. The locals said *salve* before continuing about their business, and up here I wouldn't be distracted by any fancy stores or enticing exhibitions. I had three weeks to buckle down and knock out a semester's worth of Italian. The order was a tall one, but in such a pretty, peaceful town, I wouldn't have any obstacles.

Except maybe Henrietta.

Chapter Five

Ten minutes into class, my head hurt. I knew verbs were important, the cornerstones to speaking the language, but they made my head spin. I knew enough Spanish to be confused by it, so learning Italian verb endings challenged my every brain cell. I could swim through present tense, but now that we were reviewing the present perfect, I couldn't juggle all the irregulars. Having a teacher who was on autoplay didn't help. I could imagine the problem. Aurelio had taught the course too many times, so it wasn't fun anymore. He wasn't making it fun for us.

Maybe it wasn't his fault. My fellow students and I hadn't yet settled into Orvieto. Our senses had been dulled by the long introductory meeting which lasted an hour and a half when ten minutes would have been plenty. Lucia droned on and on, careful to mention anything remotely useful. She gave us little cards that listed emergency numbers for the police and the ambulance and the hospital and even her home phone. She warned us that if we did anything that went against Italian law we'd land in jail. She reminded us that there were NO excuses for missing exams and NO makeups, that we needed to show special respect to the locals since, as in her family's case, many came from noble heritage, and that the funicular between the train station and the hilltop ran until eight-thirty p.m. No matter if we went to Rome to visit the pope or Florence to climb Brunelleschi's dome, we couldn't miss that last funicular because it was dangerous to climb up the steep hill to Orvieto in the dark.

The bars were all dangerous too. Locals might prey on us before kidnapping us and requesting large amounts of money. We'd never see our families again. And why would we waste good money on liquor? Barhopping was an immature act that we should save for Tucson.

Those weren't Lucia's only gems of advice. She also had a healthy number of warnings. Excessive public use of alcohol could get us sent straight home. We didn't want that, did we? We shouldn't think we could get away with going out to the bars even if she were out of town because the second any Americans got drunk, the bar owners assumed the students were Lucia's and called her, even in the middle of the night.

What with the gazillion rules and warnings, no wonder my classmates and I were more concentrated on the nearest source of caffeine than page ninety-five in Aurelio's book. But the man offered zero inspiration. The long nose poking out between strands of unwashed hair was one distraction, but he wore a sweater over a long-sleeved shirt even though it must have been seventy degrees outside and eighty in our tiny classroom. He spoke so softly that we kept asking him to speak up. What kind of Italian was he? All the other townspeople spoke so loudly that they could be heard from one end of Orvieto to the other.

Another problem was that we were dead tired. In my case, my roommate had worn me out. After sleeping all afternoon, Henrietta made it out to the living room, at which time she proceeded to talk, talk, talk. I came in from a pleasant walk to be bombarded by someone who had nothing to say but wouldn't stop saying it anyway. Yes, she was Italian American, so she wanted to learn some Italian, but who cared about learning the language when most people spoke English? She'd come to Italy to learn about fashion first-hand, but since we were stuck in a tiny little town, how could she learn anything at all?

I didn't mention that the tiny little town had a population of some twenty thousand and that the locals, as far as I had noticed so far, were better dressed than anybody I'd seen around Tucson. In terms of culture, food, language, and travel, my roommate was completely unprepared for a study abroad experience. She'd never studied

Italian, and any grammar that she'd learned in four years of high school French had evaporated before she left Arizona.

Meanwhile, by the time Aurelio reached the section on reflexives, I tuned out. He let us slip off a few minutes early, maybe because he couldn't handle any more mispronunciations on the same day. The others were going out for gelati, but gaining five pounds was not part of my summer mission, so I crossed the Piazza del Popolo and idly strolled down Corso Cavour, here peeking into a window, there sticking my nose into a store.

I found Enoteca Fabrizio by accident when I took a small side street instead of continuing down to the funicular. Orvieto was replete with specialty shops that sold local products, but they were outrageously expensive, such as fifteen euro for 500 milliliters of olive oil. I wasn't drawn in to this particular venue by the rows of cute wine bottles or olive oils or the packages of salami and cheeses. At the back of the shop, a door led to a sea of green.

Tentative, I stepped inside. To my left, a guy stretched his arms over the counter as if protecting it. His black, curly hair draped over a collared shirt with rolled-up sleeves. He smiled pleasantly, as if happy I interrupted his solitude. He was too close to my age to be intimidating, but I would have expected someone with his face and musculature to grace the cover of a fitness magazine.

"La posso aiutare?" The Italian sounded correct, but the accent was typically American. East coast.

I indicated the Bicocca expresso machine behind him. "Sure, you can help me. If I buy a coffee, can I sit on your patio?"

He jabbed his thumb towards the machine. "That piece of junk hasn't worked for a decade. Soda? Water? White wine?"

"Frizzante."

He whipped out a bottle of mineral water from the tall fridge beside him and handed it over.

"How did you know I spoke English?"

"Educated guess?"

"My accent gives me away. I know that."

I could sense his disappointment. "Your accent is fine, but you're not native. That's all. It's not a crime."

"Around here it might be!"

I hadn't spoken to enough townspeople to know, but I figured they were proud of their origins. "My last teacher came from Milan, so I suppose a distinctly Northern accent is worse."

"Certainly. Those Northerners can't be trusted."

I laughed. I suspected Italians everywhere were suspicious of other areas. "I take it that you didn't grow up here."

"Would you believe this is a summer job?"

"If that's what you tell me."

"That makes you easy in a good way."

We both laughed. He didn't take himself seriously enough to seem creepy. He held out his hand. "I'm Tony Bianco."

"Gina Campanello. Pleased to meet you."

"Same here. I'm running this place for my great uncle Fabrizio. He wanted my mom to come over and help him, but she's had some serious health problems lately. Since she wasn't available, I'm here instead."

Good old family expectations. I knew all about them. Sometimes they were helpful because they granted you a sense of purpose, but sometimes you couldn't escape from them.

"You were the most expendable family member," I said.

"That's right, although it doesn't sound nice when you say it like that." He grinned; he could both take it and dish it out, so we were already at ease with one another.

32

"I'm the most expendable too, but that stays between you and me," I said. "I'll never tell anybody."

"Let me guess. You're here for summer courses?"

Not fair. My backpack was a small one. "I'm that obvious, too?"

"You've been around here for a couple of days already."

What? Who would have paid attention to my comings and goings? I hadn't carried a paper map even though I'd checked my cell phone app a couple of times, so I shouldn't have been immediately obvious as a lost tourist. "Are you nosy or bored?"

He laughed, displaying white teeth that were perfectly straight. He had a black blemish under his chin as if an artist had lost track of the brush and left a dot in the wrong place. "Here on the hilltop, you notice people."

"The area isn't exactly tiny."

"True, but somehow you run into the same people again and again."

The phone rang from its perch on the wall behind him.

"Excuse me," he said as he stretched for the receiver.
"Of course."

"Enoteca Fabrizio," he said pleasantly. Then he frowned and returned the phone to its perch.

"A hangup?"

"Probably somebody who wanted to sell me wine. See how exciting it is around here?"

"I'd say it's relaxing."

"That's one opinion. What made you choose to study in Orvieto anyway?"

The question was simply that, a question rather than a judgement. I thought back to the study abroad fair, an overwhelming event where representatives of a hundred different programs shouted at us to come to their tables for glossy brochures and current information. I'd initially considered a program in Rome, but Lucia, who had flown over for the event, assured me I would love Orvieto so much that I would revisit the city again and again. It was quaint, it was safe, and the townspeople would help me learn the language. I might even fall in love. Lucia gave the example of an Orvieto boy who now worked at Roma Imports in Tucson. He'd met a University of Arizona student in Orvieto and followed her back to the States. Such things happened.

"Lucia sold me on the idea of a quiet town with zero crime."

"Gina, there's always crime. But here they don't shoot you. Maybe they steal some of your olive oil."

"Then I'm perfectly safe. I don't have any to steal!"

He pointed to some of his wares. "I can fix you right up."

"I probably can't afford anything."

"For the right bottle, no price is too high."

I pointed to a locked door behind him. "Is that why you keep the best bottles behind bars?"

He turned around. "Uncle is paranoid. And yes, you guessed it. Those are the very best bottles for the very best dinners."

"I only use olive oil on salads."

"You get the right brand, you can make anything taste good. Anything!"

"Does that mean the chefs with inferior olive oil get envious?"

"They sure do. You can't even imagine."

I couldn't. I didn't actually cook.

A woman in her forties or so entered the shop. Greens erupted from a plastic grocery bag, and she carried a cardboard bakery box in one hand. Presumably, she also needed a quality bottle of olive oil.

I pointed towards the back door that led to sunshine. "May I?"

"Of course."

"Thanks a lot!"

As the man wandered over to his customer, I scooted outside. The square space was too wild to be a garden. Filled with grassy weeds and rocks, it was bordered by tall stone buildings on three sides and a gate leading to tall trees on the fourth.

White plastic chairs were tipped against a white plastic table. I shook the dust off the closest chair and sat, content to take in the surroundings. Clotheslines stretched between a few of the windows, with sheets and underwear dotting the lines. A black and white cat emerged from an open window on what the Italians called the *primo piano*, the first floor up, used a shrub to make its way to the ground, and strolled through the grasses. Then it spotted me, or sensed me, and disappeared over the gate in a couple of jumps.

I took out my grammar book but didn't open it. In time I knew I would come to appreciate Orvieto's narrow streets and the close quarters, but now I longed for the spacious college campus I enjoyed back home. Even though the long distances between buildings could be inconvenient, the U of A offered wide open skies and the chance to breathe even during hundred-degree weather. Between a small classroom and smaller apartment, Orvieto hemmed me in. A borrowed garden was a perfect solution, and it didn't even cost much.

The smell of roasting olive oil wafted down from an open window. The irony finally struck me. In the States I was close to people in terms of feelings yet far from them physically; here I was close to them in proximity and far away in understanding. The contrast was interesting, but I wasn't sure I liked it.

"Mind if I join you?" The man had come out with his own bottle of sparkling water. "It's too quiet here in the afternoon."

I tipped back the closest chair, which he sat in. "Do you run this place by yourself?"

"Right now I sure do. But I wouldn't want to interrupt serious studying."

I tapped the closed book. "I'm sure you're more entertaining than verbs."

"But you've already studied Italian, right? You're not a beginner."

"I feel like one. Between mid-May and now I've forgotten more than I knew in the first place."

"Very funny. You're at the Centro Studi?"

"Exactly. I signed up for this ridiculous three-week class in which we're supposed to master second-semester Italian and stay sane at the same time."

"That's packing it in, but you'll manage."

"Let's hope. But tell me about your summer gig. Not everybody has the chance to come work for their Italian relatives."

"I keep trying to remind myself how lucky I am."

"You're not?"

"We'll see! And I did want to escape Hudson County for the summer. Anyway, try not to laugh, but I was hoping that being away would give me some clarity. My degree is pre-law, but I've got another year to go."

"I've got another semester, so we're almost in the same place. But here's the problem. You can't know whether or not you're going to like a profession until it's almost too late."

"I've noticed that. Meanwhile, I'm pushing the family olive oil for the summer."

"Your uncle makes his own products?"

"He owns the land, which has olive trees and grapevines. Somebody else produces the oil and the wine for him."

"I suppose his olive oil is better than what you can get at the grocery store?"

"It's three times more expensive, so let's hope it's twice as good."

"I'm no whiz, but are you sure that works out mathematically?"

"Not at all!"

I might have kept on procrastinating, but when a real customer came around and needed Tony's help, I finally opened my grammar book. It was high time to study irregulars.

*

An hour later I was plopping the book back into my bag when my new buddy came out to join me. He was even more handsome in softer light. His slender nose divided his face into perfect spheres while his brown eyes danced. He wore sharp dress pants and a complementary blue shirt with tiny white stripes. He sported a hint of cologne that reminded me of my favorite perfume, Giorgio, and a wristwatch with a black face and numerals the color of rose gold. I was sure he never dated women, but this didn't surprise me. I had a knack for making friends who would never, ever be interested in dating me.

"Done studying?"

"There's only so much I can do in a day," I said.

"Don't I know it? I learned Italian the easy way thanks to my grandparents. My grammar is messed up, but people understand me."

"You have the summer to brush up."

"How can I? Day after day, the conversations I have are about wine and olive oil!"

"That does seem limiting. But tell me this. No offense, but there are a lot of shops like yours. How do you stay in business with so much competition? I mean, you'd have to sell an awful lot of wine. Or maybe you do?"

"So-so. We make more profit on the olive oil. People around here are picky about the ingredients they use in their kitchens."

"No Pompeian?" It wasn't the cheapest brand available in Tucson, but it was on the lower end.

"No Bertolli either! But to answer your question, we have loyal customers, the kind who order a case ahead of time. That's the trick. That's how Uncle has managed to stay in business over the years. His products have a solid reputation."

"Even so, I wouldn't want to pay fifteen euro for a small bottle."

"I guess you wouldn't call yourself a gourmet."

"Let's put it this way. I never cook, and what I really like is popcorn."

"Hmm. Not a particular delicacy in Orvieto. The one movie house? Awful popcorn. Three days old. Don't even try it."

"I'll have to suffer and eat pasta instead. Could be worse."

"Sure could." He looked at his watch. "Say —"

"Closing time."

"If you don't mind."

We both stood.

"It IS your shop," I said, "at least for the summer. You should get to leave whenever you want to."

He held out his hand, and we shook.

"It was nice talking to you," he said. "Come back any time."

I indicated the garden. "Mind if I make this my summer library?"

"I'd like that."

"In that case, *a domani.*" *Until tomorrow.*

After Tony escorted me to the door, I headed back out to Corso Cavour. Even if I had a teacher so boring he would put his own mother to sleep and a roommate who didn't know an adjective from a refrigerator, at least I'd made a friend.

Chapter Six

I barely panted as I trailed the other students up the last steps of the Torre del Moro. The tower marked the practical center of town because it was at the crossroads of Orvieto's two main streets. No wonder so many tourists were inspired to climb the two hundred and forty steps to reach the top.

"Definitely not worth the view," said Henrietta, who gasped for air. She pushed two other students out of the way so she could sit on the stone ridge that lined the inner square of the observation desk. She used the sleeves of her flowing floral blouse to fan herself and the rest of us, too.

Although I disagreed about the view, I kept quiet. I'd attempted to elude her all morning, but she trailed me through the Belvedere Temple and the Etruscan Necropolis. She clung to me who knew limited Italian because she feared being questioned by an actual Italian whose simplest question would scare her worse than a slasher movie. As it was, our guide's meager English was half undecipherable, but I gathered the basics: an indigenous population called the Etruscans ruled the area for about a thousand years before succumbing to the Roman armies from the South. The tower builders lived in connected city-states. Polytheists, they adapted Greek letters to write their language, which most scholars considered pre-Indo-European.

I scooted away from Henrietta long enough to peer over the ledge of the medieval tower and orient myself. Via del Duomo led up to the Cathedral. Corso Cavour headed down to the funicular. Via della Cava led out of town. Those three streets would take me close to anywhere I needed to go in Orvieto. If I got lost, all I had to do was head for this intersection until I found my way again.

Next I focused on details: laundry swaying from rooftops, school kids playing on a basketball court, flowers drooping from windowsills. Now that summer had emerged from its winter cocoon, leaves budded green. Olive trees pushed towards the sky. Townspeople shifted to summer clothing.

My mission was not simple tourism. I was completing an assignment. Aurelio was as dull as a cancelled TV show in the classroom, but the activity he assigned us as homework was a clever one. Our task was to interact with native speakers and then write up our conversations.

I approached my first potential language victims, but they spoke some language I couldn't understand. I chose my second set more carefully after spotting a couple with an Italian-language guidebook to Umbria. I waited for a prime moment: when they needed a photographer to take their picture in front of the tower's huge bronze bell.

After I took three perfect shots, I considered them fair game. I practiced as many logical questions as I could think of. Why were they in town? They had chosen to explore the wonders of Umbria for their week-long vacation. The night before they'd stayed in Rasiglia. Hadn't I heard of that place? I couldn't even pronounce it. For my information, the nearby town dotted with aqueducts was quite worthwhile as long as I had my own vehicle. I didn't mention my sad state of being reduced to public transport. No matter. Language practice was my goal. With my next set of victims, I zipped through the same questions more smoothly. I might have even sounded confident.

I discovered an extra bonus that accompanied language practice. As long as I was babbling in Italian, I didn't have to ditch Henrietta. She was careful to stay away.

*

When I walked into the enoteca, Tony winked, but he was tied up with an American couple making a large and complicated purchase. They had bought so many bottles of olive oil that Tony had rustled up a box for them to cart everything away.

I went straight through to the garden. I told myself that I would type up notes from my dialogues without procrastinating, but I couldn't bring myself to begin the task. It was too pleasant an afternoon to do anything other than to appreciate the greenery and the chirping birds. I also needed a mental rest. Rachel had hinted at the difficulties of crash-course language learning, but the reality had still punched me in the head. The process was exhausting.

Tony headed my way with a bottle of frizzante and two glasses of white wine, which he set on the table. "We're celebrating."

"That couple must really love your olive oil."

"They run a B&B down the hill. They sell a selection of local products, ours included."

"To the envy of your local competitors."

"You've got it."

When Tony picked up his glass, I mirrored him by picking up mine.

"Cheers," he said.

We clinked glasses.

"I don't usually —" I started.

" — drink wine so early in the day. I know. And I don't usually drink wine with customers, but you're not exactly a customer, are you? Of course, if you're throwing a dinner party this weekend, you might need a bottle or two."

"We'd be the only two partiers. I haven't met anyone else besides my fellow students."

"You wouldn't party with them?"

"I'm reserving judgement." I liked the two Mexican sisters who were tackling Italian 102 with me, but I wasn't sure they ever partied.

"The other students aren't friendly?"

"They're untraveled, so they're in shock that their apartments don't include AC and there's no Chipotle nearby."

Tony ran his fingers through his hair. "Wait till they run out of their Pantene Pro-V and can't buy it anywhere. They'll go nuts."

"Exactly. But if traveling were easy, it wouldn't be a challenge."

"That's why most Americans stay home. About half hold passports, and that's up from a few years ago. That's crazy, isn't it?"

"I can't imagine <u>not</u> traveling." To me the act was as natural as it was simple: throw all the wrong things in a suitcase, hop on a plane, stagger off jetlagged hours later, and absorb completely new experiences even though they overwhelm you.

"I'm not one to stay home either," Tony said. "For most people, leaving the country is too much of a change. I overhear tourists complaining all the time."

"By next week you'll be hearing my cohorts. They'll be piling the complaints on one after another."

I'd already heard grumblings. The plumbing in the apartments was too old. The linen provided by the landlords balled up. The towels were so scratchy they caused pimples.

"Why did your friends choose to study Italian?"

"Friends? We're not that tight, trust me. But to answer your question, they're mostly knocking out their language requirement. A few are part Italian, like me."

Tony tipped his glass in my direction. "Terrific. Where are your relatives from?"

"Would you believe I'm not sure?" I sipped the wine, which was tart and fruity.

"Your grandparents already passed?"

"They're in Upstate New York somewhere. My dad left my mom years ago. That made him the black sheep of both families. I don't see his relatives, and he doesn't either."

My phone buzzed; I checked the +31 number, which was the code for the Netherlands, and ignored it.

"You probably have cousins over here, right?" Tony asked.

"I guess. I'm not sure."

"Try Facebook. Italians love it. Then you can invite them to Orvieto for one big party."

"And buy lots of your wine!"

"Exactly."

My phone buzzed again. I pretended not to hear it. "Given your uncle, you must have quite a few relatives around here yourself."

"My uncle is a blacker sheep than your father is."

"Wow. That's hard to do. Did he marry the wrong woman?"

"Worse than that. He didn't marry! Seriously, I suspect there's a property issue. As soon as somebody dies around here, the vultures come out to lay claims. Fabrizio doesn't talk to any of his cousins, so I'm sure something went sideways."

"He won't tell you what happened?"

"Are you kidding? He clams up when it comes to the farm, and now that he's on the road, forget it. Since he has a dumb phone, he sends one-word texts such as 'totals?'"

I couldn't remember the last time I'd seen a flip phone. Even my grandmother was on her second Jitterbug by now.

My phone buzzed a third time.

"Aren't you going to answer?"

I turned off the offending apparatus and set it down between us. "I'm busy talking to you."

"You could text and say you'll call later."

"I could."

"Boyfriend?"

"I don't do men anymore."

"Girlfriend?"

"Not interested. Okay, full disclosure, there's a guy who wants to be my boyfriend."

"That sounds like a story. Should I get more wine?"

Tony popped up before I could stop him. Then I decided I didn't need to stop him anyway.

I settled back into the chair. Why shouldn't I spill my guts? It was a travel phenomenon to tell strangers more than you shared with your closest friends. Tony wasn't exactly a stranger, but he didn't know me well enough to have preconceptions. If I felt too embarrassed afterwards about what I told him, I never had to return to his shop.

He brought out the wine bottle, poured me a half an inch, and poured himself a second glass. "Let's hear it."

"I'm not sure my little story is worth this much wine."

"I'm living vicariously. The more pathetic the better."

"I don't want to bore you."

"Trust me. I need this."

Tony seemed to have an answer for everything, but he was so cheerful that I didn't mind. He counterbalanced my fellow students, who didn't have any answers at all.

"Have you ever been hung up on someone only to find out they aren't hung up on you?" I asked.

"Hasn't everyone?"

"Good point. Probably. Anyway, last summer I made a fool out of myself over a guy named Vlinder."

"What kind of name is that?"

"A nickname. Dutch. Never mind. He wasn't interested because, guess what, he doesn't do women. Meanwhile, his brother is convinced that I'm the perfect partner for him."

"Unfortunately, the brother doesn't turn you on."

I shrugged.

"You don't like Holland?"

I shrugged again.

"Ah. Let me see if I got this right. You've never met the brother or been to Holland, yet this poor man is convinced you're the one."

"Something ridiculous like that."

Tony's face lit up. "I'm fond of ridiculous. Good looking, or you don't know?"

"We've WhatsApped a few times. He looks like his brother. So, yes. Good looking. Blond. Tall. Blue eyes."

"Homeless? Jobless?"

"He lives with his parents, but he works at a bank. I suppose that's responsible."

Tony nodded. "In Europe it's normal for young people to live with their parents, and he's probably not a creep looking for a Sugar Mama. So what's the big deal? Invite him down to Orvieto."

"While I'm working my butt off to learn Italian?"

"Flirting with Italian men would be better, but why not take a chance? If he's as interested in you as you say, he'd make the time to come down."

"He already offered."

Tony snatched up my phone. I jumped to my feet to reach for it. "No, you don't!"

Tony waltzed out of my reach. "I want to help you."

"You think I'm that desperate?"

He waltzed back. "Desperate? No. Fearful, yes. Cautious? Also, yes. But sometimes it's smart to take a chance."

"You just suggested I find a nice Italian boy instead."

"In theory that's true, but what's important is why someone is interested."

Tony had a point. At least Sander Van de Velde knew enough about me to be intrigued for the right reasons. He would have heard stories from his brother, whom I'd made friends with the summer before. He knew I was passionate when I had a just cause. He'd seen pictures, so he also knew I was average height, that my eyes were blue, and that I was such a sharp dresser that almost everything I wore came from Target.

"A guy from Holland is probably trustworthy," Tony added. "That's always a plus."

"Are men ever trustworthy? Besides you, I mean."

"Well, well, aren't you the gal who's been around the block?"

We laughed. Then toasted. Then I let Tony top off my glass. After all, I wasn't driving home. I wasn't even taking public transport. By the time we finished the bottle, I was ready to consider extending an invitation to a Dutchman I'd never met.

I wasn't ready to promise it.

Chapter Seven

Although the ten-feet high wooden giraffes in the mini-courtyard of Caffè Montanucci delighted me, I couldn't say the same about the company. My nine fellow students and I had spent the morning touring the famous Duomo with the Signorelli frescoes in exhausting detail followed by an equally thorough and very chilly tour of Orvieto Underground, which showcased Etruscan strongholds beneath the city. These highlights were topped by a complimentary lunch aimed to help us become better acquainted while we practiced Italian.

At least that was the program's intent. Every time Lucia turned her back, the group switched back to English, as if it were some cool, secret language that we could understand but she couldn't. Our supervisor wasn't unpleasant, but she played up being an authority figure. The others were wary of her, especially the students in Italian 101.

Those poor students were in over their heads. They were scared to attempt a word in Italian, let alone a full question. They didn't strike me as go-getters anyway, but no one warned them that completing a semester of college-level language in three weeks was a Herculean feat that could only be managed by linguists who already understood the basics about language patterns.

None of the beginners fit that category. Henrietta's classmates included a trio of sorority girls who had come to flirt with every passing man and a frat boy so dense he'd spent his first night in town WhatsApping us that he couldn't unlock the door to get out of his apartment and asking us to help him. Three hours later, he wrote back asking for help to get back in. He'd awakened two sets of neighbors, and they'd hurried over, clad in their pajamas, to bail him out so that they could get back to bed.

My own cohort was a mixed bag. I liked Becky and Michelle, the studious Mexican sisters, but Armando and Lalo were loudmouth buddies who had chosen to study Italian because they assumed the sexy language would help them land dates. They'd gotten through Italian 101 thanks to home Spanish, but after a day of Italian 102, they were more lost than three-year-olds at an amusement park.

When Lucia went across the room to greet a friend, Henrietta bent towards us conspiratorially. "When are your boyfriends coming to visit?"

"Mine is applying to med school as we speak," said Nancy. "He's coming in a few days."

"Mine is finishing grad school," said Julie. "He's coming next week."

Becky looked up from the menu. She'd probably memorized all the new vocabulary words by now. "You'd better warn them that the hotels around here cost a fortune."

Julie reeled back so fast her long brown hair slapped against the chair. "As if! He's staying with Nancy and Christie and me."

At this I looked up sharply. We'd been told that overnight guests were not, not, not allowed in our apartments, and anyone who violated that policy would be sent back to Arizona.

Michelle glanced up from her menu. "I thought—"

"We're taking turns," Christie said. "First Nancy's boyfriend, then Julie's, then mine. You see, we have it all worked out."

Becky rapped on the table. "We're not allowed to have guests."

"Lucia doesn't have to know everything," Julie said. "We've got everything perfectly arranged."

The setup sounded perfect, all right, if you were hoping for a disaster. First there were the logistics. Lucia knew everybody in town, so she'd find out about shenanigans one way or another. The next problem was that the girls assumed Italy would mean romantic nights of lovemaking, but their boyfriends might well be distracted by smart, well-dressed Italian women, that is, if they got over jetlag.

I could play the fantasy game too. I wasn't opposed to seeing Sander Van de Velde in person; I was opposed to falling for him. A few months earlier, he'd contacted me with the pretext of asking questions of a "typical American" for a master's degree class he was taking on U.S. economics. After ten minutes in which I admitted to not knowing a single useful thing about the economy, we spent an hour chatting about our studies and upcoming weekend plans. A couple of weeks later, he called with extra questions, and we talked for twice as long.

I'd enjoyed our sessions. Who minded a video chat with a handsome blond with an unending smile? His blue eyes sparkled, he asked interesting questions, and he made me laugh. As soon as I mentioned signing up for a study abroad program, however, he wanted to know when he could visit. Italy was a lot closer than the U.S., so he could hop down for a weekend without any trouble. If we found out that we couldn't stand one another, he'd hop right back.

I had carefully refused to commit. I gave the excuses that I wasn't sure what the program would be like or if Orvieto would be a nice town. I also wasn't sure how much spare time I would have, and it would be silly for him to travel all that distance to watch me do homework all weekend.

For the last two weeks, he'd texted me frequently because he wanted to buy a plane ticket.

"When is your boyfriend coming?" Nancy asked Henrietta.

My roommate stuffed a morsel of pizza crust into her mouth and chewed it exaggeratedly as if to show she had good teeth. Then she pointed at me. "We haven't had time to talk to about it, but I'm sure we can work things out. I can get him to come whenever it's convenient to me."

"He doesn't work?" joked Lalo.

"He works for his dad. He can get away with just about everything."

"That's a good job," said Armando.

"The best! But come on, Gina. What do you think? Honestly, I can design my whole schedule around you. It's no problem at all."

Sander's texts were barbs under my skin. Tony's advice was a bad angel sitting on my shoulder. But the pressure from my crazy ditz of a roommate pushed me into the Grand Canyon. Social crap invaded my system while warped worries about judgement ricocheted around my brain cells until they were soggy.

I gave into a moment of insanity. "My boyfriend is flexible too. He lives in Holland, so it's easy for him. He was hoping to come soon, but I explained that I needed to coordinate with you first."

I did it. I made the invitation public to a crowd I didn't even like. Unbelievable. But that's what drove progress, sometimes, those moments you could never understand or explain that made you leap from a tree like a carefree squirrel without noticing there weren't any sturdy branches below you.

"We haven't had much chance to talk," Henrietta explained to the others. "I've been sleeping at the funniest times."

She'd been sleeping all the time except for when I wanted to go to bed myself and didn't want to get roped into a conversation with her, but I didn't bother to mention that.

"I could ask him to come later," I said, "if that's totally more convenient. But I wouldn't want to get in your way or anything like that."

"Tell him to come soon," Henrietta said. "I'll have my boyfriend come after. We'll have so much fun!"

"What did you say about boyfriends?" Lucia asked, suddenly joining us.

The others were startled into silence, but I lived with my grandmother. I could fib on demand.

"We're thankful for zoom," I said. "That makes it easy to keep in touch with all our friends back home."

"Why, you are right!" Lucia exclaimed as if I were a genius. "That is something we must be so thankful for. Now, no one is still hungry? Then I will ask for the bill."

As soon as she left, Henrietta and the sorority girls giggled.

My smile, however, was pure show. I had no idea what I was going to tell Sander.

*

Tony poured me a second prosecco to shamelessly encourage my babbling. Luckily, we were in the garden, so he was the only one who was listening.

I flicked an ant off the table before it could approach me. "You should have heard me. First, I claimed I had a boyfriend. Second, I claimed he wanted to come as soon as possible."

"He does want to come as soon as possible."

"That's beside the point. I'm not sure I want him to! But I couldn't help myself. All the others were so smug that I fell into their trap. I blurted everything out. What do I care what those guys think? My love life is none of their business."

Tony pressed my hands around the glass. "Breathe. Drink. Relax."

"But I can't believe I—"

He tightened his grip around my hands.

"I was ridiculous. Trying to keep up with them! Trying to be them! I don't even like them!"

"You had a normal reaction."

"It was the very stupidest thing I've done this whole summer."

Tony released me and sat back against the chair. "You haven't actually done anything yet. You could totally say your friend was coming and then make up some excuse about why he couldn't."

"True enough. Why would I consider extending an invitation anyway? My mission is to squeeze in a semester of Italian. That's it. My reaction is still inexplicable, even to me."

Tony refilled his own glass with frizzante, which was what I should have been drinking too. "Why are you so scared?"

I might have blushed. That was the problem with true friends. They let you ramble like a dog without a leash before calling you back to reality with one quick kick in the butt.

"I'm not scared."

"Sure, you are. But why?"

"I'm practical. That's all. Sander hasn't met me in person. If we don't hit it off, then we'll have a miserable weekend together. Who comes all the way to Europe to have a bad time?"

"If he's that bad, you can pass him off to me. That would be a win-win situation. We'd both thank you for it. Wait and see."

"Thanks."

"I'm not kidding. After all, what's the worst that can happen?"

I polished off my prosecco. I'd have to wobble home, careful not to trip over cobblestones. "If things are a disaster, you'll have to bail me out."

He patted my hand. "I would be happy to do that. But enough about Sander, no Sander, Sander, no Sander. Can we talk about me for a minute?"

"I'm so sorry! What's up?"

Tony leaned back and laughed so hard he nearly fell off his chair, which might have served him right. "Don't worry. It was just a test."

Very funny. But when I blocked out Henrietta long enough to study vocabulary that night, I didn't get anywhere at all. To invite or not to invite.

There were probably about eighty-nine ways an invitation could go wrong.

Chapter Eight

After class I skipped down to the enoteca, where Tony was dusting off a couple of cardboard boxes. Instead of his usual stylish choices, he wore old jeans and a faded white T-shirt with a Ferris wheel logo. I wondered how badly he needed to do laundry except that he also wore flipflops, suggesting that the casual look was deliberate.

"Tony, what's up?" He'd sent an SMS asking me to drop by as soon as I got out of class.

He straightened up as if I'd spooked him. He touched the lower part of his chin. "Toothache. Bad one. I have a dentist appointment in half an hour."

"Do you have some kind of infection?"

"I don't think so. Last night I cracked a filling when I was eating a piece of bread."

"What? If your bread was that old, you should have thrown it out."

"Don't I know it? But now I need help. I begged the receptionist to work me in."

Problems did flare up at the worst possible times. I crossed my fingers that my summer vocabulary wouldn't include "cavity" or "root canal."

I glanced at the shiny rows of olive oil. "You're letting me run the store for you? Super."

I could hardly wait to take Tony's place behind the counter. I loved being in charge. I could tell tourists that Tony's uncle's olive oil was the best in town and pretend I knew so from experience. I could explain all about cold-pressed olives and regurgitate everything I'd learned from Tony.

"I wish it were that easy," he said. "But this is Italy, and Italy loves bureaucracy. Or somebody does. Here's the problem. You can't run the shop for me because you're not an official employee."

"Why can't I volunteer for a few hours? You don't have to pay me or anything."

"You're not on the employee list."

"Who says there's a list?"

"The government. You should have seen the paperwork my uncle had to go through to get me on the books."

"Why does the government care if you happen to be an employee or not?"

"It's about social security. If you're an employee, you have to receive contributions. Hand me another rag?"

I snatched one from the counter and handed it over. "That's a bit crazy."

Tony started dusting again. "Maybe it protects people in the long run, but it's not practical."

I indicated the empty street outside. "If you left me alone running the shop for an hour, who would even notice?"

"Probably nobody. But the government sends people around to check, and you have to produce the paperwork on the spot."

"Wow. They pay people for that?"

Tony gave the boxes a final whack. "Crazy, right? Never mind. That's the system, like it or not."

I refused to accept an easy explanation. "What if you need to run an errand but don't have another employee?"

"You can either leave your door open and hope nobody steals anything or close up for a few minutes."

"That's a lose-lose situation."

"Don't I know it? Look, there are plenty of things I love about Italy, but there are a dozen things I don't care for. Maybe two dozen. Never mind. That's not why I contacted you."

Tony scooted the boxes together. "Signore Baldoni wants a case of reds along with his regular order of olive oil. He'll stop by this afternoon for them or send his son."

"You need me to hand over the merchandise. That's easy enough."

"Exactly. If I had time, I'd deliver it myself, but never mind. Anyway, I'm not sure exactly what time he's coming."

"But you have to pretend to be closed."

"You catch on fast! If you're here long enough, I'll ask my uncle to make you an employee."

"Very funny. I'm not sure I'd even be worth the paperwork."

"Nobody is! The rule is completely silly, but I can't do anything about it. Anyway, you don't mind hanging around for a while?"

"Not at all. But will this Baldoni guy text when he's on his way? In that case I can hang out in the garden."

"Yes. I explained I might be closed, so he knows to knock loudly."

I patted the boxes. "One more detail. What do they owe you?"

"They already paid."

"Darn! I was going to grab the cash and hop down to Rome for the evening. Night clubs are expensive."

Tony laughed. "I was worried about that!"

"Seriously, why didn't you just tell the guy to come tomorrow instead?"

And risk a sale?"

Oh, right. In a competitive market, each sale counted. I glanced over the rows of wine bottles, the shelves of olive oils, and the cheeses. The idea of running a little shop was romantic, but I wouldn't want to be chained to such a place.

"Where did you say your uncle went?"

"*Boh.* Somewhere in Italy."

"You don't know?"

"Italians either go to the mountains or the beach. He went to one or the other."

"That narrows things down. Maybe your uncle went off to find himself."

"He went to find something!"

Around the corner, a church bell chimed.

"Listen, I have to go," Tony said. "If I'm not close to on time, they'll cancel my appointment, and we don't want that."

"Not at all. But speaking of which, kind of, in case you're gone for a while, I don't suppose you have a bathroom I could use?"

"Right!" He wiggled a metal key from his pocket and walked me to a door behind the counter, which opened to a hallway that culminated in a set of stairs. "The apartment is above the shop. Make yourself at home. The place isn't much to look at, but please help yourself to drinks and stuff."

"Will do. Good luck with the tooth."

"Thanks. I'll need it."

I was glad we didn't have to switch places. Dentist visits could be treacherous. I knew that first-hand. I had three fillings so big that the hygienist, always an optimist, constantly warned me that they would someday require crowns.

*

Even though the afternoon turned chilly and the clouds threatened rain, I stubbornly remained in the garden. I was glad to help Tony out; he'd listened to all my petty complaints without showing signs of fatigue and plied me with prosecco. I owed him this much. And I loved the garden. I'd never realized how much I appreciated outside space. Then again, I'd never lived in an apartment. Now I never wanted to. Living in just a couple of rooms was impossibly constrictive. How could you think clearly in a place where you were bombarded by your own possessions twenty-four-seven? I couldn't even stay out of snacks I hid across the room.

Of course, it wouldn't help to have a house with a garden in a place that suffered winters. I would need to find a job in Tucson or maybe California.

I heard a bang on the door and ran through the enoteca to open it.

A bald man with a face as wide as a pumpkin pushed his way inside. He might have been forty, but he was stooped. *"Chi sei?"* Who are you? His tone was accusatory.

"Mi dispiace, ma —"

"Dame la roba per Vittorio." Give me Vittorio's stuff.

The man had cut me right off. He might have stopped to realize that I was doing him a favor, but instead he pushed past me. He uttered a few sentences I couldn't understand before picking up the case of wine, which he struggled with, and heading back outside. I followed with the box of olive oil.

No wonder the man was in a hurry. He'd left his white sedan running, blocking the narrow street. He situated the wine and showed me where to place the olive oil. Then he slammed the trunk shut, inserted himself into the driver's seat, and took off.

"Mille grazie," I said even though he didn't hear it and I didn't mean it. A thousand thanks for someone to be so rude to me? *Mamma mia.*

I re-entered the enoteca and locked the door behind me. Now would be a good time to study. But first, perhaps a snack. I followed the stairs up to a small wooden door. At first I thought Tony had given me the wrong key, but when I jiggled it more vigorously, the lock gave way.

I loved entering unfamiliar living rooms. It was fascinating to see how people organized their lives, especially when you hadn't met them. Fabrizio's rectangular space featured an ancient green couch and matching armchair that faced an entertainment center with a wide TV screen. Two empty ashtrays, a small notebook, and a pen graced a low coffee table. Photographs on the walls presumably included Fabrizio as a teen, Fabrizio in the army, Fabrizio in Times Square, and an older Fabrizio with even older relatives.

I was ready to inspect the kitchen when I heard a car pull up outside the shop. Too late! Closed for Italian authorities!

The doorbell rang. I jumped at the exaggerated sound. Only a deaf person needed a warning that obnoxious.

Then the bell rang again. But I wasn't Tony, let alone Fabrizio, and I wasn't expecting any visitors.

Then the bell rang six or seven times in a row. I put my index fingers in my ears. I didn't dare press the intercom button. Whoever it was, I couldn't help them anyway. Instead, I ran over to the window. I couldn't stick my head out without giving myself away, but I could angle myself enough to view the street below.

Two men stood outside beside a white Fiat. Both had white shirts, one short-sleeved, one long-sleeved. They spoke in quick, soft sentences amongst themselves, and each jangled a set of keys. *Oddio.* What if I'd given the merchandise to the wrong person? No. Mr. Grump knew exactly what he was coming for.

That left me with two unhappy men. Obviously, the shop was closed. Why wouldn't they go away? Instead, they fumbled with keys. Evidently, they intended to enter the enoteca. Suppliers or thieves?

I needed to create a distraction. I dialed +113, which I thought was the Italian emergency number. Nothing.

Think!

I tried +114. Not that either.

+112. Bingo. A woman rattled off questions, but I was too nervous to catch them.

"Uomo ruba negozio, Via Manzoni e Corso Cavour." Man *robs store, Manzoni and Cavour Streets,* I declared in garbled Italian. Then I hung up, irritated with my rudimentary words. Couldn't be helped. Only a foreigner who was a

true pessimist would have learned the phrase for "crime in progress."

Anyway, what would a couple of troublemakers want? A cheese wheel?

Too much trouble. They'd be after cash instead. I stole downstairs as quietly as possible and entered the enoteca. I opened the register, which made a dangerously loud binging sound, and grabbed fifty- and hundred-euro bills as I heard the sound of a key working the lock. I dashed back to the hallway and bolted the door behind me. I was running back upstairs when I heard sirens. Then I heard a car door slam as a vehicle screeched off down the street.

I looked out the bedroom window as a police car sauntered down the street with flashing lights. It came to a halt at the intersection of Corso Cavour and Manzoni Street. A couple of officers got out of the car and walked up and down the street barking questions such as, "Who's there?"

Nobody answered.

Mentally, I patted myself on the back. I'd managed to scare off a couple of guys without getting involved with the authorities, who might have asked pesky questions about who I was and why I had a key to someone's apartment.

Who needed that?

Chapter Nine

Tony stroked the side of his swollen jaw while I nestled myself deeper into Fabrizio's armchair. My poor friend looked like a chipmunk that spent all day chewing on one side of its mouth.

"You risked your life for the cash in the drawer," he said. "That didn't seem crazy?"

"I didn't think. I reacted. I was mad, to tell you the truth. If you have to steal from somebody, chose somebody rich, somebody who won't even notice."

"True, but protecting me wasn't your job. All you had to do was hand over the wine and the olive oil."

"That went great. Then there were those other guys."

I'd already thought through the scenario a hundred times, but my conclusion was always the same. The robbery attempt wasn't random. The men had targeted Fabrizio's enoteca. "You have to figure out why your uncle would be a target."

"What do you mean?"

"You don't just drive up to some building and think, wow, let's try our luck at getting into this one. They had keys that worked in the lock."

"Crime has increased around here."

Tony was in denial. I understood the problem, but I couldn't let him give in to it.

"Listen, Tony. Face up to what happened here. This was a deliberate attack by two jerks who assumed they knew what they were doing. They rang the bell long enough to convince themselves that Fabrizio wasn't around and proceeded to try the door. They had a plan. They were after your uncle."

"Nah. Everybody loves him."

I considered turning on the voice recorder app on my cell phone so that Tony could hear himself afterwards.

"Or they were after you," I said.

"Me? That's even crazier."

Tony shrank back. I'd caught him off guard with a logical point that he didn't want to admit to.

This was understandable. Since he was new in town, he didn't know how things worked. He might have offended someone without knowing it. His uncle might have forgotten to warn him about certain customers or neighbors. That made him vulnerable.

Or there might have been something more personal. "Have you dated anybody?"

"I told you. I've sworn off men," Tony said.

"Uh huh. But you didn't swear off glancing at them if they came your way. Couldn't you have insulted someone without trying to?"

"I guess? Anybody can do that."

"You haven't made friends here?"

"No, but Fabrizio introduced me to some of his."

"Spent any evenings in bars?"

"Maybe one or two."

According to Lucia, they were the most dangerous places in all of Italy.

"Try to think of anything that seemed off," I said.

"What are you, a lawyer hoping to trip me up on my own words? If I'd had time to go look for trouble, I'd be happy to admit it. Instead, I've been too tired."

"Tony, I'm on your side here, but I need you to understand that what happened today was not natural. Think of the situation like a car tire that needs air. You can ignore it all you want to, but at some point, the tire goes flat, and you wind up on foot."

Tony wasn't convinced, but I knew well enough that problems never got up and left of their own accord. You had to shovel them out of the garden.

"Maybe I need better locks," Tony said.

Finally, a hint that I might somehow be exactly right.

"That would be a good place to start. The other good place to start would be figuring out more about your uncle."

"What's to figure? He's a great guy."

"You keep saying that. Proof?"

"What do you need? When I came in from the States, he picked me up at Fiumicino."

"Yes, yes, he fetched you from the airport outside Rome. Nice gesture, but it was the least he could do."

"For the next two weeks he took me everywhere in town. He taught me which bakery to use. Which butcher to buy meat from. Which coffee shop had honest baristas."

I hated delivering bad news, but when I smelled a rat, I knew to keep looking around for a tail. "I'm glad you found the perfect tour guide, but there's something you've got to remember. Everyone has a dark side. Even your uncle."

"You're wrong. He's a quiet guy. Nothing special. A little boring, really. He's got his shop, he's got his soccer team, he's got his card games, and, well, that's all, really."

I pointed in the direction of the bedroom. "There must be information right here in this apartment. Look through his drawers. Check out old letters, you know? That kind of thing."

"Not even old people write letters anymore."

He was right. My mother herself had "progressed" to texts, which she mostly dictated.

"Something weird is going on," I said. "Believe me or not."

"I'll trust you when I have proof."

Your burglary, I wanted to say, but I stopped myself in time. "Look, be careful, all right? That's all I'm asking of you."

He stroked his chin again, but he grimaced. Maybe he needed to take another painkiller. "I appreciate your help. Really. But you're wrong about Uncle, all right? Never mind about him. I'm a good judge of character. If there had been a problem, I would have picked up on it."

"If you insist."

"I do. And listen, as a little thanks, I wanted to take you out for dinner tonight, but my mouth hurts too much for me to eat anything. I'd be happy to take you out, though."

"Aren't you worried about leaving the apartment?"

"No."

"You don't think your little friends will return? It's not like the police are posted outside your door."

"They won't come back. They're too chicken shit."

While I agreed with Tony in theory, in his place I wouldn't have felt so optimistic. On the other hand, self-ishly, I felt a little spooked. Or maybe intimidated.

"I'll tell you what. In lieu of dinner, I'd be happy to settle for a drink," I said. "Can I talk you into going to a café?"

"You're on. That's always the best solution anyway."

I popped up. "Then let's get out of here."

Tony held out his hand, and I pulled him to his feet.

"Can you find your keys in the dark?" I asked.

"No need." We crossed the room, and he showed me how he'd left his key in the lock.

"Smart," I said.

"Helpful. If the key is right here, I can't get locked in."

I laughed. I'd told him all about my classmate Dennis and his pleas on WhatsApp.

"Have any place in mind?" I asked as I tripped down the stairs.

He checked his watch. "Piazza del Popolo. When it comes to people watching, that's always the best spot."

Great idea. I wanted to do some people watching my-self. But mostly I wanted to watch for Fabrizio's enemies.

I knew he had some.

*

We ambled down the main drag and took a right after the clock tower. The Piazza del Popolo was a huge rectangle that stretched several blocks. A tall stone government building divided the space in two, but its heart was the west end, where two cafés looked out at two fancy restaurants, the kind that used tablecloths and charged more for less. By day, the piazza was filled with parked cars, but by evening the vehicles melted away and the townspeople emerged.

The square was comfortable because it was slightly off the main drag, which meant it was easy to reach, but few tourists noticed it. Here the Orvietani came to hang out with one another and kick back after a long day of explaining to people which way to go to find the Cathedral. I'd crisscrossed the space bunches of times in my hurry to get to and from class.

Tony led me to the Palace Cafè, the establishment that hugged the walls of the government building. During the day, its several umbrellas protected customers from the bright summer rays, but by now the sun had disappeared, and the umbrellas were closed. Relief filled the space.

"Choose a table," Tony said.

Two were vacant. I chose one that jutted into the square. Pedestrians walked back and forth, but by now, their pace had slowed. No one was late for work or school. The few locals who weren't home preparing dinner had come to relax.

Tony returned empty-handed.

"Forget your wallet?" I reached for my purse. "It's my turn. You keep giving me prosecco."

"No, no," Tony said. "I ordered. They'll bring stuff out."

I sat back, wondering if I would ever get used to having people serve me things as opposed to simply going up and getting them myself. Probably not. The process was inefficient, which was part of its charm. The back and forth.

The forced waiting. Having to take a moment's pause when I wasn't used to doing so.

A teen with purple-tipped hair braids brought out a tray with two bright orange drinks and a bowl of peanuts.

"*Ecco, Tonio,*" she said.

Tony thanked the server as if he'd known her all his life, winked at me, and held up his glass. "*Salute!*"

We toasted, making loud clinking sounds.

I tasted the sweet, smooth liquid and set down the glass. "*Salute* to you, too. But I thought we were having a coffee."

"Too boring. Ever heard of a Crodino?"

"This orange stuff? No."

"Might be hard to find in Arizona. Anyway, we're having Crodini. Or if you don't like it, I'll drink yours and get you something else."

"I'm glad to try something new. But should you be drinking when you're on painkillers?"

Tony tapped his glass. "These are non-alcoholic."

I took another sip. "Even better. What's in these things?"

"Hmm. I have no idea. But if you're at a bar and want to avoid alcohol, this is the best alternative."

"Economical too, I presume."

"Exactly."

"Unlike those restaurants across from us, I suppose."

"True." He pointed to a brightly lit restaurant across the piazza. "Il Capitano is a modern place with a young female chef who isn't afraid to try new combinations."

"I thought everyone was old-fashioned around here. That's what Lucia says. People have their traditions, and they stick to them no matter what."

"That's almost always the case. There's nothing more important around here than good old family loyalty, for example."

"And customer loyalty! I hope that modern chef uses your uncle's olive oil."

"She does! Her assistant bought seven liters on Tuesday."

"In that case, I might splurge and have dinner there sometime. What about the place next to it?"

"Mamma Angela is a decent too, even though they don't buy supplies from us."

"What? What's the matter with them?"

"They've been in business longer than my uncle has, so they're forgiven."

"Good excuse. How's their food?"

"They're great with *cinghiale*."

"You expect me to eat boar's meat?"

Tony laughed. "It's a little tough! But it's a local specialty."

"Eating it would make me feel prehistoric. Or I might go wild and attack — wait, what do wild boars eat?"

"Anything they can get."

"Okay. I might go really crazy and attack ducks or something."

Tony crossed his legs, accidentally bumping the table in the process. "It's a good thing I'm not hungry tonight. With that kind of attitude, I can't take you anywhere at all!"

I pointed vaguely in the direction of the funicular. "I suppose there are restaurants down below the hill as well."

"In Orvieto Scalo? Sure. Lots of them."

"We could pop down there and eat incognito."

"We might have to. Otherwise, you'd sabotage my business."

"I'd try, but I've got too much homework."

We both laughed.

"Seriously," I said, "I'm happy just to be outside." The evening air hovered around seventy, which was a relief from the ninety-degree weather I'd been experiencing back in Tucson. "Back home it's already hot, which is only convenient if you're next to a swimming pool."

"Uncle says that the townspeople wait all winter for the chance to be outdoors."

"Ciao, Tony," said an older man as he passed by. He waved at us brightly.

Tony smiled as he waved back.

"Who was that?"

Tony watched the man disappear across the piazza. "That's the butcher who works at Caponeri. Or maybe he owns it."

"You buy so much meat that he even knows you by name?"

"Oh, no. He's a friend of Uncle's."

"Ciao, Tony," said a woman who passed from the other direction.

Tony waved, and since he did, I did, too. *"Buona sera."*

She marched decisively, her heels clicking against the pavement.

"And that would be?"

"The woman who cuts Uncle's hair. I accompanied him the other day. He swears she's the best stylist in town."

I ran my fingers through my hair, which stretched down to my shoulders. I couldn't remember the last time Rachel had trimmed off my split ends, so I knew I had a bunch of them. "I'll keep that in mind."

"Ciao," called out a younger man.

"Ciao!" Tony tapped my sleeve. "He sells cheese at the shop near the Duomo."

"You know everybody," I said.

"Oh, no. Uncle knows everybody. You can't imagine how long it takes to walk across town with him. You know how it is around here. The shopkeepers love to chat. If you run across someone you know, you have to exchange a few words."

I did know. I appreciated the phenomenon. That gave me more time to practice Italian. The locals were a lot more fun than my grammar book.

Two guys my age passed. They both greeted Tony, and one winked at him. Or was that at me? Next came a trio: two women and a man. Arms linked, they said *salve* as they ambled by.

"How long have you been here?"

Tony laughed. "They're Uncle's friends."

"But they all remember you."

"I'm a new face! In a small town, people appreciate novelty. Think of Orvieto as a kind of island. They need new blood around here."

"That sounds painful."

"It can be."

"Or maybe they just like you."

"Maybe, maybe not. They have to pretend to like me whether they do or not. Why? Because we'll keep running into one another. It's unavoidable."

The idea of living in a small community was a bit comforting on the surface, but I wasn't sure I could handle it. Too many people knew your business. The residents probably told you what to do as soon as they noticed you moving in. I was safe because I was here temporarily. They didn't have long to put up with me.

"You understand that your knowing everyone is a problem, don't you?" I asked.

"How's that?"

"Fabrizio knows everybody, but somehow he made an enemy."

"You're back on that again? You're wrong."

"There's got to be an explanation."

"*Boh.*"

I understood the problem. Tony wanted to think the best of his uncle. I would too.

"Even if Uncle made somebody angry, they wouldn't have a reason to take it out on me."

I didn't press my point because Tony wasn't ready to hear it. Why should I ruin his evening just because I was right? Maybe everything would blow over, like a quick summer storm.

Or maybe not.

Chapter Ten

Henrietta lifted her head from her iOS 18 long enough to frown. "You were gone long enough."

My roommate was sprawled over the couch, her books spread over the coffee table. I knew what her main problems were: she was lonely, and she suffered from FOMO, fear of missing out. I hadn't mentioned that I was heading over to Tony's after class, let alone that I'd been summoned.

"It's Friday," I said. "I can afford to let loose."

"Out with that friend of yours again?"

She didn't care that I'd been out with someone. What irritated her was that she hadn't been invited to join in. She expected the world to revolve around her, presumably the way it had in high school. Although she might have had an entourage at Catalina Foothills, by now she was down to Christie, Julie, and Nancy, and I wasn't sure they liked her either.

"I was just out and about," I said. Vague was way good enough. While I had blurted out too much about Sander, I hadn't said much about Tony. Either I was protecting him or protecting something that was mine. Invasive people made me put up shields I kept in a closet otherwise even though I knew I was irrational about it.

"I just got home too," Henrietta said. "I was shopping. Not that I bought anything. I'm waiting for Florence."

"I might shop a bit there myself." Lucia had explained that Florence was the place to buy authentic leather goods, so we should take advantage of the opportunity.

"Is the field trip on Tuesday?" she asked.

"Not until Wednesday."

"Right." She struggled to a sitting position. "You got here just in time. We're all meeting up at Charlie's for pizza. Want to come?"

I'd been planning on having two pieces of bread and some cheese, but I felt too antsy to stay inside. Tony's troublemakers unnerved me. Besides, I'd managed to stay in Italy a whole week without having pizza. I wasn't exactly inspired by the restaurant's name, but how bad could it be?

"Let's do it."

Hopefully, I'd be able to sit far away from Henrietta, where I could pretend to care about her, but no matter. Even if the company were marginal, I always chose going out over staying in.

*

The large patio at Charlie Pizzeria Ristorante was so swamped that we crossed over the pebbled walkway and headed to the indoor dining area. I assumed anyone stuck inside on a fine night would be disgruntled, but the atmosphere inside the restaurant was joyous. As we passed through the hallway and entered the main dining area, we heard the sounds of a dozen contented groups: several long tables of tourists, smaller tables of families, here and there quiet couples out on a rare Friday night date. The white walls cheered the room, the waiters smiled appropriately without faking it, and the locals made up half the crowd, meaning the food would be decent. I hadn't realized I was hungry until the aromas of rosemary and olive oil wafted through the room. Maybe one pizza wouldn't even be enough.

Nancy waved to us from the far corner of the restaurant. My fellow students were already seated, but I slipped in beside Becky and Michelle by taking a spot at the head of the table.

"We're glad you came out," Becky said. "You didn't reply to the WhatsApp."

Right, I ignored the constant stream generated principally by Henrietta. Somehow, the afternoon had gotten away from me, but I couldn't explain that to the dedicated sisters who had come to Italy to study, study, and study.

They would probably finish the program knowing grammar rules more precisely than our dear teacher did. Instead of grammar, I would be the one to learn more colorful vocabulary. I'd duly looked up *reato in corso*, "crime in progress," for the next time I unwittingly spent a busy afternoon at Tony's.

"Henrietta talked me into coming," I whispered.

"Eating out is expensive," Michelle said, "but once in a while, we deserve it."

I assumed the sisters were on the kind of strict budget that meant they wouldn't owe a million dollars when they finally finished their degrees. I was on a budget myself, but my grandmother had promised to fund "incidentals" as long as I didn't get too crazy.

"To tell you the truth, my indecision wasn't the money," I whispered. "I'm here to learn Italian. That's my main goal. And our classmates, well, I'm not sure what they're here to learn."

"Me either," said Michelle. "All Julie and Nancy talk about is how they're going to spend the night with their boyfriends."

"Not allowed!" Becky and Michelle and I whispered together.

"Let's be practical," I said. "If you want to sleep with someone, be sure to choose a guy who doesn't speak English!"

We giggled like practiced conspirators.

Michelle pointed at her sister. "She flirted with the guy at Meta."

"What's wrong with that?" I asked. The grocery store had the best prices in town, and the two young owners both seemed friendly.

Becky pointed at Michelle. "She talked to the flower lady so long that the woman started smoking a cigarette to get rid of us!"

"We were having a nice conversation. I made her laugh thanks to all of my mistakes."

I didn't doubt it. The tiny flower shop in the Piazza della Repubblica was mostly open air, but the dark-haired woman who ran it always smiled and said hello.

"Shopkeepers are fair game," I said. "Like Lucia said, 'practice is practice.' But anyway, you guys are doing a great job. You're getting ahead of me."

"We already did the homework for Monday," Becky said. "Guess what? More verbs!"

"But we've been listening to those YouTube videos you told us about, the ones on Easy Italian," said Becky. "I finally understand why I'm not supposed to order a cappuccino after lunch."

I'd been too busy to supplement my language skills with videos even though I'd wanted to. "I give up. Why not?"

"Italians think that milk is too heavy," Becky said.

"It's too much liquid after lunch," added Michelle. "Here's something else. You shouldn't have a cocktail with dinner, not that I would!"

"Because they're too expensive?" I asked.

"That's a smart reason for students on a budget," said Michelle. "But Italians don't drink cocktails with dinner because the intense flavors interfere with the food. They switch to wine instead."

As if she could hear from the other end of the table, Henrietta snapped her fingers. "How many bottles of wine should we order?"

"I don't want any," I said quickly.

"It's Friday night," Henrietta announced. "So why not?"

"We don't want any either," said Michelle.

"What's wrong with you?" asked Lalo. "You don't drink yet?"

"Afraid you'll get caught?" asked Armando.

I didn't appreciate the condescending tone. The sisters were polite in class and didn't deserve any nonsense from a couple of guys who thought they were special just because most of the girls in Orvieto turned their heads when they walked by.

"We don't feel like it," I said. "What's it to you?"

"Just trying to help you relax a little," said Armando. "Not that I care one way or another."

He turned away as if I'd snubbed him. Good. That was the exact reaction I wanted.

"We drink a little with our parents," Becky said, "but alcohol is expensive. We're on a budget."

"We have to spend all our money on food," said Michelle.

Lalo gave a smirk that said *You're lying,* but he turned his back to us and picked up the wine menu as if it were his calling card to an Ivy-league school he didn't have the grades to attend.

Enough of listening to the third degree. Sure, I could have splurged on a single glass. Even two. That was not the point. I wasn't going to be tricked into drinking just so the others would feel better about their own questionable decisions.

I'd also learned my lesson the hard way back in Tucson. The numbers didn't work in my favor. If all ten of us shared a bottle, the others would guzzle a lot more wine than I would. It was one thing to pay for my own wine. Another to pay for a friend's. But to pay for irritating classmates? I could quote Lucia: *No, no, e no.*

"If we all chip in, it's not too expensive," Henrietta said. "Come on, guys! We're in Italy to have fun. That's why we came."

"You don't have to shout," Becky said quietly. "We're not the only customers."

"Lighten up," Henrietta said.

"Lucia said that Italian diners—" Michelle began.

75

Henrietta closed the menu with a *thud*. Never mind about Lucia! She's not back in town until Tuesday. Now, white wine or red?"

"No wine for us three," I said clearly. "You want it, you pay for it."

"If we buy wine, we don't need as many pizzas," Henrietta said, as if everyone in the world would be able to follow and approve of her "logic."

I was surrounded by first-year college students even though they'd somehow made it to the end of their junior year.

"That's not how it's done," I said.

"What do you mean, 'How it's done?'" Armando asked.

"It's not like at home where everybody shares," I said. "Here people order their own pizzas."

"They do not," Henrietta snapped. "Anyway, what makes you an expert? You've never been to Italy before if I remember right."

How did I know? Because my fellow hostelers in Rome had explained the whole system. Sometimes two people shared a pizza, but mostly everyone ordered an individual one. That was the best thing about a hostel. Sleeping in a roomful of strangers could be unnerving, especially if they snored, but they all knew more about the target destination than you did.

Henrietta waved the menu through the air. "Well, I'm ordering five pizzas and three bottles of wine so that we can all share them. If you don't like that, you can leave."

I popped to my feet. "I will."

Henrietta looked stunned. Probably no one had stood up to her in recent history, so she'd forgotten what it felt like. "You don't have to be rude about it!" she shouted.

Nearby diners turned and stared.

"You don't have to shout," I said quietly. "All of us have good hearing."

I turned and left the room. To my surprise, because I hadn't so much as consulted them, Becky and Michelle trailed me.

We were out the door and onto the patio when the waiter rushed over to us as if we'd left our purses behind. "Is some problem?"

I pointed behind me. *That group over there? They're our classmates. They're a problem.*

"Americani," he said. *"They are often too noisy and too drunk.* But you don't eat? You must be hungry. Come on. I show you a place outside."

The sisters and I beamed at one another. We were being looked after by our own personal waiter, and all three of us were ready to adopt him for the remainder of the summer.

Even though the patio was dominated by a huge crowd of German speakers, the waiter led us to a little table for two that he said would work well enough for three. As soon as he left us with menus, we laughed uncontrollably. We might be Americans with imperfect language skills, but we were a lot cooler than our colleagues who had stayed inside.

*

My cell phone buzzed as I let myself into my apartment. The enoteca? Tony? Either one might be in crisis. Instead of ignoring the vibration, as usual, I answered the phone.

"Finally!" Sander said. "You are a busy person!"

I was caught in several ways at once. I wasn't busy, I was alone, and given WhatsApp, I could speak long-distance to someone in another country without it costing a fortune.

True, I wouldn't have answered the phone if I'd noticed who had called. I would have made up yet another excuse. Maybe I had a FODA—fear of doing anything, an acronym that I made up myself and that was only used by me.

I slid two of Henrietta's bags, a backpack and a grocery sack, off the couch and plopped down myself. Then I kicked her makeup supplies off the coffee table and used it as a footstool. "Just getting in."

"Lovely evening out?"

I was astonished to notice that it was after midnight. Becky and Michelle and I had indeed enjoyed a memorable, slow dinner. Our waiter, Marco, had explained every unfamiliar word on the menu even though it took him several visits to do so. The huge German group had ordered before we did, so we had to wait nearly an hour for our food, but we didn't mind at all. We were comfortable outside because the air temperature was perfect, and the laughter from nearby tables boosted our own mood. Marco felt so bad for us that he brought us a breadbasket for free, a treat that didn't normally accompany pizza.

We were still munching our grissini when our classmates marched out in a parade led by Henrietta. Even from a distance, I could tell her face was flushed. Their waiter escorted them from the restaurant entrance through the patio and out to the street. Momentarily I wondered if they hadn't paid, or tried to pay less, or took off without leaving the smallest tip, but when Marco caught me looking over at them, he laughed.

"They were asked to leave," he said. "Too noisy!"

Becky and Michelle and I toasted one another with acqua frizzante. Then we took pictures. Michelle attempted to document every moment of our meal. I was more camera shy. We were at dinner, after all, performing a simple daily event. But why not celebrate the moment? We were on an extended tourist visa. Good enough.

The huge pies were worth waiting for, and we took our sweet time eating them. They were so tasty that we wanted to finish every bite, something that Matteo on Easy Italian called a personal accomplishment. Even though the sisters assured me that, according to the language videos,

Italians did NOT do this, we exchanged slices so that we could try one another's combination of ingredients: pesto and tomato, porcini mushrooms and bacon, four cheese.

At first we resisted asking for espressos, another Italian thing, coffee after dinner no matter the time, because we feared we were keeping Marco from going home for the night. After he assured us that he had to clean up, we realized we didn't need to rush. He labeled us his favorite customers of the evening and brought over shot glasses of chilled limoncello on the house as a chaser for the coffee.

When we finally left, trailing the last of the customers, Marco thanked us for coming and reminded us to come back soon. I thought he meant it.

My thoughts turned back to Sander. "We wound up having a really long, enjoyable dinner."

"That is Italian style. You're falling right in with the culture."

"As opposed to most of my classmates. I think their goal was to see how much wine they could drink in one night."

"Perhaps that will help them speak Italian."

"It might if they were trying. Becky and Michelle do, though. They're sincere. They're in my same class, and we're always helping one another."

"It's great to have worthwhile classmates."

"That's for sure. They're trying to get the most out of their studies, so we're on the same page."

"More importantly, do they know how to order tasty dishes?"

"We're on student budgets, so we had pizzas. I ate every bite of my *bo, bo, bosca* —" I got stuck. I couldn't remember how to say the word.

"Perhaps a Pizza *Boscaiola*?"

Boh-sky-OH-la. I could barely say the word, yet it rolled off Sander's tongue as if he repeated it to himself five times a day.

"When did you ever have time to study Italian?" I asked.

"I only speak food. We have many Italian restaurants around Amsterdam. I believe that I have tried most of them!"

It was a poor excuse. His English was terrific, and he said that he'd studied French. His brother was good at languages too. I might have complained that such skills were genetic except that languages came easily to my sister Rachel while my stabs at Italian had cracked up our patient waiter every single time.

"Sander, you need to come down here so that I don't make a fool of myself every time I eat out."

"I was hoping you would say that. You won't mind if I come next Friday?"

When I'd finally extended an invitation to Sander, I'd made a lot of conditions. He couldn't stay with me because it was not allowed. I would have to go on a field trip, but he couldn't come because it was not allowed. I would have to go to every single class because absences were also not allowed.

All that should have deterred any normal would-be visitor, yet he said that he would immediately look for flights, that he didn't mind staying at a B & B, and that he would be happy for any time we could spend together. Uff! He was bending over so far backwards it was lucky he wasn't standing on the edge of a canal.

I still had my hesitations, but maybe having an escort would be fun. Maybe Sander would get along well with Tony and the three of us would bond. Sander might also enchant one of the sisters. They were too studious to date, but what could possibly be better than a nice, steady Dutch boy?

"Friday would be fine," I said. "If I can, I'll meet you at Fiumicino."

I couldn't believe my ears. Me travel to Rome to go to the airport to meet up with somebody who knew how to get around Europe a lot easier than I did?

"It would be fine if you came to the airport," Sander said, "but it's not necessary. If you are busy with your classes, we might meet in Rome. Or Orvieto."

Something had to be wrong. Normal men didn't accommodate me, nor I them. Later in the week I'd have to make some excuse for not meeting Sander in Rome. For the time being, I kicked Henrietta's sweaters off the couch and asked Sander about his life in the Netherlands.

From what he told me, it sounded quite a lot less complicated than life in Orvieto.

Chapter Eleven

I descended the steep path through the green forest, fully aware that any easy descent meant a hard ascent later on. I told myself to suck it up. *L'anello della rupe*, the ring around the cliff, offered more than exercise. Smack in the heat of the afternoon, the path was quiet, and I had it mostly to myself. For a Tucsonan, strolling amidst deciduous trees was a welcome novelty. It afforded me an outsider's perspective of the city. It was one place in Orvieto I would never, ever find Henrietta or Lucia either.

I felt triumphant to be out on a trail stretching my legs and challenging my breathing. Back in Tucson I swam a couple of times a week and attended a weekly gymnastics class, which meant I could almost say I stayed in shape. At the moment, however, my calves reminded me that I could do better if I tried. But I wasn't on the trail for the exercise. I needed to clear my mind.

Henrietta had straggled home at four in the morning. She didn't mean to disturb me; she was completely unaware of me. However, after she swore at the couch for running into her and the coffee table for kicking her, I was awake. Then there were the explosive sounds shooting out from the bathroom. Henrietta was five seven or so and weighed some hundred and thirty pounds. While she pretended to be a practiced drinker, her capacity would naturally be limited. I estimated that she'd reached that limit several hours earlier.

At ten a.m., her bedroom door was still securely shut. I enjoyed a lovely, quiet morning. After shopping at the Saturday market, I had coffee in the shade at Palace Cafè, where I chatted with some of the staff from the night before. I brought my few greens, consisting of various kinds of salad and veggies, back to the apartment.

By then it was two o'clock, and Henrietta was stirring. That was my cue to clear out rather than to get trapped into a long conversation about my roommate's latest exploits. Since I'd heard about the cliff walk days earlier, its time had come.

When I came upon the rose garden, I left the path long enough to take pictures. The white roses had big, beautiful bulbs that said, yes, spring has conquered another winter. The reds were pretty, but the pinks, especially those with stripes, won the beauty contest. Since they were at their peak, I felt the need to photograph each one.

My study abroad trip was like a rose itself: beautiful, impossible, unexpected, soft, thorny, brief. Since the time would flash by, I needed to appreciate every moment in its own way.

What I didn't appreciate were the clouds bunching up overhead on a day when I hadn't brought along an umbrella or even a raincoat. When the *rupe* was interrupted by a parking lot that boasted an escalator leading back up to town, I opted for retreat. I went straight to the ticket office. *"Quant'è?"* How much?

The man looked up from his cell phone. *"Per quanto tempo?"* How long?

His question baffled me. How long could an escalator take?

When I shrugged, he pointed to his watch. *"Per quante ore avete lasciata la macchina?"*

The one word I caught was *macchina*, which meant "car." Silly man! Couldn't he see that I was on foot? With my fingers I mimicked walking. He laughed out loud before covering his mouth with his hand.

Of course, I was the silly one. While visitors had to pay for parking, the escalator was free. It was also a marvel, a huge underground structure whose ascent was accomplished with the help of four separate escalators, an accompanying walkway for those who were in a hurry, and photographs of local hot spots. Lucia had failed to explain this important shortcut up to the city. The next time she reminded me about a rule I broke, I'd ask her to add this unique set of escalators to her list of essential information, right between the police station and the tourist center.

Best of all, the passageway spit me out close to the center of town, around the corner from Charlie Pizzeria, which meant I didn't have to fight the magnet that was Enoteca Fabrizio. A brief walk took me straight to it.

Tony stood at the counter pouring over a notebook, in other words, his uncle's sophisticated non-digitalized accounting system.

"Gina! I expected you hours ago."

"Give me credit for figuring out something to do on my own instead of coming straight here to bother you."

We kissed the traditional Italian way, two cheek kisses starting right to right.

"I'm glad you came around," he said. "I need someone to break up the monotony."

"No amusing customers?"

"You would be the first one."

I indicated an empty shelf where bottles of olive oil had stood sentry the day before. "Looks like you made some sales."

"It's by far our most popular product. I'll have to restock."

"I don't understand how you can beat out your competition. Don't your customers ever worry about price?"

Tony leaned forward as if telling me a secret. "Eating is important around here. It's hard for you and me to appreciate what a big deal it is."

"I know that extra virgin olive oil is better quality and all that, but isn't expensive olive oil a bit like expensive wine? I'm not convinced I can tell the difference."

"We'll have to do a taste test, one of Uncle's bottles in contrast to the cheapest one from the grocery store. But not today. I'm too lazy to do anything productive."

"But your customers will be disappointed because of your empty shelves."

"No. They'll be tantalized. That's good for them, don't you think?"

"Absolutely!" I'd known some crazy soccer fans, moviegoers, and even stamp collectors. I couldn't think of anything equivalent in the food world, but that was my own limitation.

"But what's the matter with you? Worried about What's-His-Name from up north?"

"That would be a garden story."

"Of course!"

Tony led me outside, where I immediately moved a chair to the shade while he plopped himself down in the sun.

"I don't have to worry about Sander until the end of the week," I said. "Actually, I'm not as bad as 'worried.' We might have a wonderful time together or we might not."

"Ouch!"

"What? A bee sting?"

"No. Your positive attitude knocked me right over."

"Very funny. I'm merely practical. But I hope we have fun at least. I hope he's not boring." Really what I was afraid of was that he might want something I didn't, which could make for some awkward conversations.

"He sounds fascinating if you ask me. A friendly man who is willing to take a chance. You don't find one every day."

"No, you don't." I did appreciate his willingness to travel. None of my friends back home were willing to come visit me, and neither were my relatives. "How's your tooth, by the way?"

"I'm taking tomorrow off. That's how it is. I plan to take several painkillers and sleep all day long and then all night."

"That bad?"

"On and off. The real reason I couldn't sleep last night was that I kept imagining someone was trying to break in."

"Maybe they were."

"I ran to the window a couple of times. Nothing."

"Maybe somebody was around the corner just out of sight."

Tony tapped his chest. "Nobody was there. Blame an inner fear."

"Right now, I'm ready to blame an inner hunger. I thought I might pick up a panino somewhere. Should I bring you one?"

"The crust would be too hard for my gums. Hang on. I have a better idea."

While I scooted my chair farther from the sun, he brought out three different cheese rounds and then sliced a piece from the biggest one. "Pecorino di Orvieto. Sheep's cheese."

Delicious. Maybe a little salty. "Made in the area?"

"The surrounding fields, somehow. It's DOP, which is a crazy big deal."

"A what?"

"A designated origin of production, which is like swearing that it's local and not just brought in from somewhere else."

"I guess that's terribly important."

"Around here it is." He pointed the knife at the cheese. "It's supposed to have a nutty taste. Do you detect that?"

The most I knew was that it wasn't cheddar. "When it comes to cheese, I'm not that discerning."

"Hang around here for a while and you will be. Anyway, the quality depends on the aging, which might be up to a year." He sliced a piece from the next wheel. "This one is a little different. Caciotta di Norcia. Also local, but it's a blend."

"Cow and sheep?"

"Sheep and goat."

The semi-soft cheese was just as delicious as the previous one. "Do you sell a lot of these wheels?"

"Hardly ever. People buy a little at a time."

It was self-defense. Otherwise, they would look like wheels themselves.

"That's the way people shop around here," Tony continued. "They think about the day, not the whole week, like we might back in the States."

Usually, my mom made one grocery store run during the week, but on the weekends, she sent me and Grandma. There were plenty of specialty stores in Tucson, but we weren't motivated to use them, so it was Safeway or bust.

"I could bring out some salami," Tony offered.

I tapped the soft cheese round. "This is enough. Otherwise, I might chomp up everything in sight."

He laughed as he cut another small slice. "Funny. You don't look like a lawn mower to me."

"I'm from Tucson. We don't have such things."

"I suppose not. Anyway, why are you worried? You're at a perfect weight, somewhere between fat and anorexic."

"Very funny. I'm trying to hold steady. Not easy with temptations around every corner."

"You're exaggerating. Food is not so dangerous. It's everything else we should be worried about."

I knew what I was worried about, prepositions. They were even harder to tell apart than cheese.

Chapter Twelve

Aurelio dragged us through exercises as if he enjoyed them. Maybe he did. He was only forty-something, but I imagined that his life consisted of grammar books with the occasional dictionary thrown in. Whenever his nose was buried in our textbook, which was often, Lalo and Armando amused one another by imitating the teacher's serious scowl.

In contrast, Michelle and Becky listened attentively, taking notes whenever they got confused. I tried to do the same. Italian grammar confused me too, but sometimes my mind wandered, and the window captured my attention instead. I wanted to be on the street instead of in a classroom, learning the gradual way, the way I'd learned Spanish, rather than forcing myself to acquire details.

Maybe I was spoiled. I'd had a whole sixteen weeks to gradually master Italian 101. The class had been a welcome break in my regular set of lectures. The teacher had been patient and funny. She'd recognized that language learning was a game. In contrast, Aurelio was married to the book. We reviewed rules before completing accompanying exercises. Repeat. He called on us in order, so we could easily calculate to see which blank we'd have to fill in.

I was so disengaged that I didn't mind at all when Lucia marched in and interrupted me halfway through a response. She herded all the Italian 101 students, Henrietta, Nancy, Christie, Dennis, and Julie, into the room with us.

"Find seats!" Lucia snapped.

She pointed her finger at me. *"Fuori!"*

Before I could turn to Becky and Michelle for an explanation, she pointed her finger at them too. *"Fuori!"*

Even Aurelio could sense the tension along with our total confusion. He nodded towards the door.

How were we supposed to know that *fuori* meant "out?" Happy to oblige, I slid my text and notebook into my backpack and stood. Becky and Michelle did the same. All eyes were on us as we headed out. Then Michelle dropped her pencil case, which popped open and spewed its contents in every direction. Even though Becky and I stooped to help her, we needed several seconds to collect ourselves and leave.

Once in the hall, we huddled together. We might have been in middle school.

"Why don't we get to stay?" Becky asked. "What did we do wrong?"

Becky and Michelle were not the type to do anything wrong ever. Application for the summer program? Submitted over a month before the deadline. Passport photocopy? Completed online. Obligatory housing deposit? They handed it to Lucia as they stepped off the train.

I was lackadaisical. I respected deadlines, but I used them. The program deadline had fallen on a Friday evening at 11:59. My application? Submitted safely at 11:54. Etc. Passport photocopy? Submitted in the Phoenix Airport while I was changing planes. To Lucia's irritation, I wasn't able to cough up enough cash for the housing deposit until the first day of class.

Such lapses were minor. Becky and Michelle wouldn't have any. They were responsible to the point of giving everyone else a complex.

"I'm sure you didn't do anything wrong," I said. "I might have."

"You thought you passed the test, didn't you?" asked Michelle.

I might have reversed the rules for the participles. Some verbs formed the past tense with the helping verb *avere* while others took *essere*. Surely confusing the two was only a misdemeanor.

"Lucia was out of town over the weekend," I said. "She wouldn't know about test scores."

Then it finally dawned on us. "Charlie Pizzeria!" We whispered at the same time.

"Lucia knows everybody in town," Becky said.

"The townspeople even call her in the middle of the night," added Michelle. "What do you think happened?"

I tiptoed to the door and held my ear against it. Was I above eavesdropping? I was not.

"How is it possible?" Lucia asked. "You have the rules! You have the protocols!"

I smiled; even in English, Lucia sounded Italian.

"So! Tell me what happened!"

No one spoke, but Becky and Michelle silently joined me at the door.

"You don't like to tell me? No, of course you don't. Where would you like me to start?"

A longer silence.

"I will start myself. You made a spectacle of yourselves!"

"We were just having dinner," said a female student, maybe Christie.

"It was Friday night," said Armando, or maybe it was Lalo. "We were drinking. So what? It's legal."

"Our students are not allowed to drink!"

"What are you going to do, call my parents?" asked Dennis. "My dad lets me drink beer at home all the time."

"You can't prevent us from living in Orvieto like normal people," said Lalo. "So unless you want to refund all our money, stop talking about dumb rules that you can't enforce."

"You are ambassadors in this town! You are guests! You must respect all of the townspeople as well as the establishments!"

"So what if we were loud?" asked Henrietta. "The whole damned place was noisy."

"You will not use such words when you are speaking with me," Lucia said.

Then the other students chimed in at once: they weren't terribly loud, they were like the other customers, they spent good money, the restaurant should be thankful.

"What did Marco say to you?"

Lucia knew the waiter by name? That couldn't be good.

"He says to you, please be quiet! The waiter! He must tell you this!"

"He was culturally insensitive," said my especially clueless roommate. "He should know that Americans are naturally loud. We probably learned it from the Italians."

"You are not naturally loud!" Lucia cried. "You are loud when you feel like being loud!"

"You know what, I didn't notice," said Armando. "Are you sure we were the ones making noise?"

Lucia's heels clacked against the floor. "I am sure! And after Marco asks you to be more quiet, what do you say to him?"

Silence.

"You tell him you are the customers! So Marco gives up. He sends the owner to talk to you! And you are rude even to him!"

"You don't have proof," Henrietta said. "You weren't there."

"But I hear every part of what happened! The owner is my friend, now perhaps he is not my friend because my students, who are very bad students, no, very bad people, make trouble in his restaurant! Three groups of customers came to the dining room, heard you yelling, and left! Do you know how much business my friend lost?"

"We bought five bottles of wine," said Dennis. "He should have been happy."

"No, you bought six bottles of wine for seven people! But are you too simple to understand? This is his business!

He runs this restaurant! He is there all the days! If the customers have a terrible experience, they don't come back! You lose him the business for one night, and maybe for many nights! The other customers are local. They want a peaceful place to eat, but can they find it? They must give their business to somebody else."

"We're sorry," said Henrietta without sounding one bit sorry. "We didn't know it was such a big deal."

"Then I will need the rest of the day to explain it to you!"

Footsteps neared the door. Michelle and Becky and I stumbled over one another as we dove for the nearest chairs. I looked down at the floor, as if lost in the deepest kinds of grammatical thoughts.

"You may go home," Lucia said. "No more class today."

I stood. "Thanks. We waited because—"

"Yes, yes. Goodbye."

She shut herself inside the classroom again before we could say anything else. We clasped our hands over our mouths to muffle our laughter. Becky politely took two paces down the hall, but I returned to the door. Henrietta was my roommate. I had to know what kind of trouble she was in.

"But then you continue the party!" Lucia shouted. By now, her throat should have been raw.

"That damned pizza made us thirsty," said Dennis.

"Enough of your excuses! The owner of Blue Bar is also my friend! When his customers drink too much, he stops serving them. When there is a problem, he calls me. Guess what time he woke me up from a beautiful sleep? Eh? You don't know? As I have taken the trouble to warn you so many times, one call to your parents and you are leaving the program."

"Don't you have to give us at least one warning?" asked Armando.

"You already had your warning. This is your second warning. Third warning, you go home!"

"But we paid —"

"That is not my problem. You are temporary citizens of my hometown. Finally, there is a matter of safety. If you are all drunk at two in the morning, how can you walk one another home? You cannot. This behavior of yours is not acceptable!"

"What are you going to do?" Henrietta asked. "Send all of us home? Then you won't have any students!"

I didn't doubt that Lucia could send everyone home. By now, our fees were nonrefundable. But even for a control freak, the threat seemed extreme.

Heavy steps, probably Aurelio's, approached the door. I scurried down the hall with Becky and Michelle in tow. Amusing as it was, we had no reason to get caught up in Lucia's personal war against the partiers of Orvieto.

We hit the street and continued well out of earshot.

"Can you even believe that?" Michelle asked.

"I've never been in that much trouble in my life," said Becky. She looked at her watch. "Now what are we going to do?"

I headed south, which was uphill. "Let's do what the locals do."

"What's that?" asked Michelle.

I went around the corner and through the arch, which opened onto the Piazza del Popolo.

"Sit and have an espresso," I said.

Since the tables at Palace Cafè were vacant, I pointed Michelle and Becky to the one in the shade. Then I went inside and ordered coffees.

Chapter Thirteen

That night when the girls and I reached the entrance to Mezza Luna, a basement trattoria catty corner to the parking lot escalator, I assumed Tony had made a mistake. He claimed that he'd made a reservation for four, but when I peeked inside, I didn't see any way we would fit. The rectangular tables were filled with diners who were packed so closely together that if they hadn't come as relatives, they would leave as partners. To add to the chaos, two waiters crisscrossed the narrow aisles, one with an appetizer tray the size of Italy and one juggling bottles of mineral water as if he were practicing for the circus.

"There aren't any tourists here," Becky whispered. "This is so cool."

Michelle nodded. I hadn't planned on asking them to dinner, but since we were still at the café snickering about our silly companions when Tony texted me an invitation, I felt inspired. Tony assured me that he didn't mind extra company as long as they were friends of mine. Now I was glad I'd included them. Their enthusiasm spread over the room like a rainbow.

The water-bearing waiter hurried over. He was about to wave us away when he saw Tony coming up behind us. *"Ciao, giovanott'!"*

He greeted Tony like an old friend and led us among the clusters of eaters to a tiny square table below the cashier station. We squeezed into its chairs. Not only was every other seat taken, but the ambient noise was louder than crashing waves on a beach. While a handful of people chewed, the others talked at the same time, loudly, because that was the only way to be heard. The patrons were like bees trapped in a jar, crowding the air with ZZ's. The aromas were nearly as overwhelming: roasted meats, garlic, marinara sauce, and more garlic.

"I love this," Michelle gushed. "It's the real Italy. The one we've been looking for."

"I guess you've been here often?" asked Becky.

Tony smiled brightly, which made him even more handsome than usual. He seemed glad for the extra company. Even though he knew a lot of people around town, they were acquaintances rather than friends.

"If I eat out, I usually eat here. It's local and the prices are moderate. Also, Antonio cares about whether his customers are satisfied or not." Tony tapped the laminated menu. "There aren't many choices, but a limited menu is common in Italy. That way the kitchen crew concentrates on doing a few things well."

I appreciated the idea. Back home too many eateries tried to be everything for everybody and failed to be anything for anybody. In Tucson, my favorite Italian restaurant was Perché No?, a downtown eatery run by an Italian chef. Come to think of it, that menu was limited too, but all the items were delicious.

A roly-poly aproned man sauntered over and greeted Tony with a hug. They joked about having the same name, which meant they were also kindred spirits. Their *onomastico* was coming right up on June 13th, so they would have to celebrate it together. As in Mexico, name days were often as important as birthdays, probably because they were easier to remember.

The connection between Tony's uncle and Antonio went way back. The latter had bought the restaurant from the original owner a couple of years earlier, but Fabrizio had always been a steady customer, often bringing in regional vendors as well as various relatives and friends. Tony was eager to continue the family tradition of embracing the establishment.

"What has happened to the nice boy I met?" Antonio boomed. "Before you didn't bring enough girls. Now you bring too many!"

"We're testing his limits," I said.

"We want to keep him out as late as possible," said Michelle.

"If we don't like the food, he promised to pay himself," said Becky.

Antonio looked us over before winking at Tony. "I hope you have a good evening! But now, let's talk the important thing. What are you eating?"

The girls protested that they'd barely looked at the menu. Antonio smiled indulgently at their halting efforts to make themselves understood.

"You look the menu," he said. "But this is the best carbonara in the world." He rushed off to other customers.

"The 'best in the world' is a tall order," I said.

Tony pointed at the menu, where, indeed, the second pasta dish read *Spaghetti alla carbonara (number one)*. "He might be right. You'll have to try for yourselves. I'll warn you, though. The carbonara is heavy. You won't be able to get through it."

"I'll order vegetables," said Michelle.

"And I'll order carbonara," said Becky. "That way we both get to try."

"Smart idea." I turned to Tony. "Can we do the same? I know, I know. That's probably not done here."

"Family style! Not so uncommon. Besides, here I know everybody, and they know we're from the States. Even if we know the rules, we don't always pay attention to them!"

We also violated protocol with our wrong phrases, but Tony made us order for ourselves. Despite Lucia's warnings, or maybe because of them, we agreed to have wine. The house wine was light, and though I worried no price was listed for it, Tony assured us that the local white was in our budget.

Meanwhile I observed the bunches of Orvietani out for the evening. Several groups were mixed ages: kids, parents, grandkids all out together. Participants in other groups were closer to the same age: friends or colleagues. As the sisters had noticed, not a single tourist was in sight with the exception of a couple who wandered in and asked for a table but were invited to return the following evening when there might be more space.

A typical Italian night on the town was precisely this: having dinner with friends. Life was shared through food and drink. Everyone cared about such important common denominators.

They cared about family and friends, too. That was evident in their exuberant interactions. Family members passed around plates, babies, and baskets of bread, never once pausing their streams of dialogue. They laughed and giggled, high on the evening and one another's company. They weren't celebrating specific occasions; any get-together was special.

They did make me wonder why my father hadn't kept in better touch with his own relatives. Even though my mother had never asked for or received alimony, he hadn't kept much in touch with us either: me, my sister, my mom, her mom. When I was five, he'd taken an engineering job in Mexico even though Mom refused to go with him. That choice ended their marriage. Once in a while he bothered to contact us, but he lived in Monterrey, an industrial town none of us were fond of. He'd severed ties with his other family members as well, both those in the States and those in Italy. If he'd been friendlier to people, maybe I'd be eating with my own relatives at this very moment. At least I might know something about them.

I was doubly thankful for Tony and the girls. We bonded over common interests mixed with human decency. While we'd come to Italy for specific purposes, we were also flexible in our thinking and open-minded enough to embrace new opportunities. Ironically, because we'd known each other such a short period of time, I already knew that if I got sick or ran short on money or was scared to walk home alone at night, they'd bail me out. With them around, I didn't have to worry about anything. We were a small clan, but we weren't alone.

"What are you going to do with Sander all weekend?" Tony asked as he chose a slice of *soppressata*, a cured, prepared meat, from an appetizer tray.

"Who's Sander?" asked Becky.

"Her boyfriend!" squealed Michelle. I'd shared few details, but Michelle had put the facts together all on her own.

"Not a boyfriend," I said quickly.

"Not yet!" quipped Tony. "After this weekend, who knows?"

"Are you sure you're doing the right thing?" Becky asked. "A local boyfriend would help you learn more Italian."

"And help you dress better!" added Michelle.

"And choose better wine!" quipped Tony. "But tell us a little more about this guy before it's too late and you go to Rome and get kidnapped and we never hear from you again."

"There's not much to tell," I said.

"Come on," Becky said. "You can trust us to keep a secret."

We giggled because Lucia had warned us that we did not, under any circumstances, have time for boyfriends. We were to concentrate on our studies a thousand percent despite the fact that learning language from a native would be the most efficient way.

I snatched up a piece of bread. "I'm not kidding. I can't tell you much because I haven't met him yet. How crazy is that?"

"A blind date from another country!" exclaimed Michelle. "I love that!"

"It's very romantic," added Becky.

"He's not a blind date at all. He's a friend of the family."

My exaggeration was slight, depending on one's definition. I didn't have to spell out everything.

"It still sounds romantic," said Becky.

"Nearly dangerous!" quipped Michelle.

Tony huddled with the sisters. "How much will you pay us to not say anything to Lucia?"

I took a piece of bread from the basket and tore it in half. "Stop. You guys are making a big deal of this."

"But it is a big deal," said Becky. "We don't have anything exciting planned this weekend."

"We're going to the Etruscan Museum." Michelle yawned. "I can hardly wait."

"Look, I agreed to meet this guy in Rome. That's it."

"Where are you staying?" asked Michelle. "At a hotel?"

"A hostel?" asked Becky.

Tony waved a bread stick. "Get this. They're staying at his friend's place. How convenient is that?"

"It's terrific," said Becky. "That's exactly the right price!"

Tony helped himself to more prosciutto. "They might have to share a bed."

"A tiny one!" added Michelle.

I took the last two pieces of asiago myself, out of spite. "Okay, you guys, enough. Sander and I might not hit it off, in which case I might come back to Orvieto early."

"And miss out on Rome?" Becky asked. "Sure, we've got that field trip coming up, but how much can Lucia cram down our throats in a single day? There's a ton of stuff to see in Rome. You could spend a day at the Capitoline Museum alone."

"Or the Castel Sant'Angelo," said Michelle.

I waved my fork. "He likes Bernini. I got us tickets for the Borghese."

"Oh! That's where they have the famous statue of Daphne and Apollo," said Michelle.

"Right!" said Becky. "The one where she's running away."

"Gina, you're not supposed to plan to run away before you even meet the guy!" Tony laughed.

Enough of the silly questions. As the waiter walked by, I beckoned to him. At first I thought I'd ask for a bottle of water. Then I thought about asking for more bread. Then I spotted a copy of the menu. I placed my finger under the restaurant's name. *"Perché Mezza Luna?"* I asked. "Why Half Moon?"

The waiter paused for a moment before shrugging. *"Boh!"*

Of course he didn't know. Antonio might have offered a decent explanation, but he was busy with other customers. So what that the name had nothing to do with eating? At least I'd managed to change the subject long enough for my friends to stop asking pesky questions. By the time the pasta arrived, we drifted to other aspects of life in Italy, such as the slow pace despite frequent stops for coffee, and the fashionable clothes despite the dearth of clothing stores atop the hill.

As we laughed and chatted, I felt that, in our own way, we belonged. Although the "number one carbonara" in the world was so heavy a forklift wouldn't have budged it, the combination of eggs, *guanciale* (cured pork cheeks), and *pecorino romano* (a salty sheep's cheese), was not only different from any carbonara I'd tasted in the States, but a divine combination of hedonistic ingredients. I felt each calorie cling to my stomach and laughed about it.

Maybe the wine helped us along, but Becky and Michelle opened up about their fears about getting into med school because the competition was so fierce that perfect grades didn't guarantee you a spot. Tony explained that he was so fed up with his friends' expectations for excessive partying that he would have done almost any-thing to get out of Jersey City for the summer. We shared stories about aspirations we hadn't attained, silly relatives that drove us crazy, and mistakes we'd made that proved we were the stupidest tourists ever. We were so busy talk-ing that we didn't have time to gossip or speculate about the other customers.

When the waiter suggested dessert and Tony said we'd share a *tartufo nero,* a black truffle, I didn't blink. He knew best how to help us enjoy a full experience. Then we had an espresso, the expected finish to every fine Italian meal, and then, just when I thought we couldn't possibly have an excuse to stay any longer, Antonio brought out lit-tle shot glasses of liqueur on the house.

No one had to mention that refusing a complimentary after-dinner drink would be rude. We gratefully accepted the surprising treat.

"What is this?" Michelle asked happily. She'd already declared that this was the best evening of their trip, and Becky seconded the opinion.

"It's walnut liqueur," Tony said. "Another local spe-cialty."

Hurray for specialties. The strong, sweet drink nearly took my breath away before leaving a nutty flavor in my mouth. It was a perfect finish to our impromptu banquet. I could hardly wait to write my relatives and make their mouths water.

Perfection screeched to a halt after we split the bill, said good nights all around, and moved towards the door. At that moment, I noticed that Antonio beckoned Tony back to the cashier's station.

I halted in place and watched. Antonio didn't say a word, but he placed his index finger below his eye and pulled his skin downward. Then he tapped his ear and raised his eyebrow. He quickly turned away as if the ges-tures never happened.

I couldn't catch Tony's expression, but I held up my end of the farce by holding my tongue the whole time we walked Becky and Michelle to their apartment, which was in the medieval quarter, and then Tony and I headed to mine, which was close by.

I waited until we crossed the Piazza della Repubblica, where the lights were so bright that I could see my friend's expression even if he preferred to hide it. "What was all that about?"

"What do you mean?"

"Between you and Antonio."

"Oh, nothing."

"He was telling you something."

"Nah."

I stopped short in front of the Santandrea Bar, where spotlights illuminated every inch of Tony's face. "I'm trying to help you here."

My friend stopped reluctantly and backtracked a couple of steps. "I appreciate that. But I don't want to get you in trouble."

"You're going to be the one in trouble if you don't come clean."

"The message wasn't obvious?"

"I'm not conversant in Italian sign language yet."

Tony shrugged. Between the seeming nonchalance and the Barba Napoli shirt, he didn't look one bit American. He might have passed for a native in any of Italy's twenty regions. "Antonio was telling me to be careful. He's heard something."

"About what?"

"He didn't say."

I didn't know enough to understand the context. "I thought this little town was too quaint for crime. Was he trying to scare you?"

"Definitely not. He's my friend. He was telling me to pay attention."

"That's not much help."

Tony edged off, and I followed.

"Can't you explain more than that?"

"Antonio heard something, but he can't or won't talk about it. Hence the warning."

A light bulb went on. "It's not about you. He knows something about your uncle."

"He seems to. But maybe not him. Maybe one of his customers. The original owner of Mezza Luna is Fabrizio's age. They went to elementary school together. That might be the connection."

I hadn't bonded with a single person in my elementary school. I was barely in contact with anyone from high school either, but it was different to grow up in a big town rather than a small one. "What do you think is going on?"

"Look, Uncle probably shortchanged somebody by accident or maybe he somehow sold them a bad bottle of wine."

"Why wouldn't they just say so?"

"Maybe they're waiting for the right moment. Maybe they realize he's out of town."

"Fabrizio didn't warn you about any possible problems?"

Tony started walking again, and I took big steps to keep up with him. "Uncle told me the basics about the business, but that's it. I almost felt like he didn't want to share secrets of the trade. Know what I mean? I needed to know enough to keep the enoteca on its feet, but he didn't tell me anything extra."

"No gossip, you mean?"

"No problems. If something was wrong, though, maybe he didn't know it."

I turned on the speed to match Tony's stride. His pace matched his hurry to change topics. "Now you're being defensive."

"I know. The truth is that I couldn't get him to talk much, not about himself." Tony pointed out the tall buildings towering over us along Corso Cavour. "He explained that foreigners have bought up so much real estate that the locals have to move to the cheaper areas below town. He told me about Corpus Christi, the big religious event." Tony pointed to a poster along a side wall. "He told me about the summer music concerts."

"He filled your head with useless information."

"I wouldn't say that either, but he didn't level with me. He was anxious to get out of town. Did he need a break? I don't know. Was he bored with the shop? I would be, but I didn't get that vibe. Was he worried about creditors? That's the most likely possibility."

"Or maybe a post mid-life crisis?"

"I don't know. It's harder to live in Italy without a partner. Or maybe not harder, but let's say it makes you suspect because nearly everyone has a spouse whether they still love them or not. Or maybe Uncle regrets not staying in the States. Can you imagine living in this town your whole life? It's sweet and picturesque and the food is the best you've ever had, but the town doesn't offer much world experience. That's not helpful in the long run. At some point, you'd get tired of the place."

"Being in the same business year after year wouldn't be great either," I added.

"Exactly. Olive oil is important and all that, but after a few decades, I'd be through with it."

"Me too."

If I were in Fabrizio's shoes, I knew I'd get tired of reaching out to tourists hoping they would buy my products. I'd get tired of the same two main streets that served the town. I'd get tired of the old-style architecture. But who was to say how the career had affected Fabrizio?

I'd spent most of my twenty-one years in Tucson, but excursions to Mexico, Thailand, and the Midwest had shown me different ways of thinking. They had given me an appreciation for different religions and landscapes and histories. I was thankful for that range of experiences.

I wasn't sure they'd be any help with deciphering Orvieto.

Chapter Fourteen

Our van pulled into Autogrill Chianti Ovest behind two huge tourist buses.

"*Accidenti!*" Lucia said. "*Vi sbrigate, ragazzi!* Hurry!"

I understood her concern. The highway gas station had limited services, and if the kids from the school bus beat us inside, we'd be waiting forever.

"Come on!" I grabbed Becky's hand and pulled her up from her seat. Michelle was already waiting outside.

"What's the matter?' Becky asked.

"Nothing's the matter, but look over there."

Small children with matching baseball caps poured from the next bus like ants rushing over a hill with bits of leaves.

"They're adorable," Becky exclaimed. "Like cats but with better language skills."

Adorable? Not that good. Cute, maybe. Menacing, surely. But Becky had awakened from a nap, so she might have still been dreaming.

"We need to get ahead of the line." I ran Becky and Michelle over to the building and up its short flight of stairs.

"But I really have to go to the bathroom," protested Michelle.

"After!"

I rushed them past the stacks of cookies and chocolates and through the turnstile to reach the bar area. Heavy duty coffee machines towered behind showcases of pastries and sandwiches. I looked for the *cassa* sign, which, if there was one, was hidden, and instead headed for the cashier, who stood off to the right.

"What do you want?" I asked the girls.

"A coffee, I guess," said Becky. "Maybe a croissant?"

"*Tre caffè, per piacere,*" I told the cashier. "*E tre cornetti.*"

The woman smiled brightly. She had a wide face with rosy cheeks. She might have spent most days over a hot stove.

"Qui al nord, sono brioche."

I smiled back weakly. I hadn't understood anything besides *nord*, which meant "north," but the last thing I needed were traffic directions.

Becky pushed forward with a ten-euro note. *"Grazie mille!"*

"What did I miss?" I whispered.

"Croissants are called by their French name here," Michelle said. "As you go farther south, they're *cornetti* instead."

"How did you know that?"

"A YouTube video, of course!"

The woman rang us up, handed me the receipt, and waved towards the counter where two young guys dressed in matching Autogrill shirts pounded coffee into the portafilters. At nine-thirty a.m., the guys looked exhausted. I wondered how many coffees they'd already made that morning.

I handed the nearest worker our receipt. He nodded and threw it back on the counter.

"You know your way around these places," Becky said.

"It's my first Autogrill, but Tony warned me what to expect."

He'd spent twenty minutes explaining the whole system. He joked that nobody could say they'd genuinely visited Italy until they'd made a pilgrimage to the roadside gas station chain that monopolized the highways of the whole country.

Behind us, a handful of women herded the impossible number of children towards the cashier. The kids held hands in twos, but they squirmed in line and murmured complaints I couldn't catch.

"Look at this mob!" said Michelle. "Why is there one cashier?"

"And two baristas?" added Becky.

Perhaps there were long periods of time without any customers at all, but even that seemed unlikely. We were on the A1, the main road between Rome and Florence.

"We'll never have time to use the restroom," Becky said.

"That's the irony," I said. "Plenty of toilets, one cashier."

"It's another mystery," said Michelle. "Italy is full of them!"

I would have taken the time to agree, but by then the barista motioned to us and slapped our coffees on the counter.

"*I nostri cornetti?*" I asked. Whoops. "*Le nostre brioche?*" I asked, correcting myself.

He sent us to the next counter, where a woman with mauve lips tossed the customers pastries as if they were Frisbees. Three middle-aged Italian men pushed their way in front of me before I could reach the woman, but Michelle, who was taller than I was, stretched over, and the woman, who had seen the others trying to sneak ahead of us, took our receipt.

"*Ah, tre cornetti,*" she said. Couldn't anybody in this country decide which word to use for a croissant? Evidently not. The woman used a paper-thin napkin to pick up the first treat, which she handed to me, and then another to Becky, and the final one to Michellle.

"Not even Italians agree on what to call these things," Becky said as we bit into the soft dough.

As I reached the rich Nutella inside, I didn't care.

*

I'd read about Dante and the Renaissance. I'd watched and read *A Room with a View* multiple times. I'd heard so much about the wonders of Florence that I knew there was no way one poor little city could live up to anyone's expectations. But it wasn't that I didn't know enough about architecture to appreciate the Brunelleschi dome or the copies of the Ghiberti and Pisano doors on the Baptistry.

What I couldn't get past were all the people. Being a tourist myself, I could hardly complain, but the town was swarming. Marta, our city tour guide, blamed the cruise ships, which anchored in Livorno but hustled their passengers over for day trips. Even though she waved a flag as high as she could hold it, we could barely navigate the crowded streets long enough to follow her. Since there were ten of us plus Lucia, we had a fighting chance to stay together, but I could hardly absorb the history lesson when focused on not falling over people. "There is the Mercato del Porcellino," Marta said. "And there is the Fontana." The city passed in a swirl.

When we were finally granted freedom by a reluctant Lucia, Becky and Michelle and I didn't even attempt to join the long line of tourists hoping to enter the Duomo. Instead, we headed towards the Ponte Vecchio, the famous old bridge lined with jewelry shops, the one bridge that was spared during World War II. We paused half-way across and watched the parade marching by. People speaking languages I couldn't identify herded past with kinds of dogs I'd never seen before. I wasn't sure whether to admire the city's fame or to be horrified by the ridiculous number of visitors. Had my fellow tourists come to appreciate the city or check it off their lists? Was it important to say, "I've been to Florence" or to think, *the Vasari corridor is a secret passage overhead?*

While I was content to observe the world from the relative safety of the midpoint of the bridge, a few feet out of the stream of humanity, Becky suggested visiting Dante's house while Michelle wanted to try the Museum of Illusions. I sent them off on their own because the real showcase strutted before me. The scene was as joyous as it was crazy. It was as if every single tourist's biggest ambition in the whole wide world was to be right at this very spot, crossing the bridge, turning around, and crossing it again.

Enjoying Florence? texted Sander.

Trying to breathe. You can't believe the crowds.

Of course, Italy is popular, especially in a Jubilee Year.

I could hardly forget. A Jubilee Year, celebrated by the Catholic church four times a century, signified extra prayer, special masses, and a renewal of faith. While most of the attention turned to Rome, other cities anticipated higher tourism rates as well.

Rome is going to be crazy.

The city is expecting thirty-five million visitors this year! But don't worry. They won't all come this weekend.

Are you sure?

Rome is a big area. The tourists will be spread further apart! Besides, we can walk past the most famous places at night when no one else is around.

Oh, dear. A clear hint at romance. I wasn't sure if I would be ready for it or open to it, but maybe I wouldn't have to worry. There was no guarantee I could survive a day in Florence.

*

The restaurateur shook his head so fast I couldn't even distinguish his facial features. *"Siamo completi."* We're full.

"That's it," I said. "I'm buying a salad at the grocery store. You guys can keep trying if you want to."

"I've had enough," said Michelle. "But didn't we pass a Spar a few blocks back?"

"Three blocks," said Becky. "I've been keeping track in case we needed other options."

We did. All the tourists in the city had decided they were hungry at the same moment we had, but some had been clever enough to make reservations.

It had never occurred to us that we needed one. Hadn't Marta complained that all the tourists had come from cruise ships, ones that certainly provided free meals to all their guests?

I might have enjoyed a nice relaxing dinner at a quaint restaurant, but the famous Florentine *lampredotto panino*, a sandwich made from cow stomach, didn't entice me anyway. I probably couldn't afford a Florentine steak, and *pappa al pomodoro*, tomato and bread soup, was something I could make back in Tucson given enough motivation.

"A Spar salad," I said. "They can't be that bad."

In fact, we all agreed that they were tasty, especially for the reasonable price. More importantly, grabbing a bite at a grocery store gave us a chance to eat outside Santa Croce, the train station, where the traffic slowed down to such a trickle that we could pretend we nearly had the city to ourselves even though we knew it wasn't true.

At least by nightfall, we could walk down the streets without tripping over fellow tourists. That was already a big improvement.

Chapter Fifteen

As Lucia alternated between stomping on the pavement and flinging her arms up and down, which did equal amounts of zero good, the Uffizi guards eyed her suspiciously. When they finally asked what was wrong, she shot out words faster than a firing squad shoots bullets. At first I couldn't catch a single one, but wait, had she really called my fellow students *delinquenti?* I couldn't have agreed more.

Lucia turned from the guards to the three of us: me, Becky, and Michelle. "Where are they? Why do you think we spent the money for you to stay overnight in Florence? To make it easy for you! So that we could enter the Uffizi right on time! The first slot!"

Holding ten student tickets to the Uffizi and seeing three show up would have disheartened any art lover, but the woman needed to consider the source. The bar owners back in Orvieto all had Lucia's number on speed dial. Florence offered countless options where my classmates were happily anonymous. To set them loose on the city and expect them to show up for an eight-fifteen museum entrance was expecting way too much. No matter her enthusiasm, Lucia should have known better. Maybe her previous groups of students had been more serious, but I doubted it. Art museum or unchaperoned drinking? That was a tough one.

"Well?" Lucia asked me. "You know Henrietta quite well. Where do you think she is?"

"I haven't seen her since the end of yesterday's walking tour," I said. Since I'd offered to stay in the triple with Michelle and Becky, I'd been able to dump Henrietta on Christie for a change.

"Maybe the others didn't hear their alarms," Michelle said.

Even if they'd remembered to set them, and even if they'd heard them, they wouldn't have obeyed them. They would have ignored the ringing, turned over, and gone right back to sleep to nurse their precious Italian hangovers. Lucia shouldn't have needed much help to understand that.

"Never mind, *ragazze*," Lucia said. "We don't wait. Our guide is already here."

Marta arrived one second before the museum doors opened and helped Lucia manage the electronic tickets while herding the three of us inside.

For the next two hours we were under Marta's control. I protested that I preferred to see the museum's rooms in order, but Marta refused my request in both Italian and English. Finally, I caught on. Marta made a beeline through the medieval rooms and the Early Renaissance so that we could see Sandro Botticelli's famous works and even take selfies before the room filled top to bottom with tourists doing the Indy 500.

I couldn't blame the other tourists. I didn't know how to appreciate art myself. Instead of jumping up and down at *The Birth of Venus*, I tried to imagine why, in a country of mostly dark-haired people, Venus was blonde. And to be accurate, the painting showed Venus arriving on shore, not actually being born.

Those were technicalities. I could appreciate the wind god blowing his brains out and Venus's flowing hair and garments. The classical scene was peaceful and gentle, a celebration of beauty, an escape from the harsh realities of the times.

"Isn't this great?" Becky asked.

"Great," I said, halfway meaning what I said. I didn't mind looking at the famous Michelangelo or the da Vinci or even the Gentileschi, but I didn't connect with the paintings or wear out my phone taking pictures of them. I was tempted to blame myself for failing to appreciate highlights. I didn't fare any better once we'd escaped the huge institution and poured into the Piazza della Signoria. While most of the famous statues under the Loggia were brutal scenes of rape or death, the Poseidon in the fountain beside the Palazzo Vecchio made me laugh. Not only did the god have a quizzical look on his face as if he couldn't understand what was going on right in front of him, but he had to suffer being photographed all day long with a pigeon on top of his head.

Now that was art.

*

Tony asked me to stop by after I returned from our field trip, but when I reached his flat, the windows were all dark.

Are you at Mezza Luna or Palace Cafè? I texted. *Tell me where and I'll catch up to you.*

Moments later Tony peeked out the window. I would have shouted a greeting, but he put his index finger to his lip and buzzed me in.

I rushed upstairs, but before I could knock, Tony opened the door and pulled me inside. The lights were off, but the living room was illuminated by the streetlight outside the window.

"What's wrong?"

"I don't know. Maybe nothing. Maybe just my wild imagination."

"You've been sitting in the dark?"

"I don't want to deal with anybody. Besides you, I mean. Not that I have to deal with you. You know what I mean."

He led me over to the sofa, and I sat close to him. Even in the semi-dark, I noticed the drooped shoulders and deep-set eyes.

"What happened around here?"

"Nothing. I mean, well, I'm not sure."

Tony didn't sound like himself. I'd never seen him so uncertain.

"Tell me."

"I'm not even sure what happened."

"Try to explain."

"This afternoon, I'd already closed up when someone banged on the enoteca door real loud, like they were trying to force their way inside."

"That door might belong to a castle. There's no way somebody could get in without a key or a battering ram."

"I wasn't worried they would break in, but they yelled *vecchio stronzo* and took off."

"Old . . . what?"

He took a deep breath. "A *stronzo* is a stupid person. A real idiot. It's not quite a swear word, but it's strong."

.   "They were referring to your uncle?'

"Even if they wanted to call me a jerk, they wouldn't have put 'old' with it."

Of course not. They were insulting Fabrizio. They had to be. While that seemed as childish as it was out of line, I wouldn't have thought twice about it. Tony, however, was bent out of shape all the way back to New Jersey.

"Okay, that wasn't nice, and it's not that great for your neighbors either, but why are you so worried?"

"It was weird, you know? You don't expect someone to bang on your door, shout, and run. Actually, I heard a car door slam, so they were too lazy to come on foot."

"A drive-by insult. That's a new one. It's not mentioned in any of the guidebooks."

"And it's never happened before."

I thought back to Mezza Luna. "Think this has to do with Antonio's warning?"

"I guess? There was something else last night."

"I missed it while I was busy dining in Florence. Someone trying to break in?"

Tony shrugged. "I don't know. Some kind of banging sound woke me up. I figured it was out on the street, but I couldn't see anything out the window."

"That's strange, all right."

"Oh. I almost forgot."

He fished a key chain from a ceramic jar. A soccer ball dangled from one end.

"Your spare keys?"

He handed them over. "As promised. One opens the enoteca, one opens the door into the hallway, and the third opens the door to the apartment. Come use the garden whenever you want, even if I'm not here."

I was touched. Although he'd promised, I wasn't sure he'd follow through. Not everybody felt comfortable opening up their house to their best friends, let alone to people they'd barely met.

"I appreciate it. I really do. And if I come by and your lights are out, I can still get in!"

"Exactly."

He didn't even crack a smile.

"Tony, I was kidding, you know. You can't just sit around in the dark."

"I know. But I need a chance to get my bearings. To feel sure of things."

"And to talk to your uncle."

"I've tried more than once. Never mind." He popped to his feet. "Say, I should have offered you something to drink. A little wine?"

"No thanks. I have more homework to do later. How about a little frizzante?"

"Coming up."

"That would be perfect."

While Tony stumbled through his kitchen in the dark, I fumed. Who left his own nephew in charge of a mess without explaining what was wrong? It was unfair as well as dangerous. People should at least know what they were getting into. They needed time to digest the information enough to develop a plan of action.

Tony stumbled back with tall glasses of water and handed me one.

"No offense," I said, "but I've lost patience with your uncle. This is way too much responsibility for a summer job."

"You're right."

"He's paying you, I hope."

"We didn't exactly talk about it."

"What?"

"I know. I should have asked, right? But the moment I arrived seemed like the wrong time, and then we were always out with other people, and then, I don't know, he left before I had a chance to bring the subject up again."

"You're too nice."

"Maybe."

"For a day, fine. For a week. But that's enough!"

"I don't know what I was thinking, but it's kind of too late now. I mean, I wouldn't walk out on him."

"But he doesn't respond to your calls. I'm not sure you owe him anything."

"I know. He's eccentric and all, but this silence is extreme."

"It's impolite. Extremely impolite."

"Like your classmates not showing up for the Uffizi tour?"

I'd texted Tony highlights. "You should have heard Lucia on the way home! But never mind. I earned brownie points. Let's hope I don't need them."

"What would you do wrong?"

"I could think of something."

"Like inviting your friend to stay in Orvieto overnight?"

"Not that!" I'd told him all about Lucia's rules and my classmates' plans to thwart them.

"How are you feeling about it?" Tony asked. "Are you glad you invited Sander to visit you or not?"

I'd thought about Sander on and off ever since extending the invitation to him. I alternated thinking I was an idiot with thinking I was merely crazy. Who invited a friend they barely knew to visit? Yes, I knew about his family. Yes, I was friends with his brother. That didn't mean we would hit it off. Staying with his friends would make the situation even stickier.

On the other hand, if you didn't take a chance at things, how would you ever manage a fun life?

"I'm meeting him in Rome tomorrow," I said. "That's all I can tell you for sure."

Tony wiggled his shoulders. "Excited?"

"More like apprehensive."

"You'll have a great time. I'm sure of it."

We heard a sudden *thud* so loud we both turned towards the window. Then we ran and looked out. No people. No cars. Not even a bike.

"Same sound you heard last night?" I whispered.

"I'm a heavy sleeper, but a loud noise woke me up. That's the most I know."

We retreated to the living room. "You don't think someone was trying to break in?" I asked.

"No. I think someone was being a pain in the ass."

Teens played tricks. Bad friends played tricks. Criminals were more aggressive, and they accomplished their goals much more often.

"What did Fabrizio tell you about the neighbors?"

"Nothing."

"Want to try calling him again?"

"I sent three texts. He'll either answer or he won't. I'm guessing he won't."

I couldn't imagine not responding to something so important, but I wanted to give Fabrizio the benefit of the doubt—for the moment. "He might have gone out for the evening. Maybe he'll contact you when he returns to his hotel."

Tony shook his head. "I'd like to think that's true, but it's more likely that I'm on my own."

"Doesn't he care about his business?"

Tony paused. "Maybe he's ready to quit but not ready to admit it. Retiring is a hard decision for people. It means giving up their lives and starting over. That would be a scary proposition for anybody."

"I get all that. There are a million reasons somebody wouldn't want to let go. But Fabrizio is far away anyway. He couldn't help you tonight if he wanted to. Meanwhile, why not contact the police?"

"And tell them what, that someone I can't identify might have thrown something at my window which, luckily, didn't break?"

"I see what you mean." I pointed to the bookshelves. "Promise you'll look through some of his papers while I'm gone?"

"I promise. It's pretty dull around here when you're not around. Who else would entertain me?"

Your neighbors, I wanted to say. Your uncle's enemies. Jerks from around town—every town had at least one. "It's Dullsville, all right. That will give you extra time to look around."

"For what?"

"You'll know it when you see it."

"Right, right," Tony answered.

He didn't believe me, and maybe there was nothing to find anyway. That didn't mean he shouldn't look.

Chapter Sixteen

Passengers crossed Roma Termini in such a confused mass that I was surprised anyone reached the correct platform. The electronic board explained which trains were leaving or arriving from the twenty or so *binari*, but everybody seemed to enter the station from the wrong side. Some of the train tracks weren't posted until ten minutes before departure, so parents held onto children and businesspeople clung to briefcases until they knew which direction to run.

As soon as I spotted an escalator, I escaped to the second floor. The airy space held both eateries and cafés, and big picture windows emitted light. Although I'd offered to meet Sander at the airport, he insisted that we meet at the train station instead, and he was the one who suggested the upstairs hideaway.

Smart man. He was practical, and he knew about traveling. Those were positive signs even though I was still nervous. He was convinced that we would enjoy spending time with one another, but he had no way of knowing that. No way at all.

I will take the next Leonardo Express, texted Sander. *I should arrive in thirty minutes.*

Perfect. Good to have a heads up. I took out the vocabulary list I kept in my pocket for extra moments like this and repeated the new words to myself.

My cell phone buzzed; maybe the train was already delayed. No matter. It wouldn't arrive ahead of schedule, so I could relax for half an hour. I didn't need Sander to update me a hundred times. Once would have been plenty. I wasn't glued to my phone the way my classmates were. I had no intention of giving in to the constant need to check my device.

One *ping* followed another.

I still resisted checking. I didn't need the blow-by-blow. How old was I, five?

Instead, I needed my word list. *Scorciatoia*, I said aloud. Score-cha-TOY-ah. Did the word for *shortcut* need to be four syllables? I went through the list of two dozen words, crossing off the ones I remembered. Cramming a semester's worth of Italian into three weeks was crazy. I'd known that at the outset. I'd prepared by reviewing beforehand. By now, I couldn't catch up with myself. I had to power through.

Ping.

Sander was scheduled to arrive within five minutes. Great! Let him arrive. I had a comfortable table at the coffee shop. Let him find me. If our initial meeting was awful, so be it. At least we tried. But because he might have been delayed, I troubled myself long enough to check my messages.

There were zero from Sander, but there were several from Tony.

Being detained. May need your help.

Contact my uncle. +39-347-490-1847

He won't text. Keep calling until he answers.

What?!

I read the texts again. Tony knew I had plenty to deal with. He wouldn't have played a practical joke on me while I was on my way to meet Sander. Something else was going on.

Detained where?

No answer. I called the store phone and let it ring twenty times. Nothing.

Detained? As in by the police? The idea was crazy. He couldn't have done anything that bad. He didn't have a car, so he couldn't have run somebody over. He barely drank, so he wouldn't have been drunk and disorderly, especially not during the day. He could have gotten mad and taken a swing at somebody, but that too was out of character. He could have miscounted money, though, and a customer might have assumed he was being cheated.

The message made no sense. If Tony were detained, what could I do? Even if I contacted Fabrizio, what would I tell him?

"Gina!" A tall blond with a bright smile suddenly towered over me.

I sprang to my feet. We had an awkward moment of confusion, but then I greeted him with a small hug, which was easy since all I had to do was lean into his chest as he towered over me.

"I apologize," he said. "European flights usually run very much on time."

I couldn't speak. Too many conflicting thoughts. Tony, what? Meanwhile, a more melodious voice than I noticed on the phone. A handsome, well-built man who looked more attractive in person than on WhatsApp. Muscles bulging through the short-sleeved Polo shirt. Dressed for comfort in walking shorts and summer sandals. A neat haircut that allowed for waves of blond.

I should have felt like the luckiest person on the planet.

"How are you?" His rosy cheeks shone.

"Uh, uh, okay."

"I do apologize about the delay."

"That's all right."

"You might have taken a later train down from Orvieto and then not had to rush away from school."

Leaving school quickly was a pleasure, not an inconvenience. But Tony? What could I do? Where could I do it from?

"You seem tired. Perhaps you are weary from your studies?" he asked.

"Not tired." I was too stunned to speak. I might have been a zombie.

"Perhaps you're not feeling well?"

I felt like I'd been knocked down by one of those obnoxious little cars rattling around the narrow streets of Orvieto and run over.

"Feeling okay." I sank back into my seat.

Sander sat across from me. "If you have come up with a more important plan for the weekend, that's perfectly all right. I'll still have a lovely time with my friend."

"Stop. I'm glad you're here," I said slowly. "I'm happy to spend time with you. But I might need to go right back to Orvieto."

"That is fine. We can change our plans. I'm sure we can find a hotel."

I shook my head. "Remember a year ago, that first time we talked on the phone?"

The occasion was memorable. I contacted Sander in such a panic that he assumed I was crazy. I had a valid reason to be worried about his brother, but he didn't have any way to know that at the time.

"I cannot forget! I'm sorry I was so unfriendly. I had no idea you were telling me the truth. I'm still ashamed about my reactions. Perhaps you cannot put my insults out of your mind. I completely understand. Don't worry for it! You came all the way to Rome to meet me, and then you realized you shouldn't have. It's perfectly all right."

I held up my hand as if it were a stop sign. "Okay, two things. One, your mind is working faster than mine right now. I'm not mad at you or even reacting to you. I need to tell you a bit of a story."

He grinned until I thought his teeth might burst from his mouth. "That's three things."

What was he, a math major? Maybe, since he managed a bank. After opting not to punch him, I offered a weak smile.

He nodded towards the bar counter. "Coffee?"

I shook my head. "I may be too caffeinated already."

He nodded. Again, his practicality was a good sign. As he led me outside and over to the closest bench, he took my craziness right in stride.

*

An hour and a short bus ride later, Sander and I climbed three flights of stairs to reach a flat on Via della Luce, the Street of Light. A tall and graceful Dutch woman opened the door for us. She seemed ageless, but she might have been fifty or sixty. She had high cheek bones, white skin, and a slender build. She had plenty of blonde hair, but it was wrapped up in a cloth on top of her head.

"So good to see you, Sander," she said in clear, crisp English as she gave him a hug.

Sander nudged me forward. "This is my friend Gina."

"I'm Fleur," the woman said. To my surprise, for she wasn't Italian, she also hugged me. "Good to meet you."

"It's awfully nice of you to let us stay here," I stammered. In my experience, fellow students put you up in their living rooms on hard floors and loaned you ratty towels while adults gave you lists of nearby hotels. "Are you sure we're no trouble?"

"I'm happy for the company. Come on in. I have prepared a little tea."

She motioned for us to leave our bags at the door and led us through a corridor that opened into a pleasant rectangle. Light streamed in from a double-paned window that stretched to a high ceiling. The modern furniture, probably from Ikea, consisted of light-colored wood and simple lines. A pot of tea and cups and water glasses waited for us alongside hazelnut wafers. The woman couldn't have done a single thing to make us feel more welcome. I would have been overwhelmed if Sander hadn't explained the close connection. Fleur's older sister had attended school with Sander's mom. The two families had been close friends ever since, which meant for the past several decades.

"I hope you're enjoying your study program," Fleur said. "What no one warns you is that language learning is much harder than you would imagine, especially in a compressed period of time."

I could have kissed her. She understood my situation exactly without my having to explain it. I wrestled my word list from my pocket and waved it through the air like a flag. "Some days nothing sticks."

She laughed. "I had that same experience for the first few years."

This incompetency was going to last? No. She wanted to make me feel better. Bless her. "Sander said that you've lived in Italy for a while."

"A decade by now. But the agency I work for is governed by the EU. In theory they send us to various countries, but I've elected to stay in Rome, at least for a while."

"She helps with international law so that companies can branch out to new locations," Sander explained. "She travels extensively."

"I do indeed," Fleur said as she poured us tea. "Sometimes too much!"

"But you love to travel," Sander said.

"Yes. I'm a dedicated hodophile. But I'm ready to hear about your trip, Sander, and Gina's experiences in Orvieto. Believe it or not, that's one city I haven't visited."

"You wouldn't find lots of international businesses," I said. "But I'm afraid I can't be a good guest, and we might have to return to Orvieto."

"Oh, dear, I hope not! I've made a dinner reservation at one of my favorite restaurants. But that doesn't matter. What's troubling you?"

I looked over at Sander, but he nodded. I hadn't wanted to burden his friend, but he'd insisted that I tell her everything I was willing to share. "I guess a friend of mine might be in jail."

Fleur set down the teapot as if it suddenly weighed three times as much as it had the moment before. "Oh, dear! There are so many things you can do wrong, especially in Italy. Is your friend one of your fellow students?"

I gave Fleur the whole story, a detailed version of what I'd already told Sander. The longer I talked, the sillier I felt. The situation was ridiculous. Tony couldn't have been detained. He hadn't done anything wrong. I knew him well enough to know that.

"I don't even know where the jail is," I said. "I don't know if they'd let me in. I don't know anything!"

Fleur calmly drew the tea bags from the pot. "It is often hard to deal with Italian authorities. To our minds, they might seem complex and inefficient. However, it won't do you any good to return to Orvieto."

"Why not? I should try to help him."

Fleur held out the tray of wafers, and I snatched one up.

"Yes, I can see that would be the case," Fleur said. "But your friend has an American passport, correct?"

I nodded.

"He won't be held in Orvieto." Fleur pointed out the window. "He'll be held here."

"In Rome?" I exclaimed. "But why?"

Sander held up his index finger. "Because of the consulate?"

"Exactly," said Fleur. "No matter what he did, the authorities will contact the consulate before they do anything else."

"And bring Tony to Rome?"

"Yes," Fleur said. "They won't have a choice. For U.S. citizens studying in Umbria on student visas, there is a specific procedure that must be followed. I'll explain the whole process to you over dinner."

I accidentally snapped the wafer into pieces, which then flew in multiple directions. "Oh!"

"Not to worry," Fleur laughed.

But I did. I knelt on the floor. With Sander's help, I gathered up the bigger crumbs.

Unfortunately, gathering up the facts about Tony wouldn't be nearly as easy.

Chapter Seventeen

By the time we hit Trastevere, a colorful section of Rome hugging the west end of the Tiber, I would have sworn that everyone else in the capital city was already eating. Trattorie lined the streets, their tables stretching out in every direction. Since it was past eight o'clock, the traditional dinner time, locals dined alongside tourists. Anxious eaters wielded their forks defensively as if neighbors would steal their noodles. Garlic pierced the air, hovering above marinara sauces and fried fish. Here we smelled a touch of basil, there a touch of rosemary, and everywhere, extra virgin olive oil warming to a perfect temperature.

I wished I could contribute to the joyous atmosphere. Every few feet I remembered that we'd learned nothing about Tony, which meant we couldn't help him. Fleur had made numerous calls, but none of her connections at the consulate knew anything about an Italian American from New Jersey. Tony didn't seem to be anywhere, which either meant he hadn't arrived or, more likely, hadn't been processed.

I felt awful for him. He was probably scared and alone. Worst of all, I couldn't imagine he'd done anything wrong.

My two Dutch friends sympathized. They'd heard plenty of stories about people being detained for no reason. They made things easier for me by offering options: Did I prefer to spend the evening at the flat by myself? Did I prefer we all stay in? That didn't seem fair either, so I opted that we stick with Fleur's plan to have a meal out. I reminded myself at least twenty times that since I was in Rome, I needed to do as the Romans. That meant I needed to feast.

Fleur herded us a short distance to Taverna Trilussa. The waiters whisked us inside with a knowing smile that told me Fleur was a welcome regular before leading us to a reserved table on the terrace that afforded a view of the whole establishment.

Why shouldn't Fleur be a frequent diner? The eatery was a short walk from her house, and the aromas from each table we passed were so enticing that I was ready to plop down in the next empty seat and invite myself to dinner with strangers.

When Fleur recommended that I try pasta with the traditional *amatriciana* sauce, I nodded before she finished the sentence. My world might be falling apart, but at least I could eat well. After all, I needed to keep up my strength. I would probably need it.

"What do you think of your study program?" Fleur asked.

My feelings were contradictory at best, and worrying about Tony pushed school far from my mind, but I couldn't evaluate the program accurately. I couldn't blame the program for my lackadaisical colleagues, but they interfered with my overall experience. Maybe they came with the territory. They loved the idea of studying in Italy, but they hated the idea of actually studying.

"The program is more ambitious than I thought," I said. "We're supposed to breeze through Italian 102 in three short weeks. I knew the course would be challenging when I signed up for it, but the task has been harder than I expected."

"The difficulty of language learning takes most of us by surprise," Fleur said.

"But your English is flawless, and so is your Italian."

"Thank you, but you see, I use both languages all the time at work. I am forced to practice. Necessity is always the best teacher."

I turned to Sander. "What's your excuse?"

"I can't speak Italian," Sander said quickly.

"What were you using with the waiter, French?" I demanded. "You ordered flawlessly."

Sander laughed. "I know restaurant Italian. It comes in handy."

"Okay, but if you give me the excuse that you learned to speak English by frequenting English restaurants, I'll call you a liar. English food is just not that good."

Sander's cheeks turned one shade redder. "I like to watch American TV?"

Fleur and I laughed as Sander launched into a full review of favorite shows. Ever since I'd discovered that most titles were available in Italian, I'd been loyal to Netflix although I often cheated and watched the subtitles in English.

"Didn't you say you learned Spanish at home?" Sander asked. "That should make Italian a lot easier for you."

"Spanish only makes it easier when it's not causing interference."

"You didn't want to complete your studies with Spanish?" Fleur asked.

"Try not to laugh. I thought I needed a bigger challenge. Also, I have Italian grandparents."

"They speak Italian to you?"

"Actually, long dark family history, we're not close. They're in New York some place. I have relatives over here, too, but I don't know about them either. I know that sounds pathetic."

Fleur indicated the sea of diners around us. "It might be rewarding to track down such relatives. You might be invited to some home-cooked dinners!"

Maybe, but what if I had uncles who turned out to be as egotistical as Fabrizio? Sometimes it was better to leave relatives buried in their hometowns without dragging them across the highway.

"Ostensibly you could look for your relatives when you have free time at the end of the program," said Sander.

Since when did anyone on American TV use the term "ostensibly?" Sander probably learned the word reading something heavy, such as Russian novels translated into English.

"Yes, maybe," I stuttered.

"Perhaps you won't meet your relatives on this trip, but you could do so in the future," Fleur said. "You're young. You have plenty of time."

I might have protested that I didn't have enough information to take the first steps towards contacting said relatives, but once the dishes arrived, our conversation stopped dead. In Italy, pasta deserved total and immediate concentration no matter the topic. As I forked my way into the first bites of the tasty sauce made from tomatoes, onions, pecorino, and pancetta, I was glad I knew the rule.

*

Although she insisted on paying for dinner, Fleur hurried off after drinking her coffee even though the waiter brought over shot glasses of meloncello, which was an even tastier after-dinner drink than limoncello. I suspected that Fleur wasn't honestly in a hurry. She wanted to give Sander and me some time on our own. We complied by lingering over the shots until all the other customers left and the waiters started setting the tables for the next day.

We didn't go straight back to the flat, however. Wandering the streets of Trastevere was a helpful way to digest all that pasta, which wouldn't have been too bad if we hadn't used the "little shoe," the *scarpetta*, meaning that we used bread to soak up every molecule of sauce. Then there was the *Millefoglione*, the Thousand Big Leaves dessert, and we couldn't leave a crumb of that either. I swore I wouldn't need to eat for days, but that wouldn't be the case either; the very next day I knew I would want to repeat the process all over again.

Since the diners were lingering rather than eating by now, we heard animated conversations from every eatery. People who had rushed around all week were happy for a payoff, including a bit of grappa, to round out the evening. A hot day topped by a luscious meal in anticipation of a romantic night made the whole area sizzle. No wonder the Italians lived well: they enjoyed sharing long meals with one another, they took their time, they brushed away worries, and instead of bottling up their emotions, they let them bubble to the surface and jump out.

We completed the triangle around Piazza Trilussa and took the street that hugged the river.

"You didn't tell us much about your program," Sander said. "Are you finding it unsatisfactory?"

"The classes are fine. It's my classmates who need work. Three of us are here to learn Italian. The rest wanted an excuse to come to Europe. Don't get me wrong. It's great to have a reason to visit Europe, but my classmates aren't trying to learn Italian. They're satisfied spending their evenings testing out the bars, where they don't need much vocabulary. As long as they earn a C, they'll still pass."

Sander had long legs, but he modified his stride so that I could easily keep up. "You're disappointed in them."

"I guess? Maybe I shouldn't be. If they came here to get drunk all night and sleep all day, they're achieving their goals."

"Can you attribute their attitudes to the shock of living in a new culture? That's a difficult step for people if they are unaccustomed to it."

I'd considered that possibility. My classmates were so accustomed to their own ways that they couldn't think things through any differently. They'd never had a chance to try.

"Culture shock is part of the challenge. My classmates don't know enough to avoid normal mistakes such as asking for a latte and being surprised when they're handed a glass of milk instead of a coffee drink. They don't know where to start, you might say."

We reached the corner and continued to the next block.

"When we travel, we are presented with many things that are unfamiliar," Sander said.

"Exactly! That's what I love about it. Afterwards, you can pick and choose the elements you like. Do you know what I mean? You can take the best bits of different cultures and incorporate them into your own repertoire."

Sander put out his hand to stop me from walking into a fast-moving pedestrian. "What do you mean, exactly?"

"Let me give you a quick example. Back home people think a big breakfast is healthy. Here, forget it! One pastry, and off they go! Of course, they have lunch to anticipate, so it's all right. But I've never enjoyed a heavy breakfast in the morning. The Italian system is much better."

"I see."

Whoops. Remove foot from mouth. Remember that not everybody reacts the same way you do.

"I'm sorry," I said. "What I meant is that for me, the Italian system makes more sense. You probably enjoy a big breakfast!"

"The Dutch are accustomed to bigger breakfasts than the Italians. That much is true. But I eat all the time. I don't jump past any meals!"

I believed him. Anybody that tall had to fill the reserve tank. Sander wasn't heavy; he was sturdy. He could have stopped a Cinquecento by holding out one hand.

"Eating well in Italy is easy," he continued. "Vlinder said that it's much harder to find delicious meals in the U.S. I suppose that means that you must know where to look."

We walked past the third trattoria in row, all three of which looked inviting.

"We do have nice restaurants, but you have to work harder to find them. We don't have the same culture of enjoying meals. That's the difference. And a lot of people are married to fast food, but that's just what I call a bad habit."

Sander pointed out a ragged edge on the sidewalk and guided me carefully past it. "Every country has its advantages, and every region as well."

"Absolutely! Take the comparison of space. In Tucson, land is relatively cheap. I'm used to living in a house with a garden, not a tiny apartment I can't turn around in without falling over myself. My place in Orvieto is cute, but it's claustrophobic. It's up three flights of stairs and all closed in."

I craned my neck to get a glimpse of the baby young parents were parading in a stroller.

"No balcony?"

"Only windows. It's no big deal, but it does drive me crazy."

"I can understand why. My parents' garden is small, but they enjoy it. In Amsterdam, as soon as the weather turns warm, people prefer to sit outside. They have to take advantage of the opportunity."

Ironically, as soon as it turned what I would call nice in Tucson, most people retreated inside and cranked the AC. "Not only do I have a small apartment, but I'm sharing it with a narcissist who's so focused on social media that she wouldn't notice if the roof caved in unless she lost her internet connection."

"That sounds uncomfortable."

"Yes! But that's what led me to Tony. I spotted the garden in back of the enoteca, and then I went over to investigate."

We walked past three middle-aged Italian men, all wearing dress pants and short-sleeved shirts, who looked like they were out for modeling jobs.

"Perhaps it was Tony that interested you! There's no reason to be awkward about it. I'm not offended if he won your attention before I did."

"Trust me. Tony is just a friend. I could tell right away that I'm not his type, but we hit it off immediately."

"Kindred spirits?"

"We've also had a lot of similar experiences."

Sander pointed to a trio of Americans swaying back and forth outside a bar. "Tony is more mature than your fellow classmates?"

"He came to Italy to serve an actual purpose, not just to have a good time and spend his parents' money. Besides that, he's more traveled, and because of that, more aware."

"Travel is the best teacher, isn't she?"

"Absolutely," I said as we reached the river. "By the way, is that the bridge that connects Trastevere to Ancient Rome?"

"I believe it is."

We paused, admiring the arched expanse and the tranquil water below.

"If you're tired, we could turn back," Sander said. "I realize you received quite a lot of negative news today."

Sander was right, but there wasn't much I could do about it. Fleur had tried her best to help, and now our one option was to do nothing and wait. That meant I had to put Tony out of my mind and concentrate on the moment.

Positive thinking! I reminded myself. For example, it was a perfect night. The air held fast at eighty degrees, and a gentle breeze blew pockets of fresh air. Sander and I weren't on a time schedule, so we could stay out as long as we wanted to. Half of Rome paraded before us, so all we had to do for entertainment was to keep our eyes open.

"We're close to 'The Mouth of Truth,' aren't we?" Ever since watching the humorous scene from *Roman Holiday*, I'd wanted to see the stone mouth for myself. Legend had it that if you were untruthful but dumb enough to stick your hand into the gaping hole, the mask bit off your hand.

"I believe it's in a church on the other side of the bridge."

"I realize that visiting a legendary stone face is a crazy tourist thing, but as long as we're nearby, I sure wouldn't mind."

"We all have our illusions," Sander said. "Mine was to meet you in person! Allow me to satisfy one of yours."

We meandered over to the Basilica di Santa Maria in Cosmedin to follow in the footsteps of a princess. The church was closed, but through the metal railing, we could easily discern the huge marble face that nearly gobbled up the hand of journalist Joe Bradley in the 1953 movie. The Princess laughed so hard at being duped that the whole world fell in love with her.

I wasn't sure anyone would fall for me the same way, but I was ecstatic that Sander had worked hard to hear me out and worked even harder to aid a stranger. I couldn't have expected anyone to go the extra kilometer in the same way, yet he seemed to understand my predicament and appreciate the problem.

As he stood beside me with a dozen other tourists, I appreciated his calm demeanor. He took everything in stride, which was something I was still learning to do, and he was unassuming to the point of being naïve. He didn't seem to notice the women who strained to get a better look at him even though they were accompanied by men of their own, nor did he shoot smiles in their direction.

In other words, I had Sander to myself.

The possibility of a summer fling was one thing, a good thing at that. Who didn't want a romance to punctuate her summer study program? But meeting someone who could be a true friend was a zillion times more important.

Maybe I just had.

Chapter Eighteen

Gentle arms rocked me awake from what must have been a deep sleep. When I opened an eye, I thought I saw Vlinder. Then it all came back: traveling to Rome, meeting Sander, staying with Fleur. The sun streamed into the room, bathing Sander and doubling the radiance of his blond hair. I remembered too the night before. I'd worried about the implications of spending the night with Sander, but the delightful guest bedroom held twin beds separated by a nightstand. Once we'd returned from our walk, we'd shared a nightcap and a kiss on the cheek. As soon as I stretched out my legs, I fell asleep..

"You must wake up," Sander whispered.

I straightened my tank top and propped myself up on my elbows. Right. We had sightseeing duty. Lots to cover. To start with, Largo Argentina, Piazza Navona, and the Pantheon. Yet I saw no reason to hurry. The sights would be open all day, and although they weren't right next to each other, they weren't far apart. Sander probably always rose with the sun and jumped into the day, just like his brother. Maybe it was a family thing. Maybe it was cultural.

"What did you want to see first?" I asked. "Do we need to catch a bus?"

Sander squeezed my hand. "We've located Tony, but we are only allowed to speak to him if we arrive soon."

I sat up straight. "You found him?"

"He's at a detention center of sorts. But we must arrive presently, or we'll lose the chance."

"That makes no sense."

"Fleur may have misunderstood."

No. Our hostess knew more about Rome than the Romans did, especially when it came to the workings of bureaucracy. "I can be ready to leave in a few minutes."

Sander tucked in his shirt. "Coffee?"

"Please."

Within fifteen minutes, Sander, Fleur, and I scurried down the stairs. Panic had roused me quicker than the coffee had. A taxi driver who routinely worked for Fleur waited for us outside. He greeted us warmly before whisking us through town.

I lost sense of our route, but we crossed the Tiber into the heart of Rome and worked our way north for a couple of miles. Then we reached a nondescript office that stretched several floors high.

"*Aspetto?*" the taxi driver asked. "Should I wait?"

"*Meglio di no,*" said Fleur. "Better not."

He waved as he sped off.

I didn't blame him. I didn't want to be stuck at the imposing building either, but at least the uniformed guards at the door didn't shoo us away. Instead, they kindly pointed us to the longest possible set of stairs. Then after waiting in three separate offices and offering various explanations, all done expertly by Fleur in a soft, diplomatic voice, she and I, though not Sander, were led down the hall to a metal door.

We were warned not to touch Tony, but as soon as the guard opened the door, I rushed inside the room.

"Gina!"

"No loud," the guard said. He'd entered the room with us but stayed at the door. He indicated for us to sit down. Two empty plastic chairs awaited us a few feet in front of Tony, who had already been sitting when we came in.

"What happened?" I asked.

"How did you know to find me?"

I pointed at Fleur. "Sander's friend here is your new guardian angel. We'll explain about that later. Tell me why you're here."

"I can't because I don't know!"

"You're kidding," I said.

"Not at all! Police showed up at the enoteca and asked if I had sold some products to the Baldoni family. After I said 'yes,' they told me to lock the door, and then they took me away!" He looked at Fleur. "I'm sorry to bother you, ma'am! But I don't have any idea why I'm here."

"The guards won't give us much time," Fleur said softly. "As quickly as you can, tell us anything that might help explain your situation."

"I don't know! Fabrizio prepared the boxes before he left town. but maybe he miscounted the bottles, or maybe the olive oil wasn't extra virgin enough, or maybe the wine was bad."

"That's all you know?" I asked.

"I'm lucky to know that much. I heard the police mention Baldoni, so I figured they were talking about my uncle's customer."

"Have they been mean to you?" I asked.

Tony glanced at the guard, who pretended not to be listening. "Not mean. Inefficient. Paperwork, phone calls, more paperwork."

"They've contacted your parents?" asked Fleur.

"Mom is undergoing chemo, and yesterday she received a treatment. I won't bother her if I can avoid it."

I couldn't blame him. In his shoes, I would have made the same decision. "What do you need?"

"Besides to get out of here? This building was freezing last night, so a hoodie would help. Or a shirt. Or a towel. Or anything."

"Did they feed you?" Fleur asked.

"A sandwich and some water."

"*Cinque minuti,*" said the guard. "Five minutes."

"What else?" Fleur asked.

"I'm supposed to talk to some lawyer, but I don't know when. The guy in charge of this place is called Sergio, but I didn't catch a last name."

"We can't assist you legally at this point," Fleur said. "The consulate will send a lawyer, but they might not have one available. Can you think of anything you might have done wrong? Is there anything they asked you about?"

"They only asked about the oil."

"Then there was some stupid mix up," I said. "That's the explanation."

Tony waved his hands through the air Italian style. The guard took two steps forward, realized Tony was merely gesturing, and took two steps back. "It would be nice to know what I'm accused of!"

"That would help," Fleur said. "But we'll take this one step at a time. I don't work for the Italian government, but I do work for the EU. I have some connections that might be useful."

"Seeing a friendly face is already a big help."

"I'll try to learn more, but for right now, I'm afraid you may have to be patient."

"I won't have a choice."

"That's correct. For now, stay as positive as you can. We'll be back as soon as they give us the opportunity."

"Thanks!"

I blew Tony a kiss and stood when Fleur did. She smiled as she nodded at the guard, and we both said *grazie* as we slipped past him.

"I know you'll have questions," Fleur whispered, "but it's best to talk outside."

We exited the building and found Sander across the street, where he leaned against a tree shading a six-car parking lot.

"How was your meeting?" he asked.

"It was inconclusive," said Fleur. "Did you find a café?"

"I did." Sander led us around the corner to some outdoor tables that stretched into the street outside Café Luna. We took one that offered half sun, half shade.

"Sit wherever you like," Fleur said.

I immediately snagged the shade, which made my Dutch friends laugh. They both rearranged their chairs so that the sun would warm their faces.

"I live in Arizona," I said. "I get enough sun."

Sander laughed. "Last week the sun didn't appear in Leiden even once! But come. Tell me your impressions."

I looked at Fleur, but she shook her head. "You first."

"Tony's there, and he's okay, but he could use a care package." I turned to Fleur. "Is that allowed?"

"In this case."

"Don't they have to—doesn't someone have to— Well, I don't know what my question is," Sander said.

"There are certain procedures," Fleur said. "But sometimes special circumstances interrupt the rules, you might say."

I scooted my chair closer to the table so that a woman with a grocery cart could pass behind me. "Do the officials have permission to keep Tony?"

"Let me put it this way," Fleur said. "Orvieto is like any Italian town."

"Full of corruption?"

"No. Not full. But sometimes there are elements."

"You think the charges are fake."

"I've heard that some of the Orvietani family are established."

"Meaning 'powerful.'"

"It may mean that."

The waiter stopped by and took our order for three coffees.

"Tony hasn't been in town long," I said. "He hasn't had time to anger anyone. Not intentionally at least."

"People can become angry for no reason," Fleur said. "It's the same all over the world. People who have too much time on their hands envy others without reason for it. They entertain themselves by complaining."

"This happens to my parents," Sander said. "Our neighbor always complains that our bird feeder attracts too many birds. Can you imagine anything so silly?"

"Neighbors are always a problem," I said.

"Exactly," added Fleur. "When I bought my flat, I was ecstatic. Housing is precious here. I'm in a central location close to public transport. But I hadn't noticed an important factor. Only the first floor has garbage service."

"What?" Sander and I asked simultaneously.

"Yes, I know it's crazy. As usual, there are bins in the basement for the different types of garbage: organic, glass, cardboard, mixed. But they belong to the ground-floor residents ONLY."

The waiter stopped by with the coffees. I added extra sugar and stirred in quick, choppy motions, actions that matched my feelings.

"So if you live on the third floor, you're not supposed to generate any trash?" I asked.

"Excellent question! You see, there are special bins for people with no regular service. They can be found a short distance from the building."

"You have to take your garbage on a walk to get rid of it?" I asked.

Fleur laughed until she snorted. "You might think of it that way! By now, I know what to do. Every time I go out, I throw something away. But never mind. The point is that after I first moved in, I accidentally used someone's bin. The owner was so angry that he, or perhaps she, took my organic garbage, which was dripping with vegetable parts, deposited it into the hallway, and left a nasty note on the front door of the building."

"Because you used someone's garbage bin?!" I asked. "That's crazy."

"Yes. If someone had explained the system to me, I would have used it properly! Instead, the note warned against borrowing private property."

"Who composed this notice?" Sander asked.

"That is the amusing part," Fleur said. "There are four downstairs flats, but I'm not sure whose bin I borrowed!"

"Because the residents were too chicken to identify themselves," I said.

"Right! I might make a guess. But never mind. I simply avoid talking to the residents on the ground floor."

"I'm not sure that's the best strategy," Sander said. "Someday you may need them!"

"Maybe, maybe not," Fleur said. "But you understand the problem. People can become very upset here about small things that do not matter."

"You think this happened to Tony," I said.

"Yes. I think that's exactly what happened. He made a mistake somehow, and it snowballed. A local might have wiggled his way free, but Tony doesn't have the right connections."

"So now he finds himself trapped in the bed of bureaucracy," Sander said.

Fleur rotated her coffee cup. "Exactly. I do enjoy living in this country. But when it comes to legalities, some situations are ridiculous."

The woman's explanation made perfect sense. Tony walked into a cultural trap without seeing the cobwebs. His uncle should have warned him. Maybe he'd been too optimistic. Or too naïve.

I stirred my coffee one more time. Then I drank it in one gulp.

Italian-style.

*

Twenty minutes later, Fleur emerged from the detention center empty-handed, meaning that she'd delivered the emergency supplies we'd purchased, but she was frowning.

"Did you have a problem?" I asked. "You were gone a long time."

"I believe the guards will give Tony the supplies after checking them, but the situation is as I expected. We won't know anything until the lawyer arrives, but that won't be today, and tomorrow is Sunday."

"So not a single thing will happen until next week," I said.

"Yes. I'm sorry there's nothing more we can do."

"I'm really, really sorry to have dragged you guys into this," I said.

Fleur took my hands. "No. We are happy to help. But for right now, we have done the most that is possible."

I'd already assumed that would be the case. Some things you could fight. Others were beyond your control. You had to accept them and move on.

"Gina, I know it's difficult for you to concentrate," said Fleur. "But perhaps you would like to do a little sight-seeing?"

This was only my second chance to be in the vast playground of the Eternal City, and I didn't want Sander to feel that he'd come down south for nothing. The day was warm but bright, I'd already done my good deed for the day, and I had a willing companion.

"Some sightseeing would be terrific," I said.

"That is fine. I will leave you two on your own. I have a few errands to run myself, but they are not of interest. Sander, you still have the key?"

He felt in his pocket and nodded.

"Please, come and go as you wish." She indicated the approaching bus. "Meanwhile, Number 63 will take me to my stop. I will see you both tonight!"

She hurried off.

"I'm sorry I messed up her whole schedule," I said.

Sander patted my shoulder. "It's a special case. She was happy to help."

"I would have never figured out what to do on my own."

"No. It's nearly impossible to navigate the legal system of another country. And I'm sorry about Tony. He has been detained unfairly, and perhaps illegally, but there's nothing we can do about it at this time."

"I'm sorry to ruin our weekend."

"Nothing is ruined! We have the rest of the day."

"What would you most like to see?"

"Gina, I leave everything up to you. I have visited Rome a couple of times, so I have seen the main sights. I would enjoy revisiting all of them, but you might prefer to wander around with no plan at all."

I took out my phone. "You said you liked statues. I made reservations for us at the Borghese."

"The Borghese!"

"Well, you said you'd never been there."

"I haven't! That's excellent! Why didn't you say so?"

"I was afraid we wouldn't make it." I glanced down at my watch. "The time slots last for two hours, and ours starts in thirty minutes. What do you think?"

"I'm delighted to be with a fellow art lover!"

He was giving me way too much credit. I had a lousy track record with art museums, but I didn't have to appreciate art myself to enjoy Sander's enthusiasm.

"Know how to get there from here?" I asked.

He whipped out his phone and mapped the route.

If we'd had the luxury of time, I would have requested a slower pace. Instead, I pounded the pavement to keep up. The task was pleasant because I'd discovered yet another of Sander's attributes. While I would have checked Google maps every block after asking a dozen locals if I were going the right direction, Sander did neither. Fortunately for me, he had a terrific sense of direction.

Chapter Nineteen

Given my experiences at the Uffizi, I had low expectations for the Borghese Gallery. I wasn't an art person, I told myself. At least, I wasn't that kind of art person. I admired newer stuff, such as the Chihuly glass sculpture in the Oklahoma City Museum of Art. I could appreciate that art reflected useful knowledge about a society and its choices, but I couldn't make myself like things. The next best level was achieving appreciation.

Since the Borghese Gallery boasted statues and paintings from the 16th and 17th centuries, I assumed I wouldn't relate to them. I was surprised to detect palpable excitement as soon as we neared the palazzo that housed the collection. Eager patrons stood in line, obediently awaiting their time slot. They giggled as they took pictures of the building or consulted their guidebooks. They were on cultural missions.

Sander displayed similar enthusiasm. He explained that in the Netherlands he'd naturally studied art history. His ancestors had a rich history of painting, especially in the Dutch Golden Age. People flocked to Amsterdam to see paintings by Rembrandt and Hals, so the locals needed to appreciate their heritage.

While we waited our turn to go inside, he eagerly studied the ornate façade with its statuettes and four symmetrical windows. Given the limited two-hour time slots, the gallery couldn't have that extensive a collection, at least not that was on display at any one time, so visiting it wouldn't be an all-day project.

"Do you know how long I've wanted to come here?" he asked.

I politely shook my head. I'd never heard of the gallery until Sander mentioned it as a possible activity for our weekend together. "How long?"

"Since studying art history!"

I thought he might be disappointed, but as soon as we stepped inside the building, my skepticism melted. A half-naked marble woman stared out so intently that I admired the defiance of her gaze. While other tourists passed by, I studied her graceful face and the delicate folds of her sheet. Through the stone, she shouted out the confidence of a woman who knew what she wanted and would be sure to get it.

"Fine, isn't she?" Sander asked. "Pauline Bonaparte as portrayed by Antonio Canova."

I couldn't imagine a statue with more intensity. The woman might have been real. *What's it like to be worshipped all day long?* I wanted to ask. *What does it feel like to be locked into eternity?*

Sander tapped me on the shoulder and indicated that he was moving ahead. While the former statue was the epitome of feminine grace, the next room showed nearly the opposite. Bernini's depiction of David was another wonder, but this statue displayed the strength of the masculine leg, the flexibility of a gymnast, and the stubbornness that came with having an undeniable cause. As little as I knew about history, I remembered that David had bravely battled a giant.

Neither of these objects prepared me for the next room, whose centerpiece was a big white sculpture of a young man chasing a young woman uphill. Their legs were delicate poles, and their outstretched arms provided a visual line from one to the other. The man smiled in lustful triumph as he pulled back the woman's head with one hand and clutched her belly with the other. Her hair flew out behind her, and her gaping mouth suggested pain. I circled the marble, studying each example of movement.

Finally, I read the description: *Apollo and Daphne*, by Gian Lorenzo Bernini. Michelle and Becky had mentioned the statue as well. Thinking back to a humanities class, I vaguely remembered the story about the nymph who turned into a laurel tree to escape her eager male pursuer. I circled the figures again, more slowly. Was it wonderful or horrible to turn into a tree? I wanted to blame Apollo for his lustful ambitions, but his actions weren't entirely his fault. Naughty Eros had shot him up with arrows of love.

Or maybe they were poisoned darts. Was it so hard to fall in love with people that you could only do so with the help of magic? Maybe I needed a hard dose myself. What crazy Cupid had sent Sander to Rome to meet me when he certainly met beautiful Dutch girls on a regular basis, ones that would be a lot easier to spend time with? Yet here he was. I might have been Daphne myself even though I had stringier hair. I'd been running from Sander, putting him off, discouraging him from coming. Now that he was here, I could either keep running, or I could slow down long enough for him to catch me.

"This statue is very fine, don't you think?" Sander asked. "In all of Rome, this is the work that I like best. I have always admired it."

"I can't imagine that anything might be more wonderful."

"It's probably my favorite statue in the world. It resembles real life, don't you think? That is, you reach out to touch something beautiful. You almost think you have it. You're within centimetres. And then, well, you turn into a tree, or perhaps the other person does."

"Or perhaps they're from a different city."

"Or country!"

Or perhaps you didn't take the time to look at what you had, evaluate it, and value it. Here I had a man who had flown a thousand miles to meet me on a whim. I didn't want to fall into his arms and immediately change my mind about him, but I wouldn't know how I felt unless I relaxed enough to let down my guard.

That was the big problem, striking the balance, recognizing something was right for you even though you'd never before considered it.

"Thanks for bringing me here," Sander said.

"Thanks for wanting to come. If it hadn't been for you, I wouldn't have spent the weekend in Rome, and even if I had, I wouldn't have come to this gallery. Even though I'd read about it, I wouldn't have known to take the time for it."

"You haven't yet studied art history," Sander said. "Without a basis in such a large subject, it's hard to know where to begin."

My new friend was right. In my classics class, we never made it past Ancient Rome. We'd studied statues, but they consisted mostly of statesmen, usually with a broken foot or a broken arm or a broken head.

Daphne was someone I could relate to, someone who was so scared that she ran herself right out of the story. It would be easy to make such a mistake, but the problem was that you couldn't go back and redo your history. While I didn't want to jump into anything, I didn't want to make the same mistake that Daphne had.

Sometimes, having Cupid around wasn't so bad after all.

*

Sander and I dined again in Trastevere, but afterwards we retreated to our borrowed living room. Fleur had gone off to a movie with friends, so the space was our own. After a day of running around, it was pleasant to sit at leisure without an agenda.

"Tell me about living in Orvieto," Sander said. "It must be a big contrast from Tucson."

"It's different, all right."

"In good ways?"

"Mostly? Consider the pacing. Instead of dumping everything into a cart at Safeway the way I do back home, the villagers gather their items from different specialty shops, and they buy what they need for that day. Wild, huh?"

"It's a way of life. My mother does the same thing."

"It's fun for the summer, but living that way might drive me crazy. If I were in too much of a hurry, I'd just go hungry."

"You're exaggerating, but I understand your point of view."

"Here you always have to stop and talk to people you know. That can really slow you up when you're trying to get to class."

"Italians do like to converse with one another. They can't help it. What else?"

"After dinner, whole families go out for gelato!"

"Certainly you approve."

"I'm envious! But I don't know if I could live that way. What about you? Does Rome remind you of Amsterdam?"

"In some ways. Big European cities are alike in some respects, no matter the country."

"But you're managing a bank in Leiden, right? A university town?"

"I manage a small Volksbank branch."

"Too small to be challenging?"

"Oh, no. In banking, every day is different. The customers have interesting problems, but I don't have to solve too many of them in the same day."

I'd worked hard all evening to keep Tony out of my head, but he sneaked back in. "I bet the citizens of Leiden don't get hauled off for crimes they didn't know about."

Sander patted my arm. "I know you're having a hard time. It's quite understandable. How might I best help you?"

I decided that his offer was sincere enough that I could answer honestly. "Perhaps, you could just put your arm around me for a few minutes?"

Sander complied as if it were natural for him to do so. For long moments we sat in silence, but I had trouble holding myself together. He sensed I was tearing up and didn't say a thing about it. He pretended not to notice even though at least one tear slipped down my cheek and hit his arm in a gentle ping.

He realized my emotions weren't directed at him. I was responding to frustration crossed with bewilderment. I was worried about Tony and confused about what our role should be in trying to help him.

Sander sat patiently. Upon request, he escorted me to the bedroom, tucked me in, and turned off the light.

My mind buzzed in too many directions to let me sleep. I heard Fleur return from her outing, and I listened while she and Sander laughed and talked far into the night.

I was glad, for once, that I couldn't understand a single thing they were saying.

Chapter Twenty

The next evening, Fleur passed me the antipasti tray filled with meats and cheeses, but it was the pecorino that I took multiple times. The sheep cheese was so tangy and rich that I couldn't imagine a better one.

"This is terrific," I told Fleur for the second time.

"One does eat well in Italy," she said.

Sander nodded as he wrapped a piece of pecorino inside a strip of prosciutto. "I'm surprised people ever move away."

"Maybe they leave because the justice system is so bad," I said.

Fleur pushed the grissini in my direction. "I'm confident Tony's issue can be cleared up tomorrow."

I had no such confidence, but having a positive attitude beat having a negative one. At any rate, we would go back to the detention center in the morning. In theory I was supposed to be back in class, but I'd decided to cash in my Get Out of Jail free card even though I doubted that Lucia ever played Monopoly.

"I'll keep my fingers crossed for tomorrow," I said. "At least we made the best use of today."

Sander took more prosciutto. "We certainly did."

We qualified as super tourists. We took photographs around the Spanish steps, zigzagged in and out of the shopping district, lingered by the Tiber, and visited the Pantheon despite having to pay a fee. After that we picked up Pinocchio trinkets, visited Bernini's Fountain of Four Rivers, and enjoyed the artist's Vatican Square late enough in the day that the crowds had subsided. We took our time without following a list of "must-sees." I used Italian whenever I could, testing out half-remembered vocabulary words on unsuspecting passersby.

We also had a chance to relax with one another, scampering about like kids, occasionally joining in with children kicking soccer balls or splashing one another from the city's many drinking fountains. Sander shared stories about his youth, especially about growing up with a gifted musician for a brother.

I swapped stories about Rachel. My sister wasn't the most gifted musician ever, but she worked hard enough to be successful. She approached other aspects of her life with the same vivaciousness. I wasn't aimless, but I wasn't driven by the same master. I appreciated an hour of sitting in the park or at a café because rather than wasting time, in those moments I was recharging my energy level.

I turned to Fleur. "It was so kind of you to let us stay with you."

Fleur dipped a sliver of pecorino into honey. "It was my pleasure. I love having visitors, and you might be surprised by how few people accept my invitations. But now I must ask a small favor."

"Of course!" I stacked my dish on top of Sander's. "I'm a terrible cook, but I'm happy to clean up. I don't mind at all."

Fleur laughed as she took the dishes from my hand. "Nothing of the kind. I have a dishwasher, and I've already planned the pasta. I have a different problem. Usually on Sunday nights I play cards with a couple of girlfriends."

"We can get out of your hair," I said. "We'll take a long walk or maybe find a movie theatre."

"Not that either! Maria doesn't feel well this evening, so Teresa and I need you to play *buraco*. That is, if you don't mind."

"Fine with me," Sander said.

"I love card games," I said. "But what was the name — barracks?"

Fleur helped herself to a *tarallo*, a small, round, salty piece of dough. "I don't think the name means anything in

153

particular. It's a rummy game, very old, but recently it's gained popularity."

I took a *tarallo* myself even though I'd told myself to stop eating them. "Tell us how to play."

"The game is best explained through demonstration. But first, let me assemble the pasta."

Sander and I trailed her into the kitchen, which was the most compact aspect of the apartment.

Water boiled in a stainless-steel pot with a strainer lid. Fleur plopped in two-thirds of a box of *campanelle*, little bells, and added a few shakes of salt.

Despite the appetizers, I was already hungry. Then I remembered that I was supposed to be gathering information. "What can you tell me about the Roman olive oils? This is the problem in Orvieto. There is so much competition for similar products that the merchants compete for every sale."

"I don't think it's much different in this area." Fleur opened a cabinet, which was organized but jam-packed. She handed me a sleek 750-mm bottle labeled with an oversized lime-green Q. "Quattrociocchi is one of the many local olive oils."

"It's made around Rome?"

"In Viterbo, I believe. That's about an hour north of here, but it's still in Lazio. The volcanic soil is somehow auspicious for olive trees. They also make flavored varieties." She took back the original bottle and handed me smaller ones labeled Rosmarino and Limone.

"These look fun," I said.

"I love adding them to salads. I can use the same basic ingredients every day but still take advantage of variety."

"I suppose there are a lot of olive oils from this region."

Fleur put the bottles back, opened a drawer, and pointed to a liter. "Another big company is Colli Etruschi."

"Etruscan Hills," I murmured.

"Precisely. After all, the Etruscans were the first to plant olive trees around here."

"No wonder it's such an industry," said Sander.

Fleur nodded. "Exactly. In Orvieto, you're living in the heart of Etruscan territory although I believe half of Italy's production comes from Puglia, which receives warmer sun for a longer period of time."

"Tony's uncle owns an olive grove close to Orvieto," I said, "but I suppose every production is different. I'm not sure how you're supposed to choose among oils."

"I was taught to look for a dark bottle," Fleur said. "They say clear bottles detract from the quality."

Come to think of it, Fabrizio's bottles were dark. I hadn't taken the time to examine them, but at least he was selling quality goods.

Fleur opened the lid to show me the contents of the frying pan, where cubes of pesto melted. "Teresa prepared these for me. She swears by Cetrone, yet another brand of oil, but I'm not sure I can tell the difference." She turned to Sander. "Can you?"

He shook his head. "What I know about Italian cooking is when the noodles are done."

"In that case, would you mind sampling the pasta?"

"Not at all." He opened the pot and forked a bell. After running water over it, he popped the morsel in his mouth and chewed.

"Done?" Fleur asked.

"Another minute. Perhaps ninety seconds."

My friends were foodies. Fleur and Sander cared about what they ate and understood subtleties of the preparation. They chatted about the recipe each step of the way and taste-tested as they went along.

I did the tests with them, pretending to understand the nuances. I did not. But the results were so delicious that I ate far more than I needed to.

For that, I blamed the olive oil.

*

Neither Teresa nor Fleur knew the origin of *buraco*, but Sander was a quickdraw on the cell phone. The variation on Canasta had been devised by an architect and his lawyer friend in Uruguay back in the 1940s. The goal was to build sets of cards with your partner to outscore the other team. The game took its name from the Portuguese word for "hole," as in where you ended up if you played badly enough to earn a negative score.

That's exactly what happened to Sander and me during the first couple of games. There were so many rules that I couldn't keep them straight, and I was too cautious to pick up piles of cards. Although counterintuitive, that was the smartest strategy. While the conversation bounced among English, Italian, and Dutch, Sander and I made beginner mistakes. Fleur and Teresa racked up points, easily reaching two thousand to win the first set. Then they won the second set.

By then, Sander and I caught on. While I assumed I could excuse myself after an hour or so to complete my online grammar exercises, I couldn't abandon my teammate. Besides, I'd forgotten how important it was to spend an evening playing a game instead of worrying about things I couldn't change. I also needed a break from grammar. Rather than fool with compound tenses, I learned the difference between *pulito*, "clean," meaning a run of cards without a joker, and *sporco*, "dirty," which meant a run with a joker or two. I learned that the Italian word for joker was *jolly*, and in spare moments I fantasized about working that new word into my next conversation with Eduardo.

Sander and I won all the subsequent sets until Teresa gave up, wished us a good night, and rolled across the hall to her own apartment. By then it was so late that I pecked Sander on the cheek and crawled into bed without further discussion.

He didn't seem to mind crawling into his own bed; he'd been yawning for the last hour himself. But I knew one thing for sure. I never wanted to play against him in a card game. When it came to numbers, he was better than anybody.

Chapter Twenty-One

I paced outside the office where all morning we'd been told to wait, wait, wait. The administrator in charge was pleasant enough, but Sergio di Lucca insisted that he couldn't talk to us before we spoke with Tony's lawyer. Rules were rules.

When the lawyer finally arrived, acting as if he were a saint even though it had taken him forty-eight hours to present himself, he rushed up the long staircase into the back offices before we could ask questions.

I'd already missed the morning classes. I'd originally thought I could hightail it to Orvieto in time to catch my afternoon sessions, but it wasn't looking good for those either. Tell Lucia I'd skipped class to help a friend? She wouldn't sympathize. No doubt such actions were against the rules.

Suddenly the lawyer shot through the lobby as if his wife were having an emergency C-section.

"What happened with Tony?" I asked.

"Please let us know what you found out," said Fleur.

"I have to go." The lawyer might have been forty. U.S. East coast accent. Fine suit, probably Italian made. Pointy black shoes that were stylish but looked silly outside of a luxury store.

"What's going on? What can you tell us?" I asked.

He paused long enough to frown. "You're not family, so while I thank you for trying to be helpful, I can't tell you anything."

Enough. I'd spent an extra night in Rome which, under other circumstances, would have been at my own expense. I was risking my college credits and no doubt incurring the wrath of my supervisor, whose rules I was breaking. I'd inconvenienced my new friends who had kindly accompanied me to the office.

That was hassle enough no matter how expensive the lawyer's suit was or how much his feet hurt in those shoes that looked at least one size too small. His chosen wardrobe was his own problem, and he needed to get past it.

I placed myself between the lawyer and the door he planned to escape through. "We're the closest to family that Tony has! He's here working for his uncle, who has disappeared, and his mother, who is undergoing chemo treatments, is five thousand miles away. So don't tell us, oh, you're not family because, for the moment, that's exactly what we are, and we are not leaving until you explain what's going on."

The lawyer allowed a smile through his tanned face. Either his apartment had a terrace, or he spent weekends at the beach. He probably took a lot of vacation time. "You must be Italian. Or part Italian."

"My dad's family —" What? The jerk just wanted to throw me off track. "Please, tell us what Tony has done because he doesn't even know. And tell us how to help him."

"Look, it's no big deal."

"No big deal? He's been in custody all weekend! If it hadn't been for us, he would have frozen first and died of hunger second. We've been worried sick without being able to do anything about it. Don't you dare attempt to explain that it's 'no big deal' when what you're saying is a stupid lie."

The lawyer pulled out his slick leather wallet. Eduardo Phillips handed me an embossed card with an icon of a fancy pen. Italian American. Just like me but better dressed. His Italian should have been a little better too.

"Look, the charge won't hold, all right?" Eduardo said. "It might take me a few days to get the situation straightened out, but I'm sure it's nothing."

"Nothing?" I shouted. "Then explain to me why Tony is stuck here!"

"A serious charge was leveled against him, and the police are determined to check it out. But these things take time. It shouldn't be more than a week, but they're backed up right now."

"A week! That's ridiculous!" That's preposterous! That's the craziest thing I've ever heard!"

Sander stepped to my side. "You haven't told us the charge."

The lawyer put his hand to his chin as if posing for a modern version of The Thinker. "You have to realize that Italians, well, they get riled up easily. You know that. They wear their emotions on their sleeves. Then they shake their arms, and their emotions fly out like pigeons escaping a shotgun."

"Is that what Tony did?" I asked. "He yelled at some-body? Caused a fight? Punched somebody? I can't believe he'd do anything like that on purpose. In fact, I'm sure he didn't."

Eduardo took a couple of steps back; I must have looked dangerous by then. "No, no. Nothing like that. The accusation was simple. The other day he evidently sold a case of olive oil to a certain Baldoni family. Perhaps you have heard of them?"

"He did not," I said. "It was a few bottles of olive oil and a case of wine."

"Ah, yes, I believe that was the story. Anyway, Si-gnore Baldoni claims that your friend was trying to kill him."

"What?" Sander and Fleur and I chorused at the same time.

"Imagine that! It's a serious charge."

"You must be wrong," I said.

"I'm afraid not. You see, the olive oil was very bad. The Baldonis didn't realize that, and the grandfather has almost died. He's still in the hospital. He's quite lucky to be alive."

"That's one hundred percent stupid," I said. "The olive oil looked just fine."

"Maybe it looked fine, but it was so bad that the grandfather was poisoned."

"That olive oil was perfect," I said.

I really had no idea what I was saying. I hadn't even looked at the olive oil. The box had been packed up by the time I reached the enoteca. Tony probably hadn't looked at it either.

"I'm afraid to tell you that the product wasn't quite perfect."

"How can the Baldonis prove something was wrong with it? How did they measure the results? Where's the evidence they came up with? What did the doctor say?"

The lawyer laughed. "Your questions are good ones. I admit, this sounds like your basic misunderstanding. But the family has better connections than your friend does."

"It's not even his shop! It's his uncle's. Tony is just filling in, and if he's in jail all week and the shop is closed, they'll go out of business anyway."

Calm down, I told myself. Lawyers heard crazy stuff all the time, so it was important to sound rational. But really, what was going on? How could Tony be accused of poisoning some old guy who was already on his last legs?

Fleur waved her index finger back and forth. "Rancid olive oil might taste bad, but it can't kill anybody. That's scientifically impossible."

The lawyer shrugged with both shoulders. "I agree. This whole thing is ridiculous. Nevertheless, the family has pressured law enforcement, so the authorities have taken action."

"The family owns Orvieto?"

"Well, I wouldn't say—"

"Half of Orvieto, then. Three-quarters."

"Something like that. They made the accusation, so the police had to act on it. Since Tony is from the U.S., the police had to call Rome."

"It's legal to accuse your foreigners of something ridiculous?"

Eduardo tried to keep a straight face. His inability to do so told me how right I was. Lunatic things happened to visitors. Lucia had warned us about exactly that. I hadn't believed her at the time.

"Don't worry," Eduardo said. "I know this seems terrible, and it is. But it's a simple misunderstanding of one kind or another. As I said, it might take a few days, but I'll get things sorted out."

"A few days?" I asked. "You can't do better than that? We need Tony back now."

"There's a process," Eduardo said. "We all have to follow it."

"What if the old guy is sick anyway?" I asked. "What if he dies! Then what? Then Tony is a murderer?"

"There's no reason to overreact."

"But if the family is so powerful, they can pay for any conviction they want, right?"

"This isn't that kind of thing," Eduardo said, earning his position as the King of Vagueness.

"What kind of thing is it?" Fleur asked. "Please explain."

"You people wouldn't understand."

"Oh, we wouldn't, would we?" I pointed. "Sander might not understand. I might not understand. But Fleur? She would understand exactly."

"Is that right?" Eduardo said sarcastically.

I made fists automatically.

Fleur stepped forward until she was so close to Eduardo that he took a step back.

"Mr. Phillips, thanks to my job with the EU, I've lived in Italy for the past ten years," Fleur said. "I've often been in the midst of bureaucratic failures. And I do love the Italians. They're warm and loving, and they embrace life in the way most of us dream to do. But at times they become excited over small things and raise a fuss. A big fuss, in this case."

"Then what?" Sander asked.

"They want the normal things, attention and apologies. Once they feel important, the storm blows over and the sea is calm again."

"How long is that supposed to take?" I asked.

Fleur shrugged. "It shouldn't take long. The situation is not very complicated."

"But in this case, it could well take two weeks," Eduardo declared.

"That's ridiculous," I said. "It's unacceptable. It's stupid!"

Eduardo shifted his weight from one leg to another as if that would help us understand his importance. "You don't understand the process. First the police must find a health expert. Then they must send that representative to Orvieto. That person must complete all the investigations by the book along with all the paperwork. That's the beginning."

"Unless the old guy dies first," I said.

"The good news is that he's in the hospital, but he's not in critical condition. He'll make a fast recovery."

"Because he's not sick," I said. "That makes it a lot easier."

"You're jumping to conclusions," Eduardo said. "In fact, you are typically Italian. The people here blow up and make accusations. Why? Mostly because they're bored. They need something to do. They need someone to get mad at. Especially when they live in small places where nothing else is happening."

"But there's no reason for Tony to be caught up in this! No reason at all!"

"I understand your confusion. Your friend has been here for a short period of time. He's a victim of place. Wrong time, wrong place."

"The family is not mad at Tony," Sander said.

"Bravo!" exclaimed Eduardo. "No. They are not mad at Tony. They are mad at his uncle."

"How is that supposed to be his fault?" I asked. "How is blaming Tony supposed to help anything?"

Eduardo nodded. "You're right to be irritated. Tony should not have to pay for his uncle's bad actions, but that's the system. That's how it works. There's no way to sneak around it. Instead, you have to barrel through."

"Terrific," I said. "Tony's mother will be so pleased to hear all about it."

Eduardo tapped his watch without looking at it. "But I do need to go. I represent a couple of Americans who are in serious trouble, not because of something their family did but because of their own stupidity. I am sorry for your friend, and I realize he's having an unfortunate experience. But it won't last more than a couple of weeks, three at the most."

"Three!" I yelled as loudly as I could.

"I'm kidding. Let's say a week or so."

"A week?"

"That's conservative, but it's a useful starting point."

"You're kidding!"

"Afterwards Tony can look back on this whole thing and laugh. We all will. All right?"

I might have argued with Eduardo all day, but it wouldn't have helped. Down deep, I knew he was right. Italy was a country that followed its protocols. As stupid as the process sounded, we had to honor it.

Despite his terrible hurry, Eduardo took the trouble to shake our hands. He had the firm grip of a politician, meaning that he acted with too much confidence and squeezed our hands a little too hard.

That didn't make me feel any better about what might be happening to Tony.

Chapter Twenty-Two

Lucia paraded before me in an otherwise empty classroom. "You did not have permission to skip classes to stay in Rome! You have to follow the rules of the program. You have to do what I say. I have the power to send you home!"

She'd droned on saying the same things for the last few minutes. Yes, I'd missed three out of four classes that day. Yes, I'd failed to complete my online exercises. I wanted to ask whether or not learning words for Italian card games counted as extra credit, but Lucia held the floor so securely I couldn't even get in the word for joker.

Her deluge was repetitive and whiny. Didn't I know it was important to attend every class? Didn't I know that I might not succeed? Didn't I realize I had disrespected my teacher?

I considered explaining Tony's situation, but I vetoed the thought almost immediately. Lucia was from a traditional Orvietano family. Her ancestors blah, blah, blah, I couldn't remember the background she'd told us. But who knew which side of the town she was on? Orvieto was divided into quarters for a reason. The residents probably all hated each other because one stole the other's lunch bucket back in 1907 or maybe 1908.

I let Lucia rattle on telling me how I'd disappointed her and didn't deserve to be in Orvieto at all. She needed the power struggle. If chewing out students was her way to feel superior, I felt sorry for her. What she needed was a bigger challenge. Maybe kindergarteners.

"If I have to call your mother, what should I say?" she asked.

The threat was idle. I hadn't done anything that bad, and as Henrietta had pointed out the other day, the program needed us. How else could they demand tuition money from the university?

On the other hand, there was no use getting lost in details. I wanted to get back to Sander and to my own apartment, so I took the easy way out. Although I generally avoided lying, I knew the best way to thwart Lucia was to agree with her.

"You'll have to tell my mother the truth," I said. "But you know, it's all your fault."

"What?! My fault! What could you be talking about!"

"Remember at the Uffizi the other day?"

"Of course I remember! You slept too long! You—" She caught herself in time. "Oh. You came on the tour. Your questions were not too bad for someone who knows nothing about art."

Thanks for the pat on the back.

"I fell in love with that artwork," I said. Okay, slight exaggeration, but I liked some of it. "That's incredible, isn't it? I've never visited a decent art museum before. I've never taken a drawing class. You could say I've led a sheltered existence. My parents aren't into art and know nothing about it. They never taught me anything, and the stuff on their walls is all cheap prints from Walmart. But the Uffizi and then the Accademia on the same day? That was like, wow!"

Lucia nodded, which meant I knew I had her. I barely took time to breathe. "Between the paintings and the statues, I'd never seen such beautiful things. I started reading up on famous artwork in Italy. Guess what I found out? The most important statues in the world are in Rome, so I had to go."

"But we have the field trip coming up."

"Don't think I forgot about that! But the Borghese Gallery isn't on our itinerary, is it?"

"No, I'm afraid we do not have time to squeeze it in."

"That's perfectly understandable! There's so much to see! So I thought, I'll just go down to Rome for the day. That was yesterday. Silly me, I thought that if I went to the

167

museum early enough, I could get a ticket. Well, I was wrong! Some stupid tour groups had gobbled up every spot. The first slot I could get was the very last one of the day, so I snatched it right up! I paid for it without thinking twice."

"It's a Jubilee Year," Lucia admitted. "Of course, our capital is full of tourists on every single corner and in every museum. So? How was your visit?"

"Oh, my goodness! The Caravaggio! The Canova! But honestly, what totally killed me was Bernini's sculpture of Apollo and Daphne." I hit the back of my hand against my palm. "I fell in love hard with Bernini. I couldn't help it. Of course, you only have two hours for your museum visit, but I could hardly move from one room to the other. I ran past the other paintings and right back to Daphne. I watched her for such a long time that the guard became suspicious of me."

"You were overcome with the beauty."

"I was! I couldn't have imagined anything so fine, so delicate! Can I tell you something embarrassing?"

Lucia sat up straight in her chair. "Yes, yes."

"I teared up. Just a little. Nobody noticed."

I could have sworn I saw dabs of water in Lucia's eyes as well.

"Yes, yes. It has happened to me."

"I hurried back to Roma Termini, but guess what! It was so late that I couldn't get to Orvieto in time to take the funicular from the train station up to the top. You warned us to never walk up the hill or to sleep at the train station, so I was stuck."

"The funicular is a problem. I realize this."

"Guess what I did? I walked and walked and walked. I sat in the Piazza Navona for a couple of hours to study the Fountain of Four Rivers. I walked through Vatican Square when I had it to myself. I sat before the Trevi Fountain and had myself a chat with Oceanus."

"When I was young, we did the same thing. We spent the night walking in Rome and then took the first train in the morning."

"Smart choice! But at some point you do have to sleep, right? I finally checked into a hostel. My plan was to take a solid nap, but I didn't hear my alarm. I'm sorry I missed my classes, but I did get something wonderful in return. When I get back to Tucson, the first thing I'm going to do is sign up for a sculpture class. Even if I'm no good at it, even if I don't have an artistic finger in my body, I have to learn how it feels to create magic with your hands."

Lucia closed her eyes as if savoring the smell of clay.

Then she snapped to attention. "You have done a beautiful thing, but perhaps at the wrong time. It happens! But please, do not skip any more classes. And remember, you are supposed to register with us when you leave town in case anything happens."

Right. Just in case we wound up like Tony, stranded. "I'm sorry I forgot. I was so excited to travel to Rome that I couldn't think of anything else."

"Your actions were incorrect, but I understand them. This time only! But there is something else I need to talk to you about."

Good grief. Now what? I had exhausted all my excuses for errant behavior. "Yes?"

"Your roommate is having a hard time."

Henrietta? Who cared about her? Of course, she was having a hard time. She was unhappy with herself and spent most of her spare time drinking. She said she had a boyfriend yet never talked to him. She was scared to use Italian because she freaked out when she didn't understand what people said to her.

"She might not have been ready to study abroad." I prided myself on the size of the understatement.

"I agree with this. Can you tell me anything else that is affecting her experience?"

She had too much money to throw away and an addiction to social media. She had a complete aversion to any type of house organization and a severe hatred of morning. I was sure there were more factors, but those were the most obvious.

Lucia and I might have spent the rest of the day analyzing Henrietta, but Sander was waiting outside, so I went for the jugular. "Henrietta doesn't know grammar basics."

"Aha. She forgets when to use the pronouns, for example."

"She can't tell a pronoun from a past participle."

"What? That is not possible. It is so easy to know the difference. Wait! You are joking me. Very funny."

"I'm not kidding. She doesn't get it. And the whole thing about *parlo, parli, parla*? That doesn't make sense to her either."

"She does not understand how to conjugate a verb?"

"She doesn't understand why a present-tense verb has six forms. The whole idea of number and gender is foreign to her."

"But you cannot learn a language without knowing these things!"

"I tried to explain that to her, but she refuses to listen."

"This is very basic. I will begin to work on this with her immediately."

"That would help a lot. Then, if you could explain the difference between -*are*, -*ire*, and -*ere* verbs, she might make progress."

"But of course you must understand the different classes of verbs."

"That's why she's so unhappy. She's lost most of the time."

Lucia motioned for me to stand. I assumed she would walk me to the door. Instead, her unexpected hug threw me off balance, and she had to steady me to prevent me from falling down.

"Thank you so much, Gina. *Mille grazie.* We want to help our students, you know? But sometimes it is difficult. These things Henrietta does not know I learned when I was eight years old. It is hard for me to think back to this point."

It would be hard for anybody. Maybe it was even hard for Henrietta to *not* get it.

"The French students, they know the grammar," Lucia said. "So do the students from Spain. The Germans know the grammar perfectly. But the Americans, uffa! They don't know."

No, they didn't. I was glad I wasn't running a language program myself. Most of Lucia's study abroad participants were at least average students. Then there were the others.

That meant for every student who drooled over a Bernini, there was another who simply drooled.

Chapter Twenty-Three

Sander grinned when he saw me emerge from school. He jumped off his perch from the ledge across the street and headed over. He was so bright and cheerful that I couldn't help grinning back. I also enjoyed the rare sensation of knowing that someone had been waiting for me. My last couple of wanna-be boyfriends had never bothered to show that much appreciation.

"Despite what you anticipated, Lucia didn't kill you after all," Sander said.

I'd been doom and gloom heading in to see my executioner, but she'd caved in faster than I thought she would. "Thanks to you, I spouted out so much about Bernini that she softened right up."

"See? The study of art history is useful."

"It certainly is." I pointed up the street. "But how about a little real-life history? Ready to explore Orvieto?"

He followed me up towards the Piazza del Popolo. "I would love to explore the town. But perhaps I should first look for a hotel?"

On our way to school, we'd dumped his backpack at the enoteca. "Are you kidding? I have the key to Fabrizio's place, remember? Trust me, the old buzzard owes us that much."

I led Sander past the arch that led into the piazza. In the mid-afternoon, as usual, the area was deserted. Things wouldn't pick up until cocktail hour.

"We have not spoken to Tony," Sander reminded me.

"He had bigger concerns. Anyway, he would say to go right ahead. Of course, it would be more fun to sneak you into my apartment since it would not be allowed. Just think what would happen if I committed two awful transgressions the same day! It would be worse than starting a bonfire in the Duomo."

"Your supervisor might lose her mind."

I didn't have to close my eyes to imagine Lucia having a fit in the middle of the school lobby. She would stomp her feet, scrunch up her lips, and shout in a mixture of Italian and English. That would be for starters.

"It would be tempting to drive her crazy for the fun of it, but it's fine for you to stay at Fabrizio's," I said. "I'll stay there with you."

"This is fine, but if the uncle returns and finds us at his flat, what will he think?"

I could imagine that scenario too, an old guy slipping into his own home at four in the morning after various adventures and finding some form of Goldilocks in his bed.

"Giving Fabrizio a good scare would serve him right. There are plenty of things I need to ask him, starting with what hasn't he told us about his business and why didn't he hurry to Rome three days ago?"

"These would be excellent questions."

"Exactly. But since he's not here to ask, we need to improvise."

"Meaning?"

I pointed as we passed an enoteca with a fake olive tree in the window. "Remember what Fleur said about bad oil?"

"That it could not be lethal."

"Exactly. So why did those troublemakers claim that's what happened?"

"They assumed no one would know the difference."

"Probably." I pointed to enoteche coming up on either side of us. "We're surrounded by experts. Why don't we find out a bit more?"

"Why not?"

Without hesitation, we dove into the next shop. It was a copy of Fabrizio's, meaning it was full of olive oils and wines from the region, but it was squished into a smaller space. Since it lay along the main drag, it would cost more to rent but easily snare customers. Several were inside now, perusing the shelves for specialty items, including truffles, a local favorite.

While Sander studied the wine labels, I meandered over to the shelves of olive oils and inspected them up one at a time, noticing the amber colors and the variations.

"I can help you?" The fifty-something man was earnest rather than pushy. Normally I would have stuttered something in Italian for the sake of practice, but I hoped sounding like a tourist would make me easier to forget rather than to remember.

I looked towards the organized row. "I don't know how to choose the best olive oil."

He bowed. "I am Aldo, at your services. Surely, I can help you!" He pointed. "Here we have the Colli Etruschi, very good but basic. Here we have the Alfonso Priorelli, very, very good, but expensive. Here we have the Lungarotti, always the one I recommend. Is my own favorite, of course."

By then Sander joined me. "You have so many products that we don't know where to start."

I turned to Aldo. "We want to eat well, but we're on a budget. Perhaps you could explain a little more?"

The man beamed as if we'd asked his favorite question. He pointed to the Colli Etruschi. "This is twelve euro, a low price, so you can know the quality is okay but not so perfect." He pointed to the Alfonso Priorelli, decorated with a picture of farmers from maybe a hundred years ago. "This is forty-two euro but is the best olive oil you can buy in town."

"Forty-two euro!" I exclaimed. "We can't afford that!"

"Not many people can!" Aldo pointed to the bottle of Lungarotti, which was decorated with a few green leaves. "This is twenty-four euro, so you can know it is pretty good."

"What do you think?" I asked Sander as if we always made such important domestic decisions together.

"We're not the best cooks, so I think we don't use the most expensive olive oil," Sander said.

I nodded as if he always had the soundest advice. "That's exactly right. And we're just here for a couple of weeks. But Aldo, how long does it take olive oil to go bad? I mean, if we bought a bottle and couldn't finish it, could we leave it for the friend we're housesitting for? He won't be back for a few months."

"You take to America with you," the man suggested.

"We're flying," Sander said. "There are too many rules about liquids."

Aldo picked up the Priorelli. "If you no open, this can stay for long time." He imitated opening the bottle. "Once you break the seal, is best you use next six months."

"Otherwise, it goes rancid?" I asked.

"What means 'rancid?'"

"It makes you really sick," I said.

"No, no! You no get sick, but no taste so good."

"We better not buy any," I said to Sander. "What if the housekeeper took it, and didn't realize it was old, got sick, and had to go to the hospital?"

Aldo laughed until he bowled over. "No, no, no! This not happen."

"But if the shelf life is six months — "

"You have wrong the idea. Yes, the old olive oil is no taste right. Is make bad your salad. But your pasta, is make so and so. Not so good the taste, but no hurt you."

"No doctors?" I asked.

The man laughed more heartily. "You are American, no? You watch too much the comedy TV! You see the funny shows."

He imitated chugging a bottle. "You drink one liter olive oil, is bad for your stomach. But too old, only lose the taste."

"Good to know," I said. "You know, I'm American. We don't have the tradition of cooking that you do around here. I've never cooked with olive oil before in my whole life."

"That why you come to Italy. You learn be the good cook!"

Funny guy. He pretended such a thing were easy. He probably also assumed anyone could learn Italian in a month.

Sander picked up the bottle decorated with the leaves, the one that was medium-priced. "Shall we buy this one?' he asked me.

"Yes, please."

We all headed to the cash register.

"Is make good choice," Aldo said. "You see tonight when you make the dinner."

Since several more customers strolled in, I didn't ask any more annoying questions, but I let Sander pay for the oil. We thanked Aldo for his help and left him to his new business.

"Aldo and Fleur were in complete agreement about the effects of olive oil," I said as soon as we hit Corso Cavour.

"Yes, they were. Are you satisfied with what we have learned?"

While I was satisfied that we'd made progress, it was like popping on a train. It never hurt to ask a few more passengers if you were going in the right direction.

"I wouldn't mind asking a few more questions. Do you mind if we split up and try another couple of places, perhaps on our own?"

Sander pointed down the line. "We won't run out of shops. We can start down the street and compare our notes afterwards."

That would at least reinforce our findings, which would be reassuring.

"Great idea. I'll take the right if you'll take the left?"

"I would be happy to."

I slipped into the next enoteca while Sander sauntered down the lane. I tried two more locales, repeating my charade about worrying the oil would go bad. While the shopkeepers listened carefully to my concerns, each time I received the same response: While olive oil had a shelf life, it was only dangerous to the tastebuds.

*

I set the three bottles of oil that we'd accumulated in a triangle on top of Fabrizio's kitchen table. "I hope you love salads."

Sander read the labels as he rotated the bottles one by one. "I do! It is interesting that the vendors concurred, but I don't understand what Baldoni hoped to gain through his accusations."

"To ruin the business, maybe. Tony says that if he doesn't open the shop every day, it's like a slow death. Water?"

"Sure."

I filled a glass from the tap and handed it to him.

"While you're in class tomorrow, I would be happy to run the store."

"Thanks, but you can't." I explained the crazy social security rule.

"The situation is a bureaucratic nightmare," Sander said. "Back home the rules are more comprehensible, I'm happy to say."

"They're even easier in the States, and we have crazy rules too."

Sander refilled his glass. "For the moment there is little we can do for Tony. Perhaps you need some time to study?"

It wouldn't hurt one bit to review indirect and direct object pronouns. They were as tricky in Italian as they were in Spanish, meaning I could now misuse them equally in both languages. But the thought of opening a book and absorbing any information from it was beyond me.

"First I need to clear my head. How about a short walk?"

Sander brightened. "You mentioned something about a path that circles the hill?"

"I did. And there's a convenient entrance not five minutes from here."

"Then please show the way." He rinsed his glass and set it on the rack.

Note to self: if your guests rinse their own tableware, offer them a standing invitation to visit at any time.

*

The sun was still bright as we passed through the Porta Soliana, the gate at the eastern edge of town, and looked out over Orvieto Scalo. We had a view of the whole plain: the clumps of houses, the distant fields, the rolling hills, and the train station below.

"This is a wonderful sight," Sander said. "These wide spaces seem luxurious."

I'd noticed the phenomenon myself. On clear days such as today, I could see much farther than I could from anywhere close to my mom's place in Tucson. "These distant roads make me feel like I'm in *The Hobbit*."

"Ah, the Tolkien novel. I can understand that too. All the roads lie before us, and they seem to continue far in each direction." He indicated a clump of houses. "Do those residences pertain to the town of Orvieto?"

"Technically, the area below the station is called Orvieto Scalo. It's cheaper to live down there, of course." I knew that because Luisa made a big deal of explaining that while her sister and brother-in-law lived in Orvieto Scalo, she herself would never do so.

"I suppose most people prefer to live on top of the hill," Sander said.

"Sure. The action is up here, along with the best bars."

Sander pointed to a huge beige building in the distance. Dotted with rows of rectangular windows and balcony railings, it might have been eight stories high. "Is that a military operation?"

I'd stood at this same spot several times without spotting the huge structure. "I've never noticed it."

We heard rumbling, and the red funicular passed right under us, the one that had transported us from the train station to the top of the hill earlier in the day.

"You said the funicular runs until eight-thirty at night?'

"Exactly. You miss the last ride, and you get stuck down at the train station."

"There must be cabs. Or Ubers."

While that was the rational answer, it wasn't the correct one. "Good luck with that. Last Sunday, Christie and Julie didn't make it to Orvieto until ten at night. They called around for a cab but couldn't find one. Finally, they contacted Lucia."

"I'm sure she was quite pleased with them!"

"They said she yelled for fifteen minutes straight, but then she sent the neighbor boy to fetch them. Otherwise, I suppose they might have slept on the benches outside the station."

Sander studied the terrain. "It's not that far a distance. It should be possible to walk up the hill."

"I've heard that."

"But Lucia told you not to."

"Exactly."

"Ah. Private property?"

"Probably liability. We might fall and twist our ankles. We might be accosted by monsters or villains. We might get so lost we'd never find our way back again."

Sander and I stared into one another's eyes. We'd immediately matched wavelengths: *It can't be that hard.*

"Shall we try walking down?" Sander asked.

"Of course. If we get caught by angry gardeners, I'll say you made me do it!"

We headed down the concrete path, wound up at a farmhouse, and retraced our steps. Then we noticed a small handwritten sign that pointed to the left and led us over the funicular to a quiet but distinctive path. We strolled down, passing through a stretch of forest and by an unattended field. The shadows had lengthened by then, but plenty of light illuminated our solitary path.

"Do you think we're on the right trail?" Sander asked when we reached a strip of dirt.

"I can't see why not."

We continued a short distance until we came upon a concrete road. We turned left, passing several residential streets as we moseyed downhill. A minute later we came out on the Strada della Stazione, the main road that led to the train station.

We'd made it from top to bottom in seventeen minutes. Easy enough. Why had Lucia warned us not to walk up or down the hill? Probably because she never, ever walked it herself.

"Nice way to stretch our legs, don't you think?" Sander asked.

I did. But climbing down a hill for fun was one thing. Climbing up was another. "It's eight-fifteen," I said.

"You want to take the funicular back up to the top of the hill."

"When you're in Orvieto, do as the Orvietani. So what that they're lazy?"

Sander grinned. He would have been happy enough to hoof it right back up to Orvieto, but I felt generous. I didn't give him the chance to buy his own funicular ticket. Paying a couple of euro to avoid wearing myself out was a wise investment.

Chapter Twenty-Four

I stopped so short when I walked into the kitchen that Sander bumped into me and then had to grab me so that I wouldn't fall.

"I'm sorry!" Sander cried.

"My fault. But look." I approached the table, studying the bottles of olive oil. "They've been moved."

"Are you sure?"

I squatted to view the bottles at eye level before slowly straightening my legs. "No. Think the traffic outside could have shaken the bottles a little?"

Sander shook the table, but it seemed solid. "Maybe."

"Sander! Your bag! Your passport!"

He tapped his leg. "In my pocket."

"Your other stuff!"

We retreated to the living room, where Sander had dumped his backpack. He unzipped a few compartments before closing them back up again.

"Everything looks the same."

I was relieved there weren't any immediate signs of burglary, but I couldn't shake the feeling that something was wrong, that I was missing something that was directly in front of me.

"Help me look around?" I asked.

"Of course."

I went around the apartment opening cabinets and drawers, but the disorder seemed normal. I couldn't spot a single thing that was clearly suspicious.

"How's your sense of smell?" I asked.

"Regular, I suppose."

"Mine isn't all that great. Try the bedroom. See if you spot any problems."

Sander stepped inside and took deep breaths. He rejoined me in the living room. "I don't notice anything."

Neither did I.

"Let me just try the bathroom," I said. Inside the tiny but serviceable room, I found a cabinet with a stack of clean but worn towels. The drawer was filled with an array of combs, shaving equipment, and cotton balls. The bottom shelf of the rusty medicine cabinet held tubes of toothpaste and a couple of toothbrushes. Assorted vitamins and pain killers claimed the top shelf. Hand creams and three unlabeled pill bottles claimed the middle.

The first pill bottle was empty. The second held a few white pills. The third held green dust.

Pot?

"Sander, check this out."

After he squeezed into the room with me, I handed him the bottle.

"What's this?"

"Marijuana, I think."

Sander took a whiff. "I don't detect a smell."

"Neither do I, but Fabrizio is evidently an old hippie. Who knew?"

"Do you think he was taking drugs illegally?"

"Isn't marijuana illegal around here?"

Sander did a quick check on his phone. "It seems to be allowed for medicinal purposes, but having it otherwise is not a serious crime."

"Unless good old Fabrizio was selling it."

"Do you think he was?"

I took the bottle and smelled the contents a second time. "No. This seems ancient anyway. Never mind."

I returned the container to its companions. We retreated to the living room, where we had room to breathe.

"I didn't notice anything strictly wrong," I said, "but someone did try to enter the other evening. Since the shop has been closed, a potential burglar might assume that Tony and Fabrizio are both out of town."

"In that case, they would feel more confident about burglarizing the residence."

"Or the enoteca! We better go down and take a look."

I led Sander downstairs to the unlocked door leading into the enoteca. I fumbled around to find the light switch.

I'd never seen the place at night, but the rectangle was an ominous cavern lit by a single light bulb. I understood why Tony always kept the doors open during business hours.

"Do you notice anything wrong?" Sander asked.

I reviewed the rows of products, but I wouldn't have noticed if a few bottles were missing. "I think so? I never paid that much attention."

Sander studied the showcase of various cheeses.

"Fabrizio sells wines and olive oil made locally, but he purchases other products?" Sander asked.

"Right. I think the olive grove is close to here and the vineyard too. Tony's uncle doesn't do any of the work himself, but his farmhand gathers the grapes and takes them to a refinery or something like that."

"But Tony hasn't heard from his uncle lately?"

"Fabrizio sent a couple of texts with brief instructions. He's refused to answer Tony's calls and mine too."

Sander ran his hand along the smooth counter. "You said he's older?"

"Seventy-something. And stubborn."

Sander indicated the front door. "May I?"

I handed him the key ring. "Sure."

He jingled the key into the lock and opened the door. Across the street was a stone wall. In between was a sparse one-way street lined with residential buildings on either side.

"This isn't a strategic location for a shop," Sander said. "Few tourists walk this far off the main path."

"That was my reaction as well, but it turns out that Fabrizio depends on steady customers who buy in bulk.

He gets random tourist traffic, and the shop has a website, but since it's out of date, it's no help."

Sander stepped out into the street and turned around to face the establishment. I did the same. Together we reviewed the archway over the door.

"You said someone tried to break in?" Sander asked.

"I couldn't quite tell from the window, but they parked right in front of the shop. Then they tried to work the lock."

"They had a universal key of some kind?"

I ran my fingers along the rough wooden door. "Maybe? What Fabrizio needs is a camera. We have them back home. Once they're installed, you can check your front porch from your cell phone."

Sander eyed the doorway. "We have those in the Netherlands as well. I'm sure we could obtain one."

"Think we could manage to install it?"

"Why not? The early ones were complicated, but by now they're designed for the regular consumer. Do you know of an electronics store?"

"There's the Multi-Service, but that's hardware. Maybe down the hill."

"When you're at school tomorrow, I'll investigate."

"That's not fair. You're here as a tourist. You should be visiting Patrizio's Well, for example. The Orvieto Underground. The Etruscan Tombs."

Sander laughed. "Those activities sound fine, but perhaps installing a camera is more practical."

While I feared my paranoia outpaced my logic, I nodded. "If it's not too much trouble, I would appreciate that. It would put my mind at rest. Like you said, there's not much we can do for Tony, but that one little thing might help him."

"In that case, it's worthwhile."

We retreated inside and locked the door. Then I led Sander to the side of the shop beside the cash register.

"While we're down here, let me show you the garden. I really love it."

I led him halfway down the rectangle and unlatched the door.

"This isn't locked either?"

"Fabrizio never bothers to lock it." I stepped outside, and Sander followed behind.

"This is a private area."

"We're the only ones with access. Someone could crawl out to the garden through their window, I suppose."

We stepped farther into the moonlight. The only sounds were the buzz from a nearby streetlight, and, a couple of floors up, the sound of a loud TV.

Carefully, so that I wouldn't stumble over the combination of weeds and stones, I led Sander over to the round patio table so that we could sit across from one another in the dim light. Sander was so blond that he practically shone himself. His legs were so long that he had to stretch them sideways because they didn't fit under the table, yet he seemed at ease.

"A nice spot," Sander said. "I understand why you would enjoy coming here."

"It's been a sanctuary."

"I can see why. I would come here as well. Sometimes all you need is a little space to yourself. That allows you the chance to clear your head."

"That's exactly right! Here, I can get away from Henrietta and everything else."

"But not me, I hope!"

"That's different!"

It was way different. Here in the moonlight, it was a privilege to have Sander all to myself. We could relish the moment rather than having to hurry off anywhere.

He gestured towards the neighboring buildings. Out of more than a dozen, two windows showed any light. "Do you know anything about the other residents?"

"Not a thing. During the day I hear conversations sometimes. Mostly arguing." Not that I caught many words. For all I knew it was two people who couldn't hear each other discussing the day's weather.

"You've been focused on your studies."

"You can always study more, right? But after a while nothing sticks, so you're wasting your time."

"I know I've been a distraction."

"You haven't been the only one. But look at all the practice I got over the weekend. And all the words I learned playing *buraco*!"

"The weekend was memorable."

He was right on many accounts, but he'd stopped talking about tourism. I felt like he was peering inside me, scoping me out, figuring out my inner thoughts. I might have been alarmed or at least on guard, but I was also flattered. He cared about my feelings and wanted to understand them. He'd earned a whole tray of brownies, and he wasn't even trying to.

After I smiled at him, he stretched his hand across the table to meet mine and gave it a quick squeeze. "I hope you realize that I'm delighted to be here in Italy with you."

"Despite all the crazy circumstances?"

"Maybe because of them! We would have had a dull weekend if we'd played tourists the whole time rather than becoming advocates."

"The circumstances have been crazy all right. But when I think about it, I wonder what the heck I'm doing here. I mean, a semester of Italian in three weeks? What was I thinking when I signed up for this crazy course, that something miraculous would happen?"

"Something has. We've finally met in person. That was no easy feat."

Sander was so tranquil that he made me nervous. I babbled to fill the air. "I would have never signed up for this program if I'd known what it would be like."

"Don't tell me you have regrets! Then we wouldn't be sitting here having such a nice chat."

No. And I wouldn't have to wonder what might come next because I'd be sitting at home watching BritBox with Grandma all summer. I wouldn't have had the chance to stretch out my hand as an invitation. Sander wouldn't have had the chance to gently touch the tips of my fingers.

Anyone watching would have grown discouraged. Sander and I might have spent an hour slowly touching one another's hands. Then arms. Then intertwining our feet. We rose of one accord, silently agreeing, soundlessly moving upstairs.

We didn't speed up then either. We took our time as if enjoying a slow Italian dinner. Gentle relaxing on the couch, the appetizer course. The gradual move into the bedroom for the main course. Finally, lying against one another watching the play of shadows along the wall for dessert. When we finally slept, we did so by slowly melting beside one another, finding a comfortable position that allowed us to breathe as much as it allowed us to remain close.

Finally, I'd reached a moment where I didn't have to worry about Tony or school or anything else.

I didn't even have to worry about Sander.

Chapter Twenty-Five

Since it was before ten a.m., I expected to slip in and out of the apartment without Henrietta noticing. Instead, I found her at the kitchen table. Crying.

Silently, I swore at my unfortunate timing. Then I reminded myself that being kind was a virtue. "Are you all right?"

She looked up, brushed away her tears, and pulled her strands of long blonde hair out of her face. They immediately fell back again.

"Where have you been?" she asked.

"Rome, mostly. Then I was with my boyfriend. Remember?" I sank into the other chair. So much for a quick escape.

"Everything has gone wrong! Guess where I was all night?"

Normally I would have shown off by mentioning the Blue Bar, but I pretended not to have any idea.

"I had to go to the hospital! And do you know why?" She pointed to her thigh. "I burnt myself!"

A white bandage stretched along her leg. The tape looked exceptionally strong and straight.

"Did you run into an iron?" I hadn't seen one in the apartment, but I hadn't looked. Ironing was one more domestic activity I had no use for.

"Of course I didn't run into an iron! I was trying to cook!"

"But how —" Our kitchen area was a small angle with the stove on one side and the fridge on the other. A mini counter allowed food preparation. We didn't have a dishwasher, but a large drying rack beside the sink held a metal skillet.

"I was making pasta sauce! And what did I get for all my effort? Second-degree burns!"

Shockingly, Henrietta was capitalizing on the cooking class we'd had during our first week. While my group had made pesto sauce to go with ravioli, the beginning class had made tagliatelle and *ragù alla bolognese*. Although I'd enjoyed the four-hour extravaganza that included making antipasti and tiramisù, what it taught me the most was what I already suspected: I was too impatient to participate in homemade Italian cooking. Too many steps. Too tempting. But most of my classmates had an opposite reaction. They had vowed to practice before leaving Orvieto.

"I know it's ridiculous!" Henrietta shouted. "I heated the olive oil the way I was supposed to. And I even used the right kind."

I doubted that; I noticed our apartment had provided the cheapest and most basic Bertolli, but never mind. It still might have worked.

"I was about to add the sauce, but then my phone rang, and I turned around, and the handle caught my blouse, and I spilled hot oil all down my leg! It was awful! And then I had to call Lucia, and she was busy having dinner and finally she sent her sister! And by then I was in so much pain I couldn't do anything but lay down!"

Lie down. My sister would have been proud of me for noticing. She paid more attention to English grammar than I did. "Did Lucia's sister take you to a kind of urgent care?"

"At night there's one place to go—the hospital."

I thought I'd explored every inch of town. "It must be small. Where is it?"

"It's not up here! You have to circle all around to get down the hill, and then you go past the train station and a few roundabouts."

I should have guessed that any major medical facilities would be out in the countryside where there was more space. Emergency vehicles trying to get through Orvieto proper would get stuck.

"Guess what happened when we arrived?" Henrietta asked.

I imagined that Italian hospitals were a lot like the ones in Tucson: understaffed and overstuffed. "They wanted your passport?"

"They ignored us! We had to wait for hours! And my leg burned the whole time! The pain wouldn't stop!"

"Sounds awful."

"Some old guy came in, and they took him way before me even though I'm sure there was nothing wrong with him!"

He was probably another member of the Baldoni family, one who had connections with the facility coordinator and at least half the staff. My grandma had already warned me that the way to zip through lines at a health care facility was to complain of chest pains.

"We didn't leave until three in the morning, and they wanted to keep me overnight! By then Lucia was there, so she talked them out of it."

"You weren't in danger, so why would they keep you?"

"They do that here! Because maybe your relatives will try to help you, and instead they do the wrong thing! Even if you're barely sick, the hospital won't let go of you. But since I don't have any relatives, and we didn't know where you were, Lucia explained that she would be responsible for me, and she would make sure I had the right treatment."

The light bulb flashed so quickly that it gave me a headache. If Vittorio Baldoni had gone to the hospital complaining that olive oil almost killed him, he ought to still be there. At least it was a possibility.

"Can you imagine if I had to stay there all night by myself?" Henrietta asked. "Everyone barking Italian at me? It would have been awful! And the waiting room had terrible cell phone reception. I couldn't get through to a single person back home to let them know what was happening."

We would have to pretend to be relatives, but neither Sander nor I could easily pass as Italian. I needed help. I needed a team. Becky and Michelle would be good candidates. They weren't too Italian-looking either, but at least they had dark hair.

"I might have to get a skin graft!"

First we'd need to check on evening visiting hours. There should be a few. Maybe we wouldn't ask about Baldoni. We could pretend we wanted to visit our American friend, the one with the burn. Or a tourist friend. Maybe we wouldn't have to be too specific if we were pretending to struggle with Italian.

That was it. As we walked through the parking lot, we would notice which countries were represented, and claim our imaginary friend was from one of them. We'd say our friend had stomach problems because maybe that way we'd get sent to the right floor.

"I'm sorry about your leg. It's probably not too bad, though."

"I'm going to have a scar! From cooking!"

"Most scars fade with time."

"This one will be too big!"

Maybe the four of us could split up. If we could figure out the chart, look in and see the patient, make up some kind of silly excuse for who we were looking for—sure. You couldn't get in trouble for that, right? At least not too much.

"That's going to be my whole souvenir," Henrietta said. "A scar! Now I don't even have money for souvenirs. I spent it on stupid cooking stuff!"

"At least the program is almost over. You can shop more cheaply once you're back home."

"I have to eat, don't I! Since I'm not cooking ever again in my life, I'll have to eat out."

"The cheese here is pretty good, and you can buy decent bread to go with it."

"I'm lactose intolerant!"

"A lot of the cheese is aged."

"I don't know how to say that!"

"You have to ask for *stagionato*. At the market, they'll understand what you're talking about."

"I can't say a single thing in Italian that anyone can understand! It's those stupid old verbs! They keep changing!"

"The patterns are confusing, but once you get them down, they're not so bad."

"Lucia said when it's formal, the verb ends in 'e.' At the market I asked *parle italiani*, and they all laughed at me!"

Only two words in her sentence, and she'd managed to get both wrong.

"They didn't mean to laugh. They couldn't help it. Your problems surprised them. That's all. They're not used to hearing Americans try to speak their language."

"What problems?"

"First, *parlare* is an *-are* verb. *Parlo, parli, parla.*"

"But it's supposed to be 'e'!"

"That's only true with an *-ere* verb. *Scrivo, scrivi, scrive.* Oh. I guess it's true with an *–ire* verb too. *Dormo, dormi, dorme.*"

"Why do they have to have three different kinds of verbs?"

Why did I have to have this entire conversation? All I needed was a change of clothes. "Languages have lots of verbs. That's how they work."

"But it's so hard! *-are, -ere, -ire*! Who can keep that straight? Who wants to?"

Part of me wanted to explain that verbs were easier in Mandarin because the language used adverbs such as "yesterday" to indicate time, but that would have required an explanation of adverbs. I didn't have an extra hour and a half.

The sisters could pass as quasi-Italian. The other problem was me. If the sons were around, and spotted me, they'd know something was up. No matter how much I wanted to help, I might have to send Sander to the hospital with Becky and Michelle.

"But what about *dire*?" she asked. "Is the 'you' form *de*?"

"The verb for 'to tell' is irregular."

Henrietta slammed her fist on the table. "That's too much! I can't learn how to say a sentence, and I can't pass my tests and after being in this stupid place for nearly three weeks and spending all my money, I'm not even going to get credit for it! I'll have to ruin next semester too by taking Italian all over again!"

What I needed was some vague camouflage. Even a couple of touches ought to do.

"It's impossible!" Henrietta continued. "I give up! I want to go home! And my stupid boyfriend isn't even coming! His passport expires next month, so now they won't let him in! And you tell me *parle* is wrong even though Lucia said it was right! I'm going to have a nervous breakdown. Right this minute."

It was always best to feed two cats with one can of tuna. "I have an idea. Let's go take a look in your clothes closet."

"What?"

"Does it hurt to walk?"

"Not that much."

"Come on." I strutted into her room. "Look, You know a lot about fashion, right?"

"I always used to think I did, but now I'm not sure I know anything about anything!"

"Let's relate verbs to something you're good at."

"What do you mean?"

I fingered a long flowing blouse that had oranges and reds. "Let's say this is an -*are* verb. Okay?"

"That's stupid, but all right, let's say."

Then I fingered a pair of cherry-colored pants. "Do you wear these two things together?"

"Of course not. It's the wrong color group. Everybody knows that."

"Okay, then. Think of verbs as color groups. The -*are* verbs all go together. They do things the same way." I went back to the blouse. "What goes with this?"

She pointed to a pair of gold pants which, while ugly, did indeed compliment the blouse.

I pointed to athletic shoes. "Is that what you would put on your feet?"

"Of course not! It would look stupid."

I pointed to a baseball cap. "Is that what you would put on your head?"

"What does this have to do with verbs?"

"Remember this: -*are* verbs go -*o,- i, -a, -iamo, -ate, -ano.* Once you have one, you have them all."

"You said a lot of verbs were irregulars."

"Okay, okay! Except for the irregulars. Never mind about those at the moment. First let's get this down. You've got your -*are* verbs, *parlare, giocare, andare.* No wait, that one's irregular."

"Again!"

"Sorry! Okay, *parlare, giocare, organizzare, mangiare,* for example. Those all work the same way." I fingered the cherry-pink pants. "This pair over here goes with different endings. Never mind about those other clothes for now. Today, just concentrate on -*are.* Once you get those you can go on to something else. You have to be a little patient with yourself. Okay?"

"How can you expect me to be the least bit patient? I've been working on this since I came to Orvieto!"

"Take it one step at a time."

"But the test —"

"Is coming up. Right. Got that. Look, today, get down the first set of verbs. Tomorrow, the second set. Then the third set. Then the irregulars."

"But I get them all mixed up!"

"You won't. Let's take another example. You're good with clothes."

"You think so?"

Finally! A genuine question. One that wasn't a whine. And not a moment too soon.

"All your outfits look better than all of mine. In fact, I was going to ask you a favor."

"You were?"

"So, like I said, my boyfriend is in town, and he wants to take me to a nice restaurant tonight, but I don't have a single fancy thing to wear. Would you mind loaning me something?"

I'd let the clothing genie out of the bottle. Within moments she had set me up with a complete outfit: flowing blouse, wide-legged capris, summer hat. I drew the line at her high-heeled shoes, explaining that I'd fall down if I got the least bit tipsy, but I accepted everything else. I even talked her into loaning me a little makeup and a couple of hair bands. While it was true that the Baldoni son might recognize me if he looked long enough, he wouldn't recognize me at first glance. And that ought to be long enough.

*

I had the excuses ready: Becky, you need real conversation. Michelle, you always try to talk to the natives. Instead, when I invited the sisters to have a coffee with me and Sander after class and then asked if they would come to the hospital with us to sniff out old dying Baldoni, they signed up right away. They were delighted to participate in any activity that might help Tony.

"The family is full of liars," I admitted, "but I don't think they're dangerous."

"There's safety in numbers," Becky insisted. "They can't harm all four of us at once."

"We should record them," added Michelle. "We'll want proof."

End of argument. My accomplices were lined up and excited to help. After riding the funicular, we popped onto the B2 bus that traveled under the highway and circled numerous bends until it landed at Ospedale Santa Maria della Stella. We'd prepared a whole slew of phrases involving our imaginary tourist friend, and indeed the front doors opened to a check-in counter. Since no one was manning the desk, however, I herded us straight through the lobby.

That might not have been the most expedient plan. The hospital was full of lost friends and relatives. We wasted twenty minutes wandering around and dodging coughing patients. Eventually we encountered a nurse who slowed down long enough to ask if she could help us, a cheerful young woman who was as blonde as Sander and who wielded a clipboard and several thick pages of charts.

Sander didn't have to work to turn on the charm; it flowed from him naturally and to our benefit. Baldoni? Room 203. She pointed the way.

The man was not alone. The roly-poly sixty-year-old had a handful of visitors, mostly women. That was as much as I noticed as I hurried past. Despite my new look, I didn't want to confront either of Baldoni's sons, or thugs, or son-thugs. I posted myself across from Baldoni's room and crossed my fingers that no one would ask why I loitered at that particular spot.

After Sander turned on the voice recorder on his phone, Becky took charge. She stepped into the room, dragging Michelle and Sander behind her as if they were too shy to go on their own.

In shaky but correct Italian, she asked Baldoni if he owned Ristorante Orvieto Paradiso. Of course he did.

Didn't he remember her and her sister and her boyfriend from the summer before?

He nodded as he strained his memory, but by then Michelle chimed in. They'd had such a wonderful time that it was a night they would always treasure. They couldn't thank him enough.

Oh, yes, now he did remember them. How lovely that they'd had a memorable evening.

They'd posted their favorite photos on Instagram and told all their friends who were traveling to Italy to make sure to look for Baldoni's wonderful restaurant, the best in all of Umbria.

By then Baldoni was thanking them.

Becky approached the bed. What was such a strong man doing in a hospital? They'd come to visit another friend and almost walked by without noticing him. What was the matter? Was he going to be okay? Was there anything they could do for him?

Even from across the hall, I heard giggles from the other relatives in Baldoni's room.

"Your stomach?" suggested Michelle.

Laughter.

"You ate something that was bad for you?"

More laughter as Baldoni pounded on his flabby stomach.

Our suspicions were correct. Not a thing was wrong with the man. I wanted to pound his head. What a dirty liar! It was all a ruse to ruin Fabrizio, who might have even deserved it. He wasn't much of an uncle.

"My stomach is like bathtub. Can't hurt it!" Baldoni roared.

"There is nothing wrong with you?" Sander asked.

"No! I am well! I have the bad stomach maybe one day."

Clever. He'd come to the hospital claiming he was dying of stomach pain. The doctors had failed to detect anything because nothing was wrong. The staff had assigned him a hospital room because he'd insisted on it.

Not only was he playing a trick on a man who wasn't in town, but his own community was paying for his needless hospital stay.

"If you are well, then why are you still here?" Sander asked.

"In case I die!" Baldoni roared.

I'd never witnessed such a happy hospital patient.

"We'll come in for dinner next week," Becky said. *"We hope you'll be back to work by then."*

"Of course!" He pounded on his stomach. *"Really, I am fine. The nurses don't believe me."*

"What about the doctors?" Sanders asked.

"Ha! They don't believe me either! So I have a little rest."

"Can we—" Michelle stopped herself.

"What?"

"But you're in bed."

"I don't care! Come. Take the photo. You, blondie. Take a photo for us."

By then I heard the sound of loud male footsteps. In case they belonged to one of the Baldoni brothers, I decided I'd best move along. I retraced my steps long enough to find the exit and get back out to the curb.

But now we had ammunition. As Fleur expected, Baldoni was as healthy as we were.

But if he wanted to keep playing games, so would we. And it wouldn't be Solitaire.

Chapter Twenty-Six

I stepped through the metal turnstile that admitted me to Patrizio's Well. "What do they mean, that's not enough proof?"

Sander stepped through behind me. "Despite our voice recording, the police will have to send their own investigator."

We headed down the stone cylinder. The masterpiece dated from the 1520s, when Pope Clement VII had it built to ensure the town of a water supply in case of a siege. While one set of donkeys lumbered down the first staircase, another set lumbered back up. The animals could be in continuous motion without getting in one another's way.

Although the structure had nothing to do with St. Patrick, the double helix reflected the endless cave where the saint was said to have prayed. Modern tourists profited from the clever structure because people on their way down never interfered with people on their way up.

"I don't understand," I said. "What are the authorities going to do, wait until the guy is out of the hospital?"

"So it seems. Fleur will deliver Tony another care package."

I paused to take a photo. "We must be able to do something in the meantime."

"This is what we have to figure out."

We spiraled downwards, noticing several people ascending on the other set of stairs. The staircases might have symbolized my summer. I wasn't sure whether I was coming or going myself. I'd traveled to Orvieto to work on Italian only to specialize in Italian bureaucracy. What I'd gained so far wasn't an appreciation of food or climate, but of a Dutchman who offered companionship and solutions without expecting an immediate return.

Sander paused to study the design. We were about halfway between the top and the bottom, so we could look up at the sky and down into the abyss. "This is an amazing architectural feat, yet my guidebook barely mentions it."

"Around here, if it's not Etruscan, it doesn't count." I was barely kidding. Henrietta's group had discovered that if they asked Lucia about the city's ancestors, the woman would forget all about the day's grammar lesson.

We had no such luck with Aurelio. He wasn't an awful teacher, but he was dull and predictable. I'd learned more preparing for the hospital visit than I had during the day's rote exercises. Correctly combining prepositions with articles was important, but mastering a language was a hodgepodge. You had to store bits and pieces in your mental reservoir one at a time. You had to learn vocabulary and patterns. You had to speak to real people who spoke in natural ways.

But when it came to troublemakers, non-verbal cues were more important than verbal ones. I learned more by watching Baldoni pound his fist into his stomach and laugh than I had during any of my classes. The man was a happy fraud. Who wouldn't be, what with the fan club he entertained in his hospital room?

When Sander and I reached the bottom of the well, we paused on the narrow bridge between the two staircases. A wisp of daylight shone on the pool of water at the bottom of the well and illuminated the coins that had been thrown inside. Voices of other tourists reminded me that while we'd enjoyed meandering down to the bottom, we would still have to trudge back up.

"This staircase was built almost exactly five hundred years ago," Sander said. "Can you imagine that? I might be happy if I create something that lasts five years, let alone a decade."

"I don't even know what I want to create." I suppose I'd never thought about it.

Light bounced gently around Sander's face. "Your destiny will come to you. This is always what happens."

"You aren't satisfied with banking?"

"Perhaps not. But my job has allowed me to take this vacation. I have been able to save some money. That gives me multiple choices."

Having choice, or at least the illusion of choice, was important. Otherwise, you were a donkey climbing up and down staircases. What was important was to relax and appreciate the day.

On a tight Renaissance staircase, that meant taking small steps, always one at a time.

*

I would have chosen the easy way out and stopped for fast food, but while we were heading back to the apartment, Sander suggested we try our hand at cooking something local and tasty; after all, we had plenty of olive oil. I warned him that I knew a total of five food words before leading him into a small grocery shop. The establishment was so limited that it consisted of three rows of food items and a counter for meats and cheeses, but I'd noticed the friendly, aproned owner before. He waved at me whenever I passed by. Even though I hadn't been a customer, by now he took me for a semi-local.

Sander and I paced in front of the counter for long minutes. I was on the verge of formulating a question when a local woman came in, so I backed off and listened while she made a small purchase. Then another woman came in and three more after her.

Meanwhile Sander reviewed the variety of meats. "What can you tell me about these?"

He wasn't ribbing me. The question was genuine. I'd been in Italy for a couple of weeks. I should have known something. "You might have forgotten that while I'm all about eating, I'm not about cooking at all."

"Yes, I have realized this!"

The last of the customers exited, and the owner came over and gave us a smile. If I hadn't already met Sander, I might have thought the man was the most patient person in the world.

"I can help you, yes?" He pointed to the biggest item in his showcase, a hunk of red pork with white strips. "This is *guanciale di norcia,* I think you call the jaw. This the one I like the best."

"It looks fantastic," said Sander.

It was seven o'clock, which meant we still had an hour before the stores closed, but I suspected my tall Dutch package was becoming dangerously hungry, which would mean way too much food purchasing.

The man shifted over a bit and pointed out another hunk. "The *capocollo* is also good. The shoulder muscle. Then we have the *salame brado,* which means is raised in the pasture. What you are cooking?"

Sander and I looked at each other and laughed.

"Oh! You are new to the married!"

Then Sander and I laughed even harder, but I wasn't sure whether the trigger was the man's charming use of language, his romantic assumptions, or our state of clue-lessness.

"As you can see, this is difficult for us," I said. I wondered how many times a day he had such novice customers.

He bowed. "You will use the *pastasciutta* or you make the fresh noodles?"

Sander's eyes widened. "You have fresh pasta?"

"In the next small piazza." He kissed his fingers. "Is always the best."

"We'll make fresh, then," Sander said. "Please, tell us what's the best meat to use for a sauce. We don't have a clue how to choose ourselves."

When the man pointed, Sander and I nodded at the same time.

Mental note to Aurelio: Stop teaching exercises. Take your students to a grocery store. That would be a lot more useful in the long run.

*

Our cooking made the small apartment stuffier than usual, so after dinner we retreated to the garden. Moonlight shone above us, and a gentle breeze cooled us off. We sat across from one another in the quiet calm of after-dinner digestive exhaustion. Our after-dinner coffees might have awakened us had I not added a smidge of sambuca to each, which effectively counterbalanced the caffeine.

Yet I felt quite optimistic. We hadn't solved Tony's problem, but we'd made progress. Sander had installed a camera over the front door, so at least we had minimal protection and proof if somebody — a Baldoni — tried to get in. We'd agreed to study the webcam results in the morning, and Sander and I would visit Ristorante Orvieto Paradiso, Baldoni's place, for lunch. For dinner, maybe we'd drag the sisters with us.

That was the most we could do, so for the moment we could allow ourselves to enjoy the sky and the evening. I felt complete somehow, not because I was full, but because I had enjoyed cooking. After buying meat, our inexperience had continued at the next shop, but the woman behind the counter talked us into *orecchiette*, little ears, which she claimed was the most local pasta.

We'd proceeded to concoct a dish that we would never be able to recreate even if we tried. We threw in a little of everything we had, including fresh peas and zucchini, a carrot, and a dash of ricotta. We chopped up the *salame brado* and tossed it in without noticing how much we were using. We taste-tested the sauce along the way, congratulating ourselves on our efforts.

Mostly Sander's efforts. I would have been more hesitant. I might have added a few ingredients, but he threw things in without looking back. After a while, I caught on and threw in paprika merely because I'd found some on the shelf.

"I enjoyed making dinner," I said. "I'm not ready to open a *trattoria,* but at least for one night we won't die of hunger."

"Perhaps you should open a café. Certainly, Tucson could use one?"

"It would never fly. People back home are addicted to Starbucks."

"The coffee is good there?"

Now that I could finally compare, I could speak with authority. "It's acceptable. But once you have an espresso in Italy, you don't want to have it anywhere else."

"You would know how to make the best cappuccino in town."

"Coffee is too cheap. We'd have to offer something else spectacular."

"Why not sell fresh pasta on the side?'

"Most Americans would find it too expensive."

"The difference between spending two euro for pasta and spending eight has to do with quality."

Maybe I had the wrong friends, but I couldn't think of a single one who would be willing to pay four times as much for pasta. Evidently, I also had the wrong relatives.

"You have to know what to do with the pasta as well," I said.

"You truly did not know it was necessary to simmer the olive oil?"

I saw nothing wrong with tossing it right in with the pasta, but Sander had intercepted. He'd also insisted on adding salt to the boiling water rather than adding it afterwards. He claimed that made a difference too, but I wasn't convinced.

A noise startled us. We both turned towards the gate.

"Did you—" I asked.

He put his finger to his lips.

For long moments we sat quietly. I imagined that we were being watched, but by whom? I looked up at my neighbors' windows, but not even one showed a light.

Then we heard a brushing sound. Then tapping against the gate.

I crouched down, not that anyone who looked in the patio wouldn't see me, but then a big gray cat jumped into the yard and sauntered towards us.

Sander laughed. "Miao!"

The cat stopped short as we had, considered us, and retreated to the gate. The animal scaled it easily despite the five-foot jump.

"What's on the other side?" Sander asked.

"Some kind of greenery. I assumed it was somebody's garden."

Sander moseyed over to the gate, and I followed behind. He peered over the side. "You say this belongs to the next house?" he asked.

"I never paid attention."

He shone his flashlight down and around; all we could see were trees. "Shall we find out for sure?"

"Of course. But you might have to give me a boost."

I couldn't have scaled the gate by myself, but by stepping on Sander's thigh, I could hoist myself up. From there it was easy enough to scramble over to the other side.

Moments later Sander did the same. We stepped cautiously between bushes and trees, but we weren't in somebody's yard; we were in a seemingly unclaimed area between residential properties. The land was strewn with rocks, but they seemed like a natural part of the terrain. I smelled violets too even though I couldn't see them. We made our way over to a wall that bordered the property but couldn't hear any sounds inside. After we shimmied between two multi-story buildings, we were back out on Corso Cavour, the street that gently led down to the funicular.

"We've lost the cat," Sander said. "I'm sure he lives around here."

"We scared that poor thing all the way back to Florence," I said. "But now that we're on the street, there's only one remedy."

"We need a remedy?"

"You could call it that. Or you could call it gelato."

We headed up the street. Although we might have chosen among several *gelaterie* if we had been more ambitious, instead we settled for the first one.

We'd accomplished a homemade dinner, but *gianduia*, a chocolate hazelnut paste, had never tasted so good until I tried Sander's choice, which was *mandorla*, almonds.

Or maybe it was good because it was Sander's.

Chapter Twenty-Seven

I slid into the chair Sander had saved for me at a tiny table outside Ristorante Orvieto Paradiso. I'd never known paradise to be so compact. Four feet separated my elbow from the passersby cruising down the narrow street to reach the Piazza del Popolo. The space was tighter than a closet, but I appreciated the awning that jutted out above our heads, protecting us from the midday sun. I also enjoyed the challenge of jousting with the locals who pushed their grocery carts out of the square now that market day was winding up. I appreciated that the restaurant was at its maximum capacity, meaning that the few tables inside were as stuffed as the ones outside. The two waiters darted amongst us so quickly that I wanted to take bets on when they would collide.

I set my backpack on the ground at my feet, confident no one would steal my Italian grammar book even though Aurelio swore that it was our best friend. Although I noted the surroundings, including the cornflowers draping from planters between tables, the delicate white-on-blue patterns of the tablecloth, and the polished stainless-steel cutlery, the details faded into the background. Sander grinned at me, and even though I'd promised to come right after class, and had, he still acted as though I'd done something special.

"You look very nice, if you don't mind my saying."

Who minded? I'd borrowed a sun dress, which wasn't my style at all, and a different sunhat—how many head garments had my roommate brought from the States? I'd even condescended to wear her sandals even though I wobbled when I wore any kind of heel. Unlike most of Henrietta's billowy clothes, this particular dress was a little too tight and a little too short, which meant that I looked perfectly touristy.

It was a phenomenon I'd witnessed all summer. Most of the visitors I'd seen had either packed too optimistically to accommodate their actual waistlines, or they'd eaten too much pasta. It was a hazard of Italian travel.

"I paid a lot to borrow these clothes."

Sander spread his fingers over the table. "She wanted to charge you?"

"No, no. I had to listen to her." I'd timed my visit so that Henrietta would have already left for class by the time I dropped by the apartment. I hadn't counted on her being so upset by her boyfriend breaking up with her that she refused to leave the premises.

"It's not considerate of him to break with her while she's far away," Sander said.

I'd texted him the barest details.

"I'm sure he's been planning his escape for a while," I said. "He merely chose this week to do so."

"He might have mentioned this before Henrietta left Tucson."

I shook a bug off the white cloth napkin and refolded it. "He may have been trying to break up for weeks. She probably hasn't taken 'no' for an answer. The only person she listens to is herself, and she can't always manage that."

"I have known people such as this myself. I will be curious to meet her."

So far I'd managed to shield Sander from Ms Nosy, but she was bound to see us together sooner or later. "She's curious about you, but that's because she's jealous."

She would have felt worse if I'd shared details about sleeping with a handsome man who carefully asked what I wanted to do before making assumptions of his own, but I'd skipped all that.

I rummaged around in my backpack.

"Reading glasses?" he asked.

I took out my notepad. "My cheat sheet." I showed him my list of phrases, such as *Where do you buy your olive oil?*, but our overall plan was quite simple. Have lunch at Baldoni's restaurant. Make inquiries. Gather any possible information.

"Well, bless her heart!" exclaimed a lady at the table behind me. Not only was she American, but she was from the South.

Sander started to ask a question, but I held up my hand.

"Is something wrong?"

"No. What's Dutch for 'yes' and 'no'?"

"That would be *ja* and *nee*. Why do you ask?"

"I thought this through all wrong. The best way to be incognito is to be Dutch tourists."

"You don't want to practice Italian?"

"Not now. Consider the clientele. There's not a local in sight."

English speakers sat behind me. German speakers sat behind Sander. The tourists inside the restaurant spoke Spanish and French.

"We need to blend. Whenever the waiter is in earshot, speak to me in Dutch. Say anything. It doesn't matter what. It doesn't have to make sense."

"Okay, but I won't know when—"

"*Ja, ja,*" I said.

For a second, Sander was taken aback. Then he babbled while the waiter, an awkward young fellow who didn't seem to believe in washing his stringy black hair, tossed us a menu.

As soon as the waiter buzzed off, I leaned forward. "Great job. Keep it up."

"But why--?"

"To be tourists. Just to keep people off track. And you might throw on the voice recorder in case we learn something."

"Do you think—"

"*Nee,*" I said. "*Nee, nee.*"

The waiter stopped before our table and whipped out a sloppy white notepad as if he needed to take our order within the next twenty seconds or he'd be demoted to bus boy.

"Yes? You start with antipasto?"

"I have a question," I said in my best bad British accent. "Is Signore Vittorio inside?"

"Signore Vittorio? Something is wrong? I can fix for you!"

"No, no, no problem," I said quickly. "The last time we were here—what, two weeks ago? He helped us personally. He gave us a recommendation for the best lunch, and he promised to give us more recommendations if we came back on another day."

"Oh! Well, I am sorry he is not here, but he has a little problem with his health."

"Don't tell me he's sick? For a man who is not young, he is in such good condition," I said.

"Yes, yes, good condition. He is not so bad."

"I hope he didn't have a heart attack!" Sander said. "Men his age—"

"No, no," said the waiter. "He will be released soon."

"From the hospital?"

"I knew something was wrong," Sander exclaimed. He addressed the waiter. "You see, when we passed by yesterday, he wasn't here then, either."

"A heart attack," I said. "Are we right?"

"No, no."

I slapped my hands on the table. "Goodness gracious! A stroke!"

"Oh, no, signorina. He is fine. A little sick. That is all."

"But he's in the hospital! That's always serious!"

"No, is nothing! He has the—" The waiter tapped his stomach. "Some problem with the inside."

Sander shook his index finger at me. "Gout. Too much rich food. I told you this was a problem over here."

The waiter shook his head as if leaked information about his boss might affect his salary. "I promise he not so sick. Come back next week. Perhaps now you tell me what you like for the lunch?"

I hid my face in the menu so that the waiter wouldn't notice how hard I had to work to avoid laughing.

*

Sander used a piece of bread to wipe up the last drops of sauce from his plate. "What was the Italian expression?" he asked.

"*Fare la scarpetta.* Make the little shoe."

"Very useful."

"In the States, people always say you shouldn't have bread with pasta. Too much starch."

"Who says such a silly thing?"

"I must have read it somewhere. That Italians don't eat pasta with starch. Maybe it's a tourist thing."

Sander finished the bread even though he'd run out of sauce. "My Italian friends back home always have bread with their pasta."

"Do you know which olive oils are available?"

He picked up his cell phone. "I haven't paid that much attention, but I can check some retailers."

"Just to get a comparison."

I picked up the unlabeled amber bottle of olive oil that was on our table. I poured a drop on my empty salad plate and used my finger to taste it. "This is pretty good."

"Fabrizio's?"

"Let's find out."

I beckoned to the waiter, who stood in the shade of the street praying his five tables might vacate before he melted.

He popped over in a nanosecond. "You take the coffee? The dessert?"

"We have the question," I said, sure he wouldn't catch the irony of my language use. "This salad was so good, so very good, that I have to know. What is the olive oil that you used?"

"I am not so sure. Of course, we use the best—"

"Please! It was so delicious I have to talk to the chef!"

"But—"

I waltzed inside, and Sander followed me. I went straight over to a high counter that separated the kitchen from the dining area.

"Hello?" I said. "You are the chef?"

The apron-clad man glanced up from the linguini he was peppering.

"*Che c'è?*"

"Your olive oil!"

The man shrugged. I might have surpassed the sum of his English vocabulary.

I picked up a glass bottle from an empty table and held it up. "This! I must know what this is!"

The waiter came up behind us, and I quickly turned to him. "Please. Our Italian is so poor. The chef made a delicious salad. I know your ingredients are fresh, but the right olive oil makes a difference. You must tell me, where do you get it?"

I missed the quick exchange between the waiter and the chef, but I caught the word "Orvieto."

"Oh!" I said. "It's a local olive oil! Made from local olives?"

The waiter nodded. "Yes, yes. From Umbria. Is the best."

I pointed vaguely out to the street. "Can you buy it in the local shops?"

Both men nodded.

"Enoteca La Loggia? Bottega Véra?' I asked. Luckily, I'd done enough homework about Fabrizio's competition to sound genuine.

The chef shook his head. "No, no. *Un amico.*"

"A friend," the waiter told us.

"Ah," I said as if a thunder bolt had struck my brain. "Enoteca Fabrizio?"

"Fabrizio? No," said the chef. "No good is Fabrizio."

"Fabrizio?" the waiter said in Italian. *"Isn't he the guy Vittorio something something?"*

I couldn't catch more than fragments.

"Sure," said the chef. *"That's why he hasn't been coming in. Something something."*

"What a stupid guy."

"Very."

I nodded as if I'd followed the conversation.

"Where might we buy this same oil?" Sander asked. "It will make my wife so happy."

I patted Sander's shoulder. "Yes! We want to make sure to purchase exactly the same one."

The waiter shrugged as if he'd never heard a more ridiculous question. "In Orvieto, all the oil is good, and all is the same."

I held up the unlabeled bottle. "But which is the best?"

The waiter hunched over. "Well, sometimes—" He motioned pouring two things together.

"You combine the olive oils!"

The man smiled, relieved that we had understood. "Yes, is right."

"So maybe they're two different kinds."

"Sì, sì," echoed the chef.

Clever. By blending the oils, they could make the best combinations. Or maybe they combined cheap ones with expensive ones. Or maybe they were so careless that they threw things together without paying attention. Tourists wouldn't know the difference.

"Of course! That's why your olive oil is so good," I gushed. "It's also unique. I could come here ten times and the salad would be wonderful, but different. Brilliant!"

"Is true," said the chef. "Always different. You can come every day."

"No wonder your eatery is the envy of the town!"

The chef beamed.

Sander gently bumped against me. "*Schatje*, this man needs to work. Should we ask for the check?"

"Of course!" I said cheerfully.

We returned to our table, and the waiter whipped the bill from his pocket. By then three couples stood in the narrow passageway, hoping to be seated.

Sander paid cash so that our names wouldn't come up on a credit card. Our waiter thanked us and waved good-bye before squeezing four people into the small space we'd vacated.

The diners wouldn't care. Maybe they would order salad and enjoy the finest local blend.

Despite his long legs, Sander scrambled to keep up as I raced away from the restaurant in the direction of the Centro Studi.

"I'm afraid you can't avoid being late to class,' Sander said.

"I'll claim stomach issues. What did you call me, by the way?"

"*Schatje* means something like 'dear one.' I'm sorry if that seemed too familiar."

As I rounded the corner, I picked up speed. "Are you kidding? That fit the situation perfectly."

"Do you understand what they said about Fabrizio?"

"I missed quite a few words. But that little exchange confirmed that we're on the right track. Baldoni is quite all right. Now all we have to do is talk to Fabrizio."

"Didn't Tony say the man won't answer his phone?"

"He's going to."

"That's the spirit. What is your plan?"

As we reached the Centro Studi. I took Sander's hand, pulled him towards me, and kissed his cheek.

I'm not sure who was more startled.

"I'll tell you after class," I said.

I didn't turn around to check his expression, but I hoped he was thinking *schatje*.

Chapter Twenty-Eight

Sander glanced my way from across the garden table. "Aren't your fingers sore yet?"

I couldn't blame him for asking. So far I was calling Fabrizio's number, letting the phone ring a bunch of times, hanging up, doing one grammar exercise, and then calling again. I'd started with my own phone, but Sander suggested the man might have blocked it. Fair enough. Then I started using the landline. No matter how little he cared about his nephew, Fabrizio would know better than to ignore a phone call from his own business.

"After a few more attempts, I'll let you take over," I said.

"I don't know if I remember how to use such a good phone."

We both laughed. The cordless model was so old that it might have been on display in the Etruscan Museum.

"Shall I try with my phone?" Sander asked.

"Maybe a couple of times. I know. Let's triangulate."

"I'm sorry?"

"I'll call from the home phone. You keep calling from both my phone and yours. At some point he's going to give up and answer."

"Unless he's lost his phone. Or broken it."

I'd considered that possibility as well. It would have been a simple and understandable mistake. Fabrizio might have set down his phone to blow his nose, to check a price, to dig into his pocket, and walked away without it.

"You said Tony rarely talked to him?" Sander asked.

"At first we thought Fabrizio merely wanted to enjoy his vacation without distractions. Now I'm not so sure." I'd listened to the conversation we'd recorded from the restaurant two dozen times, but I was still missing some key words.

What I did catch was *ha promesso*, which meant "he promised," and *ha venduto,* which meant "he sold." Presumably, Fabrizio had made a promise he didn't keep. In a land of loyalties, such actions were serious. Despite government rigamarole for student visas and the like, I imagined that most business was still accomplished the old way, through verbal agreements. If Fabrizio had gone back on his word, no wonder the Baldoni family was so upset with him.

Or maybe they were petty.

"You could take the recording to class and ask your teacher to listen to it," Sander suggested. "That might be amusing."

"I agree, but Aurelio will assume that I'm crazy. Meanwhile, he's keyed up preparing us for tomorrow's final."

"The end of your program came quickly, didn't it?" Sander's eyes twinkled.

"Let's say I had trouble concentrating on my studies." The material would have been hard enough all on its own without overwhelming distractions. I was fortunate I hadn't been studying something more difficult, like math.

"How many points do you need to pass?"

"I'll pass. The question is whether I can earn an A or not." I still had a square shot at it. I'd completed most of the exercises along with the bonus options. If I could stuff a few hundred more vocabulary words into my tired little brain, I'd be doing all right.

"What would you say about the progress of your classmates?"

"Becky and Michelle study so much they can explain the rules better than Aurelio can. Lalo and Armando are lazy, but they use Spanish to skate by."

"I see. But you don't?"

My cheeks just might have reddened. "All the time. Sometimes it works!" Sometimes it got me into trouble instead, but it was like having a framework that was a little out of whack. At least you started with something.

"Are you nervous about the final?" Sander asked.

"I should be. It's half my grade." I picked up my cell phone and hit redial. "But when you take things into perspective, you realize that one little exam is not so important."

I still wanted the A. It would be good for my pride as well as my grade point average. But after a crazy weekend in Rome, and my thwarted efforts at being a tour guide, I also realized that nothing was more important than friendship. Achieving a high grade was an intellectual challenge, but developing life skills was more important.

"Have you ever thought about learning Dutch?" Sander asked. "It's the language most closely related to English."

Technically, that distinction belonged to Frisian, a Dutch-like Germanic language, but I didn't correct him. I knew what he was doing. Ever since lunch, he'd hinted about my coming to visit.

"Dutch is closer to English than German?" I asked.

"Yes! And it sounds better. But of course, you should come hear it for yourself."

This was his biggest hint yet, and we did have to come to a decision. I would have to vacate my apartment in another couple of days, and presumably Tony would be back in Orvieto by then. It would be the right time to move on.

I thought back to the couple I'd met on the train on my way to Orvieto. *The Dutch men are very romantic,* the woman had said. *Once you find the right one, you'll be set for life!*

I wasn't thinking that far ahead, but I didn't want to throw away the possibility in front of me.

"You want me to come back to Amsterdam with you," I said.

He smoothed a tuft of blond hair. "I can find you a cheap place to stay. Very reasonable. Good service!"

"You said your parents' house was small."

"You can have Vlinder's room. He's on tour for another month."

The thought was sweet but intimidating. Visit a lover's parents. Stay at his parents' house. Question your status with their son because the last two weeks have taken place at lightning speed.

I winked. "You should think two or three times before inviting me to your country."

"Why is that?"

"I can't promise to stay out of trouble. Mischief trails me. Somehow I manage to be with the wrong people in the wrong place at the wrong time."

"That will make your visit a challenge!"

Sander dialed again, but this time a man answered. In his hurry to give me the phone, Sander dropped it. We both lunged for the device as it slid across the mix of rubble and weeds.

"Zio Fabrizio!" I yelled when I recovered the phone.

The line was dead.

"Try again! We've almost got him!"

Sander tried again. Busy signal.

We looked at each other and frowned. This couldn't be happening. The man had to be reachable.

"Now!" I shouted.

Sander hit "redial." Fabrizio answered on the second ring. This time Sander set the phone to speaker and handed it to me so carefully that it might have been crystal, or maybe explosive.

"Ma che cavolo volete?" the shopkeerper asked.

Had Aurelio been there, he would have cheered for me. After much cajoling, we'd insisted that he teach us slang words. He hadn't taught us the bad words we wanted, but he'd taught us some soft touches, which was how I knew that Fabrizio had just demanded to know what cabbage we wanted.

"You have to go to Rome!" I shouted. "Tony is in jail, and it's all your fault!"

"*Cosa?*"

This would be the one time in his life that Fabrizio magically forgot every word of English at the very moment I couldn't think of the translation.

I opened a browser on my own phone and handed it to Sander. "Please. Right this second. Look up the word for 'jail.'"

"Tony isn't exactly in jail. It's more like —"

"Look it up!"

While Fabrizio spewed a confused mixture of Italian and English, Sander showed me his screen. Thank you, Google.

"*Prigione!*" I shouted at the phone.

"*Non è possible,*" answered Fabrizio.

I squinted at the other definitions before choosing one. "*Galera! Colpa tua!*"

"What?" cried Fabrizio. "Not my fault! I do nothing! Maybe my nephew, I don't know, maybe he do the bad drugs."

"Not at all! The Baldoni family —"

"*Non ne parlo.*"

"You might not talk about them, but they talk about you! Thanks to them, Tony's in trouble! You have to get to Rome to straighten things out!"

"I'm on vacation!"

"Not anymore! Your vacation is over! I hope you never get another one!"

"Why are you saying such things? Why are you so mean?"

Mean? I hadn't even gotten started. "How dare you make a bad business deal and leave Tony in charge knowing he would take the fall?"

"The fall?"

"Knowing he would get into trouble! You knew it would happen! So what's the deal with Baldoni?"

"Vittorio is stupid. And yes, we have a little fight. Is nothing."

I stood as if that would help me shout more loudly. "Tony has been locked up for several days thanks to you!"

"No, no. Misunderstanding."

"You need to go to Rome tonight! Right this minute! Don't delay!"

"Who you are? New girlfriend? But he doesn't like the girlfriend."

"Tony needs you. I'll find the address."

"No, no, I finish my vacation!"

I held the phone away from my mouth and pointed upstairs. "Get my purse from the couch?"

Sander jumped up and left.

"You need to head to Rome," I continued. "Where are you, anyway? Why haven't you contacted Tony? Why don't you at least answer your texts? Don't you know what human decency looks like?"

"I'm not going to Rome."

"Oh, yes, you will!"

Sander ran back out to the garden. I fished my notebook from my purse and read out the address, loudly and clearly.

"I don't like Rome," Fabrizio protested.

"I don't care what you like or what you don't. You need to go to this office tomorrow."

"Is small misunder—"

"Leave now, for God's sake!"

"You cannot make me do this."

Evidently I lacked training in dealing with selfish idiots. "Your nephew needs you. Start moving."

"Tony will be fine. They will realize that he is innocent."

"Rome! Now!"

"No!"

I wasn't a demanding kind of person. I didn't make threats. I rarely spoke loudly. I tried to help people, even Henrietta, and I tried to be nice. But Fabrizio was outside my control. I'd bent over backwards for someone I barely knew because he'd been abandoned by his own family. I'd dragged in new friends I didn't know to aid with the cause. That was going way far enough.

The problem was that I lacked leverage. I didn't know Fabrizio's location. I didn't know how far away he was or how much money he had. But I knew one thing. As a regular Italian, he cared about property. His property, that is.

"Oh, no? Either you go to Rome by tomorrow or I'll burn your shop down."

"What?"

"I'll start a fire in your bedroom and in your shop at the same time."

"No!"

"The aroma from roasting olive oil will fill the block, and your neighbors will come running to watch your fortune go up in flames."

"You won't do such a terrible thing!"

"You should have left five minutes ago." I hung up the phone. I couldn't remember ever being so brass or decisive.

Sander clapped three times and grinned ear to ear. "Wonderful."

"I wasn't trying to be mean."

"You weren't."

"He wouldn't listen to reason. He refused to budge half an inch."

"You helped him realize that the situation was serious."

"You really think so?"

Sander leaned over and kissed me on the top of the head. "He'll come running. You'll see."

I wanted to believe Sander was right, but I knew better than to take anything for granted. Fabrizio was still a wild card. I just hoped my *jolly* had trumped his hand.

*

Later that evening, Sander and I paid for our gelati and sat on the steps of the Duomo. In other cities maybe it would be disrespectful to slurp your ice cream in front of the Cathedral, but in Orvieto, we imitated the locals. The wide steps were dotted with at least seven clusters of friends, mostly high school students, who were enjoying cones of their own.

Sander licked at his pistachio cream. "So this is what the townspeople do at night. I like this system. It's very civil."

"This is what they do in the early evening. Then they gravitate to the bars."

Sander pointed to the stone ledge jutting out from the set of buildings across the piazza from us. "When I came by earlier, twenty people were squeezed onto that poor skinny ledge. Another dozen tourists were trying to take pictures, but they couldn't figure out a decent angle. You should have seen how hard they were trying."

"In Orvieto, that's the normal, everyday scene, day in, day out."

"I'm not surprised."

The Duomo in Orvieto was one of Italy's most famous. A cross between Italian Gothic and Romanesque styles, the façade was a celebration of rounded arches and pointy tips. It was protected by symbols of the Evangelists: an angel, an ox, and eagle, and, my favorite, a lion. Biblical scenes popped from the panels in bright mosaics. Even though Luisa had explained every last story during our orientation to the city, I only remembered one: the scene at the top depicted the coronation of the Virgin.

The sides of the church were striking too; they consisted of alternating panels of gray stone and white traver-
tine. Not only was the structure easy to spot from the surrounding hills, but the stripes gave the church a humorous
zebra effect. I couldn't pass by without thinking about
prison garb.

Since its inception, the Cathedral had been an important symbol, but the city founders had messed up the
real estate. Instead of giving such a famous church a big
square, the piazza was L-shaped. The edge of the rectangle
led up to the three bronze doors that spanned the church's
entrance while another leg of the piazza stretched east
along the zebra stripes. The result was that tourists who
came to the area armed with cell phones or cheap cameras
couldn't photograph the structure in just one shot. The
building simply would not fit into the frame. The huge dimensions made the process impossible.

I'd often watched frustrated photographers. They
would first take unsatisfying shots directly in front of the
Cathedral. Then they would attempt shots from either
side. Finally, they would step back into Via Maitani, from
which they could photograph the doors and the cross on
top of the coronation scene, but that meant chopping off
the church's sides.

A man strode into the piazza from Via del Duomo,
turned on his cell phone, and took a shot of a fraction of
the Cathedral.

"There goes one more wasted photo," I said.

"Maybe it will serve as a memory."

I pulled out my phone. "In that case, let's do a selfie."

Sander licked his cone. "We should finish these first."

"No. We want people to be envious." My sister would
be, at least. I'd already boasted about the *stracciatella*,
which had chocolate strands, and I'd coupled it with salted
vanilla caramel. I took out my cell phone and captured us,
ice cream and all.

Sander took a big lick to avoid dripping on his sandals. "What do you want to remember from your stay in Orvieto?"

"Me?"

Caught. Lucia would want me to go on and on about the lovely town. My friends back home would want to know about the handsome men. My grandma would want to know about the grocery store.

But the shop I knew well was the enoteca, and instead of dashing Italians, I'd gotten to know an Italian American and a Dutchman. I'd improved my Italian, but I still had a few more tenses to learn along with countless vocabulary and a zillion irregular verbs.

I scooted a few inches away so that I could better read Sander's face. "I want to remember the importance of friendships."

He grinned so broadly I could see his teeth shine. "You didn't realize that before?"

"Orvieto has been a darned good reminder." I could not have asked for a bigger one.

"By the way, I heard from Fleur. It seems that the detention center is getting tired of Tony."

I used my little green plastic spoon to scoop out the final drops of sweetness. "Oh, dear. Does that mean she learned something bad?"

"No. And by now, whenever she arrives, they wave her inside without asking for any explanations. They realize that the charges against Tony are meaningless."

"That's well and good, but how does that help?"

Sander wet a napkin and wiped the edge of my cheek. "I'm sure Fabrizio is on his way. Perhaps you'll reconsider talking to your supervisor? She might have connections with someone around town."

Earlier that day Lucia had run through the Centro Studi as if chased by a bullet, but she was merely preparing the materials for our finals. By Sunday, we'd all be leaving.

As long as she wasn't related to the Baldonis, she'd have the chance to catch her breath.

"I'll talk to Lucia if the timing ever seems right. She's so touchy that I never know when she's going to go ballistic."

"Do you think she's easily upset? Some people prefer drama."

She thrived on being in charge. The sense of authority gave her the confidence she probably wouldn't have in the normal Orvieto circles.

"She likes operating in the fast lane, which is hard to do in a town this small. But speaking of drama, you didn't notice anything strange on the webcam over at Fabrizio's?"

"A few people have looked at the sign long enough to notice that the enoteca is closed, but no one has lingered."

"No suspicious thugs hanging around for no good reason?"

"Not yet."

I wasn't sure whether to be disappointed or relieved. "We still don't have anything to go on."

"No, but we will soon. I do think so."

Maybe. But we were running out of time.

At least we wouldn't run out of gelato.

Chapter Twenty-Nine

The first sound was soft, like someone kicking a rock. The second was a car door being closed so carefully I could barely hear the click.

The bedroom was mostly dark, but light shone in from the streetlamp outside the window. I checked the mini digital clock by the bed: four a.m.

Holding my breath to avoid extra noise, I listened for more sounds.

First, nothing. Then a few footsteps, outside, on the pavement.

I slipped into the living room, where Sander slept on the couch, face down. "Sander!" I whispered.

No movement.

I sat on the couch and rocked his back. "Sander?"

He turned around so quickly that he knocked me off the couch, which made me bang into the coffee table, which made the books tumble onto the floor with a crash.

"Sorry!"

"Shhh! There's someone outside."

We ran to the bedroom. The window had been ajar, but now I opened it as wide as it would go.

Below, a car stalled. Metal clinked against the keyhole.

"Do you recognize the vehicle?" Sander asked.

I peeked out the window without sticking my nose outside it. I could barely see the white vehicle. It was bigger than most of the cars I'd seen around town. "The other one was white too, but I didn't pay much attention to it."

By then Sander had accessed his anti-burglar app. We sat on the bed and watched as two men peered at the keyhole. Then they fingered it as if trying to ascertain the depth of the hole.

"They're trying to break in!" I whispered.

Sanders poured over their movements. "No. They think they have a key."

We watched as they tried three different keys.

Finally, one of the men stood straight and took two steps back. *"Mannaggia,"*

Maybe I was glad for Aurelio's teaching after all. The mild swear word was an equivalent of "damn."

They jumped in the car and drove off.

I sank onto the bed, and Sander sank beside me. I felt a bit shaken, and for several seconds, neither of us managed to say anything.

Sander lightly touched my ear. "You have good hearing. You must commend yourself for that."

"I was sleeping lightly." I was surprised I'd been able to sleep at all.

"You're sensitive. You're aware of things."

"Not usually. There's plenty I miss. But here, in this apartment, I'm on guard."

"Given the circumstances of the last few days, you have to be. By chance did you recognize either man?"

"The driver is the one who picked up the boxes for Baldoni the other day."

"Was he driving that same vehicle?"

"I don't know. Probably. But he came alone. We spoke for a whole three seconds. Maybe fewer."

"He was in such a hurry?"

He might have been a fire fighter late to the bonfire. "That's what I assumed at the time, but now I think he didn't want me to remember him. He didn't want to leave an impression."

"The question is what they came back for."

I leaned back against the headboard and scooted over so that Sander could do the same. "That's the big question. There's nothing to steal here per se."

"Inventory. But they could do this at any wine shop."

"Maybe there's something hidden that we don't know about."

"I don't understand how they would have a key."

"Maybe they have a universal opener of some kind? But something strange is going on. There's a reason they waited until the middle of the night to make a visit. They were waiting for the night owls to go to sleep before the larks got up to chirp. I have to admit that it was smart timing."

"I agree. But you're the one with the exam. Rest for a while."

"Think they're coming back?"

"Not unless they have another kind of universal key. But you should sleep. I'll watch the monitor."

"That's not fair."

"I can remain in bed all day tomorrow, and by now, I can assure you that I am quite awake."

I stretched out. "You don't mind?"

"Not at all."

"I probably won't be able to sleep either."

"You should try."

"You'll tell me if they return?"

"Of course."

I lay flat and closed my eyes, but I couldn't turn off my brain. Two men had come to barge into the enoteca because they wanted something specific. Since they didn't get it, they'd be back.

*

Sander shoved me so hard I considered protesting. A moment later, I realized his actions were pure economy.

"Wake up." He strode towards the door.

"What are you doing?"

"They're back. I'm going to the enoteca."

Sander left the room. By the time I raced to the living room, he was quietly unlocking the main door.

"What do you think you're doing?"

"We need proof."

"We need to call the police!"

"I need to film them breaking in. Then we'll call the police."

"They might be dangerous!"

He held up a kitchen knife. "We may be more so. Stay here."

"What?"

"Stay here. I'll go downstairs."

I would have protested, but he'd already slipped from the room.

I was fumbling through my purse to find my phone when I heard a door rattle. Then open. Then I understood. They weren't entering the enoteca. They'd entered the property from the hallway around the corner, which meant they would be coming up the stairs and heading for the apartment. I shoved my purse into my backpack and flung it on my back. Then I pushed the armchair away from the wall and crept behind it.

Ten seconds later, I watched as the door unlocked and two men entered the room. They stood silently while the extra keys swished gently against the door.

"*Cosa pensi?*"

"*Non lo so.*"

They flashed their cell phones around to see where they were going.

"*Allora?*" one asked the other. "What now?"

One kicked a book, probably by accident. Poor book. They walked through to the bedroom, swung clothes from one side of the rack to the other, flashed their phones, and retreated.

"*Lo studio,*" one said to the other. "The study."

Perfect. If they thought the bottega were a study, that was their problem.

As soon as they were both inside, I sprang to the door and latched it.

"Oh!" one shouted.

"Oh!" shouted the other.

They banged on the door so hard they might have broken their hands.

"*Porca miseria!*"

"*Mannaggia!*"

Sander raced into the living room. "Where did —"

I slammed my index finger to my lips and pointed to the door the men were pounding on.

Sander held up two fingers, and I nodded. *Two people.* He made a motion of locking the door.

Right. We would trap them in the apartment as well.

"Jackets," Sander whispered. He grabbed his own and mine from the couch. We ran into the hallway, but I ran back inside and retrieved my backpack. I waited while Sander double clicked the lock.

"Now I'll call the police!" I whispered.

"No time." From the landing he pointed out to the street, where someone had pulled up in a Vespa.

"Enoteca!" we both exclaimed.

I followed Sander down the stairs but then hurried through the enoteca. "Garden!" I pushed open the door.

Sander pointed back at the enoteca. "We need proof!"

"Not on your life!" Proof wasn't worth that much. I ran outside.

"*Chi c'è?*" someone yelled angrily. "Who's there?"

"*Aiuto!*" shouted someone in the apartment. "Help!"

We sprinted through the garden to the gate at the back. Sander held his hands together so that I could use them as a stirrup, and he booted me over. Then he bolted over himself.

We looked in each direction, but all we could see was greenery.

"Separate?" he asked.

Shouts came from a distance.

"Run!"

In retrospect, I could have chosen an easier solution. At the time, my thought was to escape. I ran towards the funicular without looking back.

"Faster!" Sander shouted as he passed me up.

I struggled to catch up with him. We dashed across Piazza Cahen as the Vespa barreled towards us. We passed through the stone gate that led down from the fort.

"*Fermatevi!*" a man shouted.

"Do you want—" Sander started.

"Train station! There's a train in a few minutes."

"Can we make it?"

"Sure."

As I jogged, I dialed the local emergency number. A woman tried to ask my name, but I shouted *reato in corso*, "robbery in progress," gave her Fabrizio's address, and hung up. Then I followed Sander down the trail. We reached the forested area, which was so dark we had to flash our cell phones, but we kept running. I heard sounds behind us, so I was sure the Vespa rider was trailing us, but we had a long lead. We kept running until we reached the paved road that stretched down from the hill. We stopped to pant for several seconds before we continued down to the main road that wound around to the train station.

I put on extra speed; the adrenaline had kicked into overtime. From a distance, I saw the lights of a train heading north to Florence. It had nearly reached the station.

We reached the lobby with such speed that the two lone bystanders waiting for the early morning train looked at us as if we were thugs.

"*Buon giorno!*" I shouted.

"Which track?" Sander asked.

I didn't answer. I ran down the stairs to reach the other tracks as the train pulled into the station and came to a stop.

By then I had a change of heart. Instead of jumping onto a train we didn't have tickets for, we could pretend to catch it instead. I shook my finger at Sander so that he wouldn't spring out to the platform where anyone could spot him.

I waited until the train left the station, then peeked through the railing.

On the other side of the track, a man shouted obscenities at the departing train. Then he turned and left the station.

"Now what?" Sander asked.

"Let's go back."

We ran back downstairs, crossed through the tunnel, and dashed into the waiting room where a screen showed the various upcoming trains. A train to Rome wasn't due for another hour, but at any rate, I didn't have time to consider the range of possibilities. The man from the Vespa stood outside the train station yelling at the man who had emerged from a car labeled *carabinieri*.

I knew when I was beat. I took out my special emergency card and motioned for Sander to dial Lucia. Then I pointed at the Vespa man and yelled *"Criminale!"* so loudly I made my own ears hurt.

Chapter Thirty

I snarled at the official hiding behind the wooden desk. *"What do you mean, come back this afternoon? That's crazy!"*

The thirty-year-old offered half a smile. *"Nobody is here but me. I'm not allowed to sign anything."*

After bringing the chair three feet closer to the desk, I plopped down on it. It was one thing to spend two hours showing various policemen the mess of broken doors at Fabrizio's. It was another to put up with Lucia rushing to the police station ready to kill me only to realize that I hadn't done anything wrong. But to travel all the way to the detention center in Rome to be told to come back later was more than I could handle.

"That's it," I told Sander, who hovered behind me. "I'm not leaving this office without Tony no matter how long we have to stay here."

Sander brought over a similar chair, sat, and stretched out his long legs. "That's fine. I have no other plans this afternoon. Fleur will join us soon, and she will know how to handle the details."

The official shrugged in a lame excuse for an apology. He was only Sergio's assistant. He launched into a bureaucratic explanation, but I couldn't concentrate. I had three hours to get back to Orvieto for my exam. It was bad enough that the train we'd taken down to Rome was stalled for an hour for no apparent reason. It was an additional irritation that the temperature was nearly ninety degrees, the office wasn't air-conditioned, and I was wearing a T-shirt rather than a comfortable summer blouse. What I needed was a punching bag.

A thin man with a wiry moustache sighed as he carried a duffel into the room. He panted so hard he had to stop and catch his breath. Both the assistant and I automatically reached out to help him over to a seat.

"What can I help you with?" the assistant asked. *"Probably what you need is downstairs in Office 1B."*

"Forgive me, but I am searching for my nephew," the man panted.

"Fabrizio!" I yelled. "Where the hell have you been?"

"I, I—"

"When did you get here?"

"I came from Termini right now. It cost me twenty euros to take a taxi!" Fabrizio turned to the assistant. "I was enjoying the beach even though it is costing me a fortune, and then I get this crazy call that my nephew has been detained!"

"No thanks to you," I said. "We're the only ones who've been trying to help him!"

"But it's not my fault," Fabrizio said. "All I wanted was a little vacation for myself! Is it so much to ask? I work hard my whole life. This one time, I want to do something for me, and I spend lovely time with my new friend, and then I receive these terrible calls!"

An elderly woman puffed her way into the room; she panted even more heavily that Fabrizio had. She wore a bulky pink skirt and jacket that offset a sunburn. Her hair fell limply around her face, and sweat had smudged her makeup into streaks. *"Please. No more stairs!"*

She collapsed into the closest chair.

Fabrizio fanned her with one hand while gesturing at me with the other. "You ruined my time with Anna!"

I wasn't sure I'd ever met such a selfish man. I was ready to bop him in the nose and tell Anna to find somebody better. Tony didn't have such a luxury. Even if your relatives placed you in legal danger, you couldn't disclaim them.

I marched over to Fabrizio and spoke to him nose to nose, Italian style. "Anna, my foot! You're worrying about a friend? You should be worried about your nephew. No! You should be begging for his release. That's what you should be here for! Do you have any idea how much he's suffered because you wouldn't answer your damned phone!"

"But—"

"He's your nephew! You ignored him to do what, sit around on a beach?"

"Tony is a smart boy. He can defend himself."

"Do you even hear yourself?" I shouted.

"Anyway, what is wrong?"

"What did you do to make the Baldoni family so mad at you? What did you put in that stupid oil?"

Fabrizio started laughing but then he couldn't stop. He turned away so we wouldn't see how gleeful he was.

"What was in the oil?" I asked.

"You need to tell us now," said Sander.

"Right now!" I shouted.

Fabrizio turned to the assistant. *"Sono tutti pazzi!"*

"Oh, no you don't," I said. "We are not the least bit crazy. You are! Now, tell us what you did to Vittorio! What did you put in those stupid bottles?"

Fabrizio bobbed back and forth. "Me? Nothing!"

I appealed to the woman. "What was in the oil?"

Terrified, she held her hands before her face. "No espeak the inglis!"

It was fortunate that Sergio entered the room before I could seriously harm someone.

"It's about time you got here!" I shouted.

I dragged Sergio over to Fabrizio. "This is Tony's uncle! But he won't tell us what he put in the oil that I handed over to the Baldonis!"

"I did nothing!" Fabrizio lied.

"At first Vittorio thought he was dying."

"He always thinks he is dying."

I stomped my feet. "What did you do to the oil? Stop fooling around and tell me!"

Fabrizio laughed. "I did nothing!"

"You won't laugh when you see what his sons did to your apartment when they went to look for you."

"They broke into my flat?"

"Or maybe they were looking for compensation. Or money. Or a deed. Or better oil!"

"My flat!" Fabrizio shouted.

"When did this break-in happen?" Sergio asked.

"Last night. Or rather this morning, depending on your definition. I made a full report back in Orvieto. But the fact is that they wanted revenge for this stupid thing Fabrizio did. I can understand why they were mad, but it's not Tony's fault!"

"Slow down!" Sergio said. "My English is not so fast."

"We were staying at Fabrizio's place to keep an eye on things, but guess what? Baldoni's sons tried to kill us," I said. "Or I don't know what they would have done. We locked them in the house and then they broke down the doors to get out."

"Those doors are expensive!" Fabrizio cried.

"You totally deserve it! Now, what's in the oil?"

"Nothing. A little supplement."

"What's a supplement?" asked Sergio.

"A stupid herb or something that makes you think you're going to feel better," I said.

"But I didn't—"

I turned to Sander. "Remember that stuff I thought was marijuana?"

"Cannabis!" Sergio cried. "In Italy—"

"It was cascara sagrada," Fabrizio said. "That's all."

"What in the hell is that?" I asked.

"Just some medicine." He patted his stomach. "When you have problems."

"A mild laxative," Sander read from his phone. "Side effects may include arrhythmia and dehydration."

"You added that to your own olive oil!" Sergio asked.

"A spoonful. It's supposed to be good for you."

"How many bottles did you sabotage? Tell us the answer now!"

"One!"

"But you left Tony behind to be your fall guy while Vittorio went to the hospital!"

"He is strong like a bull. He doesn't need a doctor! Anyway, it's not your business!"

I grabbed Fabrizio by the shirt collar and rattled him. "Tony's been here all week! What's the matter with you?"

Sergio came over and gently pulled me away. "Please, little lady. Give him a chance to explain."

"And just where have you been?" I asked Sergio. "Haven't you listened to your messages either? I phoned you three times on the way to Rome."

"I'm sorry. I was at lunch, and I forgot to look at my phone."

"Forgot?"

"It was a good lunch, and I—never mind! I am the one asking the questions here." He took a pen from his shirt pocket and shook it at Fabrizio. "Explain yourself! How dare you ruin your olive oil to make an old man sick!"

Fabrizio beat his chest. "He is not an old man! He is the same like me! Not old! Okay, not so young, but not old!"

"You couldn't talk to him?"

"He is a stubborn pig! A miserable human being! He has no morals! He is more selfish than a hungry boar that is dying of starvation!"

Sergio nodded at his assistant, who left the room. Before the rest of us could offer our opinions one way or another, the assistant led the hungry boar into the room along with his two warthogs.

The shorter warthog pointed at me. *"There's the woman who locked me in!"*

I pointed right back. *"There's the man who sneaked into the house!"*

Vittorio kicked a pebble at Fabrizio. "He wouldn't sell me the land with the olive trees!"

Olive trees? This whole mess was about a bunch of plants?

Fabrizio pointed at Vittorio. "You wouldn't give me a fair price and you know it."

"Then you promised to sell the enoteca!"

"I promised to think about it! It takes a long time to make such an important decision. You were pressuring me."

"You tried to poison me!"

"I didn't use poison!"

I pointed at the Baldoni crew. "You knew Fabrizio was leaving town, so you hoped to ruin the business when Tony was in charge. Instead, he kept things going just fine."

Swirling around, I faced Sergio but pointed at Vittorio. "He wasn't seriously sick. He was pretending! He might have had a stomachache, but he didn't need to be in the hospital. He kept groaning so they would keep him there! The doctors didn't know what was wrong, so they kept him under observation at the taxpayer's expense! In the meantime, he laughed in everyone's faces."

"Fabrizio acted so stupidly I didn't have a choice," Vittorio said loudly.

"That man acted more stupidly than I did," Fabrizio shot back.

"What about Tony?" I ran over to Fabrizio. "You threw him to the wolves!" I turned to Vittorio. "And you got him into terrible trouble! He had nothing to do with either of you! You should both be ashamed of yourselves!"

"*But Fabrizio is a bastard!*" shouted Baldoni.

"*He's a bigger one!*" shouted Fabrizio.

"*I can't believe what he did!*"

"*And I can't believe what he did!*"

"*What were you thinking?*"

"The same thing you were thinking!"

Before anyone could stop them, the two old men locked into a push-pull with one another and waltzed around the room more awkwardly than lumpy cartoon characters. The official approached but couldn't decide how to break them up. The sons circled them, equally unsure.

"Lasciali stare," Sergio said. "Let them be."

The old codgers might have needed a while longer to work things out, but Anna struggled to her feet and slapped at Vittorio's back. It took both sons to pull her away. Then the two older men ogled each other like two dogs who wanted the same fire hydrant.

"Basta!" Sergio shouted. *"I've had enough! I will put you all in jail!"*

"But he — "

"But he — "

"And he said — "

"And he said — "

" Basta!"

At that moment Eduardo walked into the room accompanied by Fleur. He nodded at us collectively.

"What a nice afternoon!" he exclaimed. "It looks like I might have myself a few more clients."

"You better help your original client first," I said. "Get them to release Tony!"

"In good time — "

I planted myself in front of him. "Now is a pretty damned good time!"

Eduardo and Sergio exchanged glances, and then Sergio gestured to the official, who left the room.

"So now what?" I demanded.

"You're too American," Eduardo said. "You have to learn to be more patient."

"How can I be patient? These two kindergarteners only care about themselves!"

"Gina," Sander said quietly.

"They're stupid and old and irresponsible! Since they have too much time on their hands, they make trouble for everybody!"

"Gina," Sander repeated.

"I can't believe that two grown men would act like two clowns!"

Sander softly touched his index finger to his lips. *Shut up.* After all, I was shouting in front of a police officer, but I couldn't help myself. Silly billy goats had ruined my week as well as Tony's, and I was supposed to be patient? Little kids fought each other. That's how they learned social skills. Seventy-year-olds were supposed to have learned something along the way.

I might have launched into another unnecessary lecture, but by then, looking thinner but ecstatic, the guard led Tony into the room. We rushed towards one another and shared a hug, and suddenly I realized that no matter the trouble I'd gone to, I'd done the right thing. Assisting a friend who really needed help was worth all the trouble.

Chapter Thirty-One

Tony tapped me on the shoulder and nodded in the direction of his uncle. "I still can't believe all this."

He wasn't the only one. By then we'd all been led into a big conference room where, seated around a long rectangular table, at least the enemies couldn't hit each other. But the arguing hadn't slowed down. Given that all of them — Vittorio and his sons, Fabrizio and his friend, and occasionally the officials — shouted in half sentences at the same time, I'd given up paying attention. I huddled at the end of the table between Sander and Tony, hoping the men would wear out their voices so that we didn't need to fetch sleeping bags.

"I can't thank you enough," Tony continued softly. "I hope you know that! I'm so grateful. I didn't know what was happening. At first they didn't tell me anything." He nodded over at Fleur, who sat between Eduardo and Fabrizio. "If you hadn't known where to come, and if you hadn't brought me some clothes, I would have been wearing the same damned things all week, not to mention frozen to death."

"It's a good thing you convinced me to invite Sander to come visit," I said. "Otherwise, I'd have never met Fleur. If you ever have any more trouble with the law, she's the one to call."

"Trust me," Tony said. "As soon as I get out of here, I'm memorizing her number."

Sander nudged me. "Speaking of numbers, you might want to text Lucia."

True. Given our earlier drama at the police station, I was pretty sure Lucia would give me a chance to retake the exam, but a little brownnosing wouldn't hurt anything.

I was so concentrated that I barely looked up in time to see Vittorio slam his fist on the desk.

"But you promised to sell to me!" he shouted as the pens danced. "We shook the hands!"

Fabrizio pounded on the desk as well. "You refused to pay a fair price, so what could I do? I need the money for my old age, and you know it!"

The two men stood. I was wrong about the table being a successful buffer since they were both trying to figure out how to reach across it.

Fleur held up her hand. *"Please sit down,"* she said in a calming, measured voice. *"I am not here officially, but I am an EU negotiator, a job I have done for many years. What is the way to a solution? Always a compromise."* She turned to Sergio. *"Am I right?"*

Sergio nodded. He'd been eyeing his watch for the last fifteen minutes. He was as worried about an overnight as I was.

"Fabrizio has made a promise, but Vittorio has violated the conditions. Fabrizio has sold some bad oil, and Vittorio has made terrible accusations. His sons broke into Fabrizio's property."

"We didn't break in!" claimed the tallest son.

"We had the key!" claimed the other.

Fabrizio wrung his fist at them. *"Because you stole it from me!"*

"Because you forgot you loaned it to us!"

"Zitti!" Sergio yelled. "Quiet! Listen to the lady."

"What is the importance of a piece of land anyway?" Fleur continued. *"Will you live there? No. So you have a few more olive trees or you don't! But young Tony has paid with a week of his life because you two gentlemen have been stubborn and unforgiving. Who will repay Tony his lost time?"*

"That's exactly right," Eduardo said. "But a couple of lawsuits—"

"Yes. His mother could come over on the next plane. We could continue this fight for another few weeks until the lawyers took every last euro of everyone's money. So here is what we do. We let the bygones be bygones. You, Vittorio, will pay to repair the doors in Fabrizio's flat."

"I refuse!"

"You will do it. You, Fabrizio, will replace the olive oil and gift Vittorio an additional ten pristine bottles."

"I should give something to him? I will not!"

"You will both comply within the week." Fleur pointed in our direction. *"Tony, bless his heart, will somehow find the strength to forgive both of you. Tony, do you think you can do this?"*

Tony looked at Sander and me. After a moment, I gave a brief shrug.

"I can try," Tony said. He turned to his uncle. "But never, ever ask me to help you with the enoteca again. You're on your own."

I wasn't sure whether he was serious or not. In his shoes, I would have been ready to say goodbye to Orvieto, and my uncle, forever. No one would have blamed him for more than a second.

"At least not until he doubles the wages," I said.

"Right," Tony said. Then he winked.

That was the moment that broke the iceberg. For the first time that afternoon, everyone managed a grin even if some of them were crooked.

"To conclude, we will leave these premises as decent human beings," Fleur said. *"Isn't this the right way, Sergio?"*

Sergio's eyes flickered. On the one hand, he could have spent the next couple of weeks writing up useless reports. He could have checked with this higher up or that one to find out exactly what was expected in such a ridiculous situation.

Or he could follow Fleur's lead.

As I considered his point of view, I held my breath. Paperwork, no paperwork. Lawyer, no lawyer. Long explanations. Old people fighting over a piece of land the size of a dining room.

Perhaps it was bigger than a dining room. I'd never understood the dimensions.

Loud church bells rang out, reminding us that it was already seven o'clock in a country where we might well be relaxing at a café over a spritz.

With a sudden rush of energy, Sergio popped to his feet. *"Andiamo. Andiamo tutti!"*

He might have waved a magic wand. Suddenly, we were in high school again, packing up our materials and vacating the room as quickly as possible.

We were heading down the long staircase when I heard Vittorio let out a muffled laugh. Then came another.

Then, Anna giggled.

Then, one of Vittorio's sons did the same.

The shorter son came over to Tony and me. He held out his hand. "I sorry," he said, using English for the first time. "I know my father is exaggerate."

Tony gave the man a vigorous shake. "My uncle too."

Amid gasps for breath, Anna said, *"Fabrizio couldn't enjoy his vacation. He worried about Tony every minute."*

Fabrizio threw his arm around his nephew so energetically that they nearly tumbled down the stairs. "I know I did the wrong thing, but I was so angry. But now, I do a good thing. I change my will. When I die, I give you the enoteca!"

"I'm not sure Italy is the country for me," Tony said, "but thanks anyway."

"Italy is the country for everyone!" shouted Vittorio. He took hold of the railing and shook his finger at Sander. "You came to the hospital to trick us. Very clever."

"I had to help my friend."

"You are a good one. That is more important than anything. Eh, Fabrizio!"

Fabrizio caught up with Vittorio at the landing. "Sure. Friendship."

Vittorio slapped him on the back. "Is good now? I'm sorry I can't pay your price for the land. Don't have so good the profit this year."

"You said you never made so much money in your life!"

"I wish I made the money, but it was not true."

"I'm sorry about ruining your oil."

Vittorio held out his hand, but instead, Fabrizio hugged him.

Great. Two stubborn old men ready to kill each other now danced on the landing as if they were taking rumba lessons. *Really?* I wanted to say. *You ruined my study abroad program because you're old goats, but now everything is all right?*

I looked from one man to the other, not sure whom to scold first. "You don't get it, do you?"

"What you say?" asked Vittorio.

"You can't just make friends all of a sudden like nothing happened! I was worried sick! So was Fleur! And Sander! We all made sacrifices because of you! Instead of taking a final, I had to come back to Rome to get things straightened out because you two are old farts! And now you want to be BFFs? How is that supposed to work?"

"Gina," Sander said softly.

"Next month you'll probably get mad at one another again and call the police. Or set fire to each other's establishments."

"Gina."

"Better yet, you can smash into each other behind the Duomo. Those streets are so narrow that everyone will assume you had an accident."

"Gina." I felt Sander's fingers sink into my shoulder.

I didn't want to admit it, but just as I'd been a part of the investigation, I now had to be part of the solution. I had to accept Fleur's request about forgetting bygones because moving forward demanded it. Dammit. I would have rather held a grudge, at least for one lifetime.

"Oh, never mind." I shook my index fingers at the two old men. "No more fighting!"

"No fighting," said Fabrizio.

"Is stop," said Vittorio.

"Do you promise?" I asked.

Sergio caught up to us and bumped Fabrizio with his shoulder bag. "They promise! And now, I am going home before my wife decides she doesn't want to be my wife. Good-bye!"

With a wave of his hand, he stopped four rows of traffic and waltzed across the street, leaving the rest of us huddled on the sidewalk.

"Gina, you saved the day," Sander said.

"It was mostly Fleur."

"It was mostly everybody," Fleur said.

Tony hugged the woman so energetically that she nearly fell over. "Without you, I would have fallen apart. You knew how to handle everything."

Fleur laughed as she pulled away. "That is my job although usually the stakes are different. Never mind! We have all lost a lot of sleep and time, but everything has turned out all right in the end." She looked at Vittorio and Fabrizio, who had turned into two big Cheshire cats. "Correct?"

"Yes, yes," said Vittorio. "Everything good."

Fabrizio hugged Anna. "Now I go back to my vacation!"

"No more vacation! See all the trouble you made? You go back to the enoteca!" Anna exclaimed.

Fabrizio nodded like a sheep without bothering to *baa*. Authorities made no difference to him, Tony made no difference to him, but Anna was able to dictate his next actions without working at it.

Sander took my hand. "What would you like to do? Should we return to Orvieto tonight?"

I'd been given a reprieve until the following afternoon. I might have hurried back to Orvieto to study for an hour or two, but how could I concentrate with Sander around?

"No," I said, feeling decisive for the first time in hours. "We enjoy a Roman evening, which means we do the one responsible thing. We go to dinner."

"Together!" Fleur exclaimed. "That is exactly right."

"And Vittorio pays!" cried Fabrizio.

Vittorio pretended that his counterpart had said something vile and disgusting. Then he grinned. "Usually, people pay me to eat! Today, I pay!"

Eduardo pointed. "There happens to be a very good trattoria around the corner."

"You're sure is good?" Vittorio asked.

"I only eat at the best places. I'm sure!"

Lawyers. They did know where to eat.

While Eduardo herded the crowd, I hung back with Sander. "Thanks. I almost lost it for a minute there."

Sander threw his arm over my shoulder. "Your Italian side emerged. That's all."

"Both of those old men—" I held my tongue.

"Exactly!" Sander said. Then he herded me under an awning and into the eatery.

That was Italy. Argue, complain, whine, shout.

Then feast.

Maybe it wasn't such a bad system after all.

Chapter Thirty-Two

The student farewell dinner at Al Cordone the following night was a joyous occasion. Guests were allowed, so Sander and Tony attended along with Julie's parents, who had come to travel with her. We were packed into a small space, but the owners were friendly and helpful, and we had the establishment to ourselves. We had plenty of pizza types to choose from, and Lucia even let the owners serve tiny glasses of wine. Since almost everyone was leaving the next morning, how much trouble could we get into?

To my surprise, even Aurelio joined us. Despite their disregard for study, my fellow students had passed their course, although I knew that Henrietta's C was awarded out of compassion, and Dennis, who at least knew how to get in and out of his own building by now, had earned the same terrific grade.

I'd done all right too. I'd earned my A alongside Becky and Michelle, but I wasn't convinced Aurelio had examined ny test carefully. He'd been too busy averaging grades so that he could come out to dinner without any responsibilities hanging over him.

Lucia clanked her spoon against her glass. After a series of obnoxious *dings*, she finally earned everyone's attention. "We are so happy that you have had a wonderful time with us in Orvieto."

The students cheered. For once, I agreed with all of them.

"You have worked very hard," she said. For the first time I realized what a smooth liar she was. The owners of Al Cordone were oblivious; they smiled at us as if we were scholars rather than mediocre language students, but then, I suspected they weren't listening. This was one of the usual haunts, so Lucia brought students here on a routine basis.

In general, the program was a lovely idea: a crash course in Italian in a quaint town where the students soon felt comfortable. Its crime rate was low despite petty fights amongst the townspeople. It was quiet unless you had unwanted visitors after hours. People feigned friendship because no matter how much you disliked someone, you ran into them, sometimes several times a day.

That made you tolerant. Even if you were a stubborn old fart, at some point you let loose and enjoyed the local Orvieto Classico, maybe right before strolling up to Piazza Duomo for an extra gelato.

"Now is my favorite part of the program," Lucia said. "All of you, please, tell me your favorite things of Orvieto."

A surge of giggles confirmed what I would have guessed; most of my fellow classmates were the most delighted that bar keepers refrained from asking anyone's age, and the fact that the students could drink for three weeks straight without anyone except for Lucia or maybe Antonio, the beleaguered Blue Bar owner, hassling them about it.

"Well? Speak up!"

"I liked going to the market," said Becky. "I learned to order exactly the right number of *etti*."

"I liked buying fresh pasta," said Michelle. "I never knew there were so many kinds, and all of them are delicious."

"I liked the pizza," said Dennis. "And you never have to share!"

That generated a laugh that launched into a safe discussion of food. My fellow students seemed genuinely happy to explain their experiences trying zucchini blossoms or wild boar or even pasta flavored with truffles.

"Have you tried the truffles?" Sander asked me.

"I can't even stand the smell."

"Does that mean you haven't tried?"

"Yes!"

He laughed heartily, which was yet another confirmation that he knew a ton more about Italian cooking than I did, and that soon I would be forced to try the foul-smelling fungus that the locals claimed as a rare delicacy.

Henrietta stood and twirled, showing off yet another new outfit. "What I like most is Italian fashion. I found so many wonderful clothes that I had to buy another suitcase."

"And she's making me carry home half her stuff," said Christie.

"Not half!" Henrietta said. "Just the things I bought in Rome yesterday!"

That's when I realized I hadn't bought a single souvenir. I'd barely remembered to snap pictures.

Nancy gestured wildly in Sander's direction while addressing me. "What have you gotten out of the program besides a blond?"

I could have taken the barb several ways. I could have simply eaten it, which might have been my style a couple of weeks earlier. I could have denied it, which would have been silly with such a handsome Dutchman sitting beside me. Best to dive straight through.

"Blonds are a dime a dozen where I come from," I said. "What's important is to find a man who understands Europe." I turned to Sander. "How many countries have you visited?"

"I'm not sure."

"All right. Have many have you visited this year?"

Since we were halfway through the year, he'd only made it to half a dozen.

"But you don't speak Italian," Lucia said.

"Not yet."

"Maybe next year you join our program!" she said triumphantly.

"Maybe next year I will," he said cordially if untruthfully, making Lucia beam.

"I want to hear from Armando and Lalo," I said. "Surely they've had some interesting adventures that they'd love to share with us."

They both froze in place, as if I'd caught them thinking about their best sexual adventures. I probably had. They mumbled something about the bars, realized Luisa was listening, and clammed up again.

"What about you, Gina?" Lucia asked.

"I'm happy that I've finally learned to separate Spanish and Italian. Mostly."

"Your Italian has improved a lot," Lucia said.

"That's because Aurelio was so patient with us."

Aurelio nodded; maybe he thought he had been patient. He'd done his best, after all. He didn't know how to teach any more effectively than he had. Perhaps he'd suffered boring teachers himself.

"And Lucia," I continued. "You run a really terrific program."

"Oh, not really," she said, beaming.

"Whenever we needed help, you were right there," I continued. "We're grateful."

"I had to make several visits to Blue Bar this summer!" She pretended to be irritated, but I suspected she'd had worse groups.

"We were thirsty!" Armando cried.

"But Gina, you should have called me much earlier," Lucia said. "I could have helped with your friend." That might have been true, but Lucia was smiling as she said it. She was probably thankful I hadn't contacted her until I really needed to.

"I didn't want to bother you," I said.

"This is my job!" Lucia said.

I thought about Eduardo, who hadn't answered his phone the morning before, the inspector who hadn't inspected, and the hospital staff who hadn't noticed three strangers slipping in.

"It might be your job, Lucia," but not everybody would bother to do it." I held up my glass even though it was empty. "Cheers!"

Every single person followed my lead.

*

Inside Blue Bar, which was actually "closed," although Antonio had let us in, I clinked glasses with Tony, then Becky and Michelle, and finally with Sander. I'd discovered Disaronno, a sweet after-dinner drink, while Sander favored a liqueur made from pistachio.

Antonio pulled up a chair alongside us. "I'm sorry I can't allow your friends to drink here tonight."

"Friends might be too strong a word for those worthless classmates of mine," I said. "But they'll find somewhere else to indulge themselves. They're good at it."

"They treat drinking seriously," Tony said. "Like truffle hunting."

Becky and Michelle giggled as if they had never heard anything so funny, and maybe they hadn't. After three weeks of intensive study, they let loose. They were taking the whole week off before Italian 201 started the following week.

"They've spent a lot of money, I bet," Michelle said.

I didn't dare try to think that high.

"They'll be paying their bills for a long time," Sander said.

"I wish that were true," I said. "Mostly their parents will be paying."

"Henrietta is completely broke," Becky said. "Her flight is tomorrow morning, but she couldn't spend money on a hotel in Rome, so she's sleeping at the airport."

"Nancy went with her," Michelle said.

"That's a better plan than missing the plane," said Sander. "I might have made the same choice."

"But you wouldn't have been broke!" I exclaimed. "You're much more organized."

He brushed his hand along my arm, which he'd done a couple of times already that day, a gesture I was becoming fond of. "That's true."

"I wish my own choice had been more conscious," Tony said. "My uncle asked my mom for help. She passed along the request to me."

"You had no way to predict how crazy things would be," I said.

"Of course not! Otherwise, I wouldn't have come."

"I hope you're not going home right away," Becky said. "We've barely had a chance to meet you!"

Tony laughed. "I'll stay a little while longer. Until I figure out my next move."

"We're staying for the next Italian session," Becky said. "We want to come and study in your garden."

"You do?"

Michelle nodded. "We already know that it's a magical place."

"Here's to magic," I said as I raised my glass.

The others happily raised theirs.

*

I led Sander into the apartment that still smelled vaguely of Henrietta, or maybe her clothes.

"I thought you weren't allowed to have sleepovers," he said sternly.

I flopped onto the love seat. "Not at all. Please don't tell Lucia."

He set his backpack on the floor next to the couch. "I promise to keep quiet. She kept looking at you during the dinner, you know."

"Did she? I wasn't paying any attention."

"She's not a bad person, I don't think. She likes students in general, but there's a reason she has so many rules. She hopes to prevent every bad possibility."

I understood her concerns, but only a genius with a modern crystal ball could foresee the problems that would accompany each group of students. Because she needed to fill a quota, though, she couldn't be too picky about accepting possible candidates.

"Lucia was fortunate this session. Only a few trips to the hospital and such. Only five or six angry calls about the drunk Americans."

"I thought one of your classmates locked himself out of his apartment," Sander said.

"Three times, but that was the first week."

"Is he the one who couldn't manage to leave his building?"

"The same! He finally figured things out."

Lucia's next bunch of students would no doubt receive floor plans. The session after that, maybe she would resort to passing out compasses.

"At least the students are good for the local economy," Sander said. "Your male classmates were both wearing new leather jackets."

Lalo and Armando were so in love with their purchases that I assumed they were also sleeping with them.

"Nancy and Christie bought enough purses to carry a different one every single day of the week," I said. "They probably also purchased extra luggage."

"What souvenirs do you have?" Sander asked me.

I tapped my head. "My new knowledge of olive oil. But what are you taking away? Your Italian vacation wasn't ideal either."

"Put it this way, Gina. With you I saw things that I never expected to. My friends back home will be surprised that I visited a detention center!"

"And you visited it more than once! Of course, it was Fleur who worked nonstop. I hope she didn't mind too much. It was quite an imposition."

"You mustn't worry about her. She was quite happy last night after everything worked out. But I do have terrible news."

"Which is?"

He attempted to stretch out on the loveseat. "I don't fit on this piece of furniture. You must sleep here yourself."

"Or we can thank Henrietta for going to Fiumicino early."

"We can at that."

Sander didn't fit on the couch, but he wouldn't have fit on my small single bed either. Thank goodness somebody — me — had taken time to wash all the sheets.

He brushed a piece of hair out of my face. "You're quite a fun companion, you know."

"Are you crazy? I'm nothing but trouble. With me it's always lost relatives, kidnappers, thieves, that kind of thing. I have a nose for them. Or they follow me."

"I don't mind. You make life much more interesting. I have a routine job. But you haven't said anything about how you feel about me."

It was my usual reticence. After making lots of mistakes in the romance department, I didn't want to move too fast ever again.

I took Sander's hand and squeezed it. "Here's how I feel. You're my new best friend."

"What does that mean?"

"Everything."

He squeezed my hand right back, and for a couple of awkward moments we stared at each other.

"You haven't said anything about your free time in Europe, either. Will you come to the Netherlands with me? I'd love to show you my hometown."

"Well, why not?"

"You haven't had time to consider yourself lately."

"Last week I dictated our every action. Now it's your turn."

"You're sure? My parents will want to meet you, and so will my friends."

I didn't have everything figured out, of course. I didn't know Sander well despite the unusual experiences we'd had in the past week. But I felt sure of a few things, including that I wanted to spend some time with him away from school, and, given the circumstances, away from Orvieto.

He wouldn't merely be a convenient tour guide. We'd either be on our way to a lasting friendship or a deeper kind of relationship. It was too early to tell. But here was a man ready to follow me anywhere, get me out of any scrape, and help my friends he hadn't met. What more could anyone ask for?

"Of course, I'm sure," I said. "It's time for a new adventure."

Then I leaned over and gave my new best friend a hug.

Then a kiss.

Honestly, we both deserved it.

Acknowledgements

Many thanks to my early readers including Elise Ransdell, David Loeb, and Kathy Johnson.

Author's Note

When I was thirteen, my great-aunt organized a trip to Italy for the Italian-American relatives. Since my grandma didn't want to go (she was never much for traveling, and the thought of a bunch of boisterous relatives was too much for her), Grandpa offered to take me instead. What an opportunity!

Grandpa had grown up in Wilsonville, Illinois, in a town with a lot of other Italian immigrants from Piemonte, a region in the northwest corner of Italy. His first language was Piemontese, but he hadn't practiced much over the years. In preparation for our trip, we dove in. We checked out a copy of the Berlitz language course from the library, and each weekend we dutifully listened to a new lesson. I still remember the first one, which started with "Arriviamo a Roma!"

When we landed in the Old Country, my grandpa proceeded to communicate in a creative mix of Piemontese, Italian, and English, which our bus driver, Sante, seamlessly understood. For me, using Italian wasn't so easy. I had to think hard before I could spit out a sentence, but I remember asking our gondolier how many bridges there were in Venice. I probably had the grammar all wrong, and the gondolier admitted that he wasn't sure of the answer, but I was ecstatic; I'd used Italian!

My journey continued through a semester in Florence, subsequent efforts to read in Italian and join Italian-language groups, and frequent trips to visit my lovely relatives in Piemonte. Then I got the chance to teach English courses for the Arizona in Italy Summer Study Abroad program held in Orvieto, Italy. Terrific!

My true mission, though, was to work on my Italian. On the third day in my cozy new hometown, I was roaming the streets with a college roommate when we spotted a small store that sold beautiful, flowered ceramics. We moseyed inside.

The woman at the counter was reading a *giallo*, a mystery. (For years, Mondadori sold their mysteries as cheap paperbacks with yellow covers, so mystery novels were affectionately called "yellows.") Since I often wrote mysteries, I naturally wanted to talk to a mystery reader!

That woman turned out to be ceramist Anna Spallaccia, and that day sparked a long friendship that has extended through to Anna's lovely daughters Claudia and Elda, their kids, and even their friends. When I return to Orvieto on vacation, Claudia puts me up. On our last trip, Claudia taught my husband how to make spaghetti alla carbonara while Anna let him roll and fill her ravioli. Elda, a watercolorist, painted me a personalized birthday card. Their friends Clara and Walter have invited us for long dinners with way too much lovely food. Paola has let me practice Italian on her whenever she substitutes at the flower shop.

Orvieto is a haven to me, a nest of language learning. Over the years, I have slowly improved. The program coordinators, Alba Frascarelli and Claudio Bizzarri, have cheerfully put up with my language attempts. University of Arizona professors Beppe Cavatorta and Letizia Bellocchio have noticed that I use any excuse to use Italian, whether at the grocery store, the Autogrill, or the pool!

Thanks to Beppe and Letizia, I was offered the chance to teach Italian 101. I was ecstatic! I warned Beppe I would make mistakes, but he laughed and admitted that his English wasn't perfect. I sailed in, ready to teach my first class. I probably scared the students with my enthusiasm. Some no doubt regretted signing up for my section; as soon as I introduced present tense, we started each class by conjugating a verb! (Now, I'm teaching Italian 102. We start each class by conjugating a verb in present tense, present perfect, and the imperfect, too!) Sometimes I make mistakes that I catch myself. Sometimes the students catch me! But we all learn together, which is the best way.

This novel is a tribute to the art of language learning, of living abroad, of making slow progress towards the difficult but rewarding goal of gaining a bit of insight into another culture. But it's also a way of recognizing that people are vulnerable. They make mistakes, they sabotage their own friendships, and sometimes they grow enough to make amends. Above all, they continue learning. All of us should.

Hodophile note: For those of you who travel to Orvieto, I should admit that Baldoni's restaurant and Fabrizio's enoteca are fictional, but I hope you take the opportunity to enjoy the Number 1 carbonara at Mezza Luna and at least one *boscaiola* over at Pizzeria Charlie's. You might walk around the *rupe* and then have a few drinks over at Blue Bar. As you stroll down Corso Cavour, you might visit Elda's shop across from Teatro Mancinelli. Maybe you'll even ask her to paint you something. Just keep in mind that the *funicolare* really does stop running at eight-thirty. It's a long climb up that hill.

Linguistic note: In Italian, plurals are usually formed by a change in the vowel. *Gelato* becomes *gelati*, for example, while an *enoteca* becomes two *enoteche*. In English we usually speak of *gelato*, Italian-style ice cream, using the word collectively. In Italian it's also common to hear the plural form, *gelati*.

Mille grazie for joining Gina on her journey. Please leave a review on your favorite social media site! Read about my other novels on my website: http://www.dr-ransdell.com or send me an email about your own Italian journeys, linguistic or otherwise!

http://www.dr-ransdell.com